Grammar & Writing Practice

Let's See Grammar

Intermediate 2

彩圖中級英文文法 三版

written by Alex Rath Ph.D.

The Passive
被動語態

The coffee is brewed fresh every morning.

Relative Clauses With Prepositions
搭配介系詞的關係子句

This is my pet mouse's favorite book, at which she can look for hours.

Verbs Followed by Infinitives
要接不定詞的動詞

Don't attempt to persuade me to get rid of my favorite armchair.

Unreal Present Conditionals
與現在事實相反的條件句

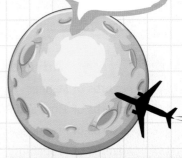

If his travel agent offered tourist trips to the moon, Jim would book tickets right away.

Intermediate 2 Contents

Intermediate 1

Let's See Grammar

Intermediate 2

彩圖中級英文文法 三版

Answers to Practice Questions

Unit 90 p. 9

1 1. be able to play   2. had to leave   3. can
4. will   5. ought to   6. shouldn't   7. Could
8. have to   9. can do

2 1. He could drink ten bowls of miso soup.
2. Jeffery will explain everything.
3. Dad must quit smoking and drinking.
4. Alison should file the documents.
5. We might get lost without a GPS system.
6. You ought to take off your dirty shoes and socks.
7. Denis can speak five languages.

Unit 91 p. 11

1 1. should go   2. Can Megan run   3. must go
4. may have left   5. should not
6. will not win   7. Shall I   8. should not
9. Could you have thrown

2 1. Karl can ride his snowboard all day.
2. Audrey will observe the lunar eclipse.
3. Elwood may have fallen off his horse.
4. Can Julio play the accordion?
5. Jasper must be feeding pigeons in the park.

Unit 92 p. 13

1 1. Can   2. be able to   3. be able to   4. can
5. be able to   6. be able to   7. can
8. be able to

2 1. can do bike tricks   2. can't swim
3. can maintain her balance   4. can't skate
5. can paint with watercolors

Unit 93 p. 15

1 1. could   2. was able to   3. could have
4. could have   5. being able to   6. could
7. could

2 1. I could see the sunrise over the ocean from my hotel window.
2. I couldn't read English newspapers before I was twelve.
3. I was not able to get out of the bed by myself. My mom helped me.
4. I managed to walk to the bathroom while holding the IV bottle above my head.
5. I could remember those crazy summers when we were hanging out together at the beach all the time.

Unit 94 p. 17

1 1. Can   2. was allowed to   3. May
4. was allowed to   5. can't   6. may

2 1. can't, can/may   2. can't   3. can't   4. may
5. can   6. may not   7. can't, are allowed
8. was not able

Unit 95 p. 19

1 1. must / have to   2. must / have to
3. have to   4. having to   5. had to
6. Must   7. have to

2 1. must have   2. must take   3. must show

3 1. have to apply   2. have to take
3. have to process

Unit 96 p. 21

1 1. have got to hurry   2. have got to eat
3. have got to give

2 1. have to   2. have got to   3. had to
4. Do you always have to   5. will have to
6. Does Nancy have to   7. have got to
8. Will you have to   9. had to

Unit 97 p. 23

1 1. mustn't   2. don't have to   3. haven't
4. needn't   5. mustn't   6. didn't have to
7. have to   8. don't have to
9. don't have to   10. must   11. don't have to

2 1. didn't need to bring
2. didn't need to go back /
needn't have gone back
3. didn't need to buy / needn't have bought
4. didn't need to call / needn't have called
5. didn't need to get up /
needn't have gotten up
6. didn't need to work

Unit 98 p. 25

1 1. I think you should go to the auction.
2. I think you ought to bid on the small statue.
3. I think you should offer $2,000 for the statue.
4. I think you ought to use an online auction company.
5. Shall I give the statue to my mother?

3

2 1. You should have brought in the laundry before it started to rain.
2. You should have simmered the sauce for five more minutes.
3. Angus shouldn't have poured too much soy sauce on the fried noodles.
4. You shouldn't have thrown away the receipt.

3 1. ought to have told
2. ought to have known

Unit 99 p. 27

1 1. had better   2. had better not   3. leave
4. Are you supposed to
5. are not supposed to
6. wasn't supposed to   7. was supposed to

2 1. I think you had better clean the house before the guests arrive.
2. You are supposed to take a number and wait for your turn.
3. You had better not invite your motorcycle club to the party.
4. You are not supposed to cut in the line.
5. I think you had better vacuum the rug.
6. You are supposed to fill out your deposit ticket while you are waiting.
7. You had better not let the dog into the house.
8. You are supposed to hand the passbook and the cash to the clerk.

Unit 100 p. 29

1 1. Bonnie may go out with us tomorrow night.
2. The plane might be delayed because of the fog.
3. The movie star could have arrived by now.
4. The police think Carl may have stolen a Ming dynasty vase.
5. The chocolate-flavored pastry might have sold out.
6. You could have sprained your ankle.

2 1. could have gotten up
2. could have presented   3. may have spent

Unit 101 p. 31

1 1. can scan   2. can connect   3. can locate
4. can sell   5. can make

2 1. should be   2. could
3. ought to have arrived
4. should have received   5. may

6. ought to contact   7. ought to hear
8. should know   9. can

Unit 102 p. 33

1 1. must   2. can't   3. can't   4. must
5. must   6. couldn't   7. couldn't   8. can
9. Could

2 1. bought this villa   2. talking with
3. made a fortune   4. drinking in the bar

Unit 103 p. 35

1 1. Can I have a cup of coffee?
2. Would you please answer the phone for me?
3. Will you turn off the air conditioner?
4. May I use the bench press when you are finished?
5. Could I take a nap on the sofa if you are not going to watch TV?
6. Can you go jogging with me tomorrow morning at 5:30?

2 1. borrow this book   2. get off the phone
3. a copy of the application form
4. open the gift   5. pass me a tissue
6. turned the light on   7. to fix the fence

Unit 104 p. 37

1 1. Will you sew this button back on my pajamas?
2. Shall I carry that big heavy suitcase for you?
3. Can I help you change that light bulb?
4. May I have your daughter's hand in marriage?
5. Would you like to go out to a French restaurant for dinner this evening?
6. Will you try a glass of white wine with the meal?

2 1. Shall I pay the phone bill at the convenience store?
2. Can I take out the garbage you put by the door?
3. Will you please have another cookie?
4. I could fry an egg for your breakfast.
5. Would you like to hear my explanation?
6. I can walk the dog for you tonight.

Unit 105　　p. 39

1. 1. shall we　2. Let's　3. Why don't we
4. Shall we　5. How about　6. We can
7. could　8. we could

2. 1. visiting the wine factory
2. waiting for five more minutes
3. make dumplings　4. go bicycling
5. take a coffee break　6. join the health club

Unit 106　　p. 41

1. 1. used to　2. spend　3. work　4. used to
5. used to go　6. loves to

2. 1. She used to drink a cup of black tea when reading a book.
2. He is used to sipping a glass of wine before going to bed.
3. Kristine used to watch horror movies.
4. Did Karl use to stay in his office overnight to work?
5. Sam used to be naive, but now he is a mature young man.
6. Where did you use to go bowling?
7. I am used to writing a journal every day.
8. Are you used to reading a newspaper before going to work?

Unit 107　　p. 43

1. 1. will　2. would　3. used to　4. will

2. 1. will often sneak onto the bed
2. will always go to the beach
3. will always sing loudly
4. will always spread a lot of peanut butter

3. 1. would often chat with friends
2. would often sit by Grandpa
3. would always eat her breakfast
4. would always doze off

Unit 108　　p. 45

1. 1. Kathy won't change her opinion.
2. Kenny won't come out of his room.
3. Yesterday I invited Lionel to the party, but he won't/wouldn't go.
4. I suggested Yvonne get a new suit for the interview, but she won't/wouldn't buy one.
5. The washing machine won't work properly.

2. 1. If you don't stay out of my room, I will tell Mom.
2. If you let me use your computer, I will be careful with it.

3. If you tell Dad what I did, I won't forget and you'll regret it.
4. I took your favorite doll. Unless you stop kicking my sheep, I won't tell you where your doll is.
5. If you tell me where Mom hid the cookies, I will buy you snacks next time.

Unit 109　　p. 47

1. 1. would rather drink
2. would rather not jump
3. would rather not hunt
4. would rather, continued

2. 1. She would rather Lisa did the dishes.
2. Joe would rather Mary didn't revise too much of his paper.
3. I would rather you went to the play with me.
4. I would rather you didn't cook chicken for dinner every day.

3. 1. may as well go　2. may as well order
3. may as well read　4. might as well ride
5. might as well have　6. might as well wash

Unit 110　　p. 49

1. 1. that I (should) consult the doctor about the bump on my leg
2. that the meat (should) be fried quickly with high heat
3. that I (should) walk around by the lavatory
4. that you (should) finish your homework every night
5. that he (should) pack the sunscreen
6. that you (should) watch the movie and not talk

2. 1. They say it is important that you drive without talking on your phone.
2. The mayor ordered that free food be distributed to the poor.

Unit 111　　p. 51

1. 1. The old man sat on the bench.
2. This tea tasted delicious.
3. The woman is 160 cm tall.
4. The large blue coat is mine.
5. We have had three weeks of hot weather.
6. The shelter has sleeping quarters on the second floor.

2. 1. The rope is ~~long~~ 45 cm long.
2. We had a ~~two hours~~ two-hour walk after dinner.

5

3. It was a lovely crystal lamp.

4. Did you see my blue Japanese silk dress?

5. I'm going to visit my ~~ill~~ sick Grandpa tomorrow.

6. Is your bird still ~~living~~ alive?

7. I fell ~~sleeping~~ asleep.

8. We have a tight schedule.

Unit 112 p. 53

1. 1. bigger   2. youngest   3. most delicious
   4. sunnier   5. farther   6. longer
2. 1. Mount Everest is the highest mountain in the world.
   2. The Louvre is one of the most famous museums in the world.
   3. The Mariana Trench is the deepest place in the ocean.
   4. Shakespeare is considered to be one of the greatest poets and dramatists.
   5. Solar energy is one of the most important sources of energy.
   6. Cirque du Soleil is the most innovative contemporary circus.

Unit 113 p. 55

1. 1. shorter   2. happiest   3. more honest
   4. most careful   5. worst   6. cheaper
   7. hotter and hotter   8. more   9. she is
2. 1. more important than
   2. the more expensive   3. the sourest
   4. as hot   5. closer (and closer)
   6. the most boring   7. more specific
3. 1. as hip   2. as smart as   3. as frugal as
   4. as fast as   5. as neat as   6. as high as

Unit 114 p. 57

1. 1. graceful   2. efficiently   3. absurd
   4. inspiring   5. in a silly way   6. impressively
   7. tentatively   8. in an ugly way   9. quickly
2. 1. as high（high 也可以當副詞，意為「（高度上的）高地」，與 highly 表「（程度上的）高地」、「非常」不同。此處指的是「跳得高」，故用 high）
   2. beautifully   3. better than
   4. the latest   5. as far as   6. carefully
   7. more intelligently   8. sooner than
   9. heavily   10. emotionlessly
3. 1. in a friendly way   2. in a lovely way

Unit 115 p. 59

1. 1. the food hungrily
   2. works in this office
   3. casually at 2:30 in the afternoon
   4. quickly in the office last week
   5. hard at the champion last night
   6. watched the fight excitedly
   7. in the south this afternoon
   8. at his brother angrily
2. 1. Trent put the box here.
   2. Sally just poured some milk into her coffee.
   3. Sonia left the library at 10 a.m.
   4. I will buy some books at the bookstore tomorrow.
   5. Mom still won't let me go to the party.
   6. Jacky jumped off the tree quickly. / Jacky quickly jumped off the tree.

Unit 116 p. 61

1. 1. Trisha usually gets up at 6:30 in the morning.
   2. Ester is never late for work.
   3. Vanessa will bring a box of donuts for her co-workers sometimes. /
      Sometimes Vanessa will bring a box of donuts for her co-workers. /
      Vanessa will sometimes bring a box of donuts for her co-workers.
   4. Does Brigit take time off work often? /
      Does Brigit often take time off work?
   5. Felix goes to a client's office once a week.
   6. Irvin writes up his sales report daily.
2. 1. goes biking every weekend
   2. have a sandwich for breakfast every day
   3. goes to a yoga class once a week
   4. have Thai food monthly
   5. has his car maintained every three months

Unit 117 p. 63

1. 1. definitely knows   2. certainly won't
   3. obviously not   4. Perhaps Stanley will
   5. is probably   6. Maybe Jill
2. 1. Beryl will probably run in the 100 meter race.
   2. Amy certainly swims faster than anybody I know.
   3. Luke is definitely in the running for a medal.
   4. Jenna obviously won't continue dancing after her injury.

5. Kathleen certainly isn't the best teacher, but she is well loved.

6. Mort is probably not going to get promoted this year.

7. Maybe Shirley can fill in for you while you're gone.

8. Perhaps Rod will play his guitar in a concert for the earthquake survivors.

Unit 118   p. 65

1 1. quite   2. fairly   3. quite   4. rather
5. rather   6. quite   7. extremely cold
8. rather   9. quite   10. almost there
11. rather   12. is quite

2 1. Antone is quite a famous chef.
2. Meg was rather satisfied with the result.
3. I feel fairly depressed.
4. Louis drove rather faster than usual.
5. Tim simply pushed the "Start" button.
6. Larry is a pretty smart person.
7. Mom's roast beef is really delicious.

Unit 119   p. 67

1 1. Not yet   2. still knits   3. is still   4. can still
5. I have already weeded
6. have already warmed up
7. already cooked   8. yet   9. yet
10. haven't gone to bed yet

2 1. already   2. yet   3. still   4. still   5. yet
6. already   7. still   8. still   9. already
10. already   11. still

Unit 120   p. 69

1 1. too   2. enough   3. too many
4. too much   5. enough
6. too small for him   7. too early to look
8. much too high   9. enough coins

2 1. enough   2. too many   3. too
4. too many / enough   5. much

Unit 121   p. 71

1 1. such   2. so   3. so   4. so   5. such
6. such   7. so   8. so

2 1. Victoria doesn't wear glasses anymore.
2. Matthew no longer watches auto racing on TV.
3. Laurie doesn't read comic books anymore.

4. Sandy is very tired. She can't drive any longer today.
5. Andy will no longer play in the Asian Cup.

Unit 122   p. 73

1 1. When   2. When   3. as soon as
4. until, before   5. as soon as   6. while

2 1. I counted the steps when I was walking home from the MRT station.
2. Do not speak when you have food in your mouth.
3. I got grains of instant coffee all over the table while I was making a cup of cappuccino.
4. The baby fell asleep while Mom was humming a lullaby.
5. The light went out as we were playing cards.
6. I lost eight pounds after I quit eating hamburgers and French fries.
7. Dad checked on the electricity, gas, and windows before we set off for our vacation.
8. I ran to my computer and checked the email as soon as I got home.

Unit 123   p. 75

1 1. Although Kathy likes toy dinosaurs, she doesn't like dinosaur movies.
2. Despite the silly plot, we enjoyed the movie. (despite 後面接名詞，所以須將形容詞 silly 放到名詞 plot 前面，變成「the silly plot」)
3. Though the movie was a little long, it was great.
4. Though we planned to have dinner in the Italian restaurant before the movie, we didn't have time.
5. In spite of the movie's bad reviews, we went to see it anyway. (in spite of 後面接名詞，所以須將句子「the movie received bad news」改成名詞「the movie's bad news」)
6. Even though Hank planned to stay up for the late movie, he fell asleep before it started.
7. Alan looks very conservative, while his wife is totally wild and artistic.
8. Jerry likes to get up at dawn, whereas his wife likes to sleep until noon.

Unit 124 p. 77

1 1. because 2. Since 3. because of
  4. due to the fact that 5. As 6. Because

2 1. Because of his miserliness, I won't ask him for help.（形容詞 miserly → 名詞 miserliness）
  2. We had to stay home because of the rain. / Because of the rain, we had to stay home.
  3. Because he was generous, we survived the hard times.（名詞 generosity → 形容詞 generous）
  4. Since they had security concerns, they decided to close the front gate after sunset.
  5. Cherries are good for our health due to their richness in vitamins.（形容詞 rich → 名詞 richness，後面都須加 in）
  6. As he has an ankle injury, he can't play tennis as well as before.
  7. As he didn't play fair in the final, he was deprived of the title two days after the match.

Unit 125 p. 79

1 1. As 2. as a result 3. so 4. As a result
  5. such 6. so

2 1. Grandma was sick. As a result, we had to put off our trip. /
  Grandma was sick. We had to put off our trip as a result.
  2. We didn't have vegetables at home. Therefore, we went out for dinner. /
  We didn't have vegetables at home. We, therefore, went out for dinner.
  3. I left home late this morning. As a result, I was caught in the traffic. /
  I left home late this morning. I was caught in the traffic as a result.

3 1. Those were such sweet peaches that I ate three of them.
  2. The scenery was so splendid that we took hundreds of pictures.
  3. It was such an amazing show that the audience applauded the performers for three minutes.

Unit 126 p. 81

1 1. William brought his own bag to carry his groceries.
  2. The dog wants to go for a walk so as to go to the bathroom.
  3. Lauren got to the store early in order to avoid the rush.

4. Kevin often eats dinner out so as not to mess up his kitchen.
5. Paulina bought some shrimp for lunch.
6. Lawrence has a knife with a serrated edge for cutting bread.
7. Nadia will give you some money so that you can buy a new dress.
8. Tamara closed the window so that it wouldn't get too cold.

Unit 127 p. 83

1 1. in case 2. in case 3. in case 4. in case
  5. if 6. in case

2 1. Take your purse with you in case you want to buy anything while walking the dog.
  2. Give me your phone number in case I need to reach you.
  3. Call him later in case he hasn't arrived at the office.
  4. Lock your cell phone keypad in case you accidentally make a call.
  5. Give Mary a call in case she's forgotten about her promise to buy some frozen pizzas for tonight.
  6. Back up your files every day in case your computer crashes.

Unit 128 p. 85

1 1. at 2. on 3. at 4. in 5. on 6. on
2 1. on 2. in 3. at 4. on 5. at

Unit 129 p. 87

1 1. in/at 2. in 3. on 4. in 5. in 6. in
  7. at 8. on
2 1. on 2. at/in 3. at 4. in 5. in

Unit 130 p. 89

1 1. under 2. over 3. under 4. above
  5. over 6. below
2 1. over 2. under 3. above 4. below
  5. under 6. under

Unit 131 p. 91

1 1. in front of 2. among 3. between
  4. behind
2 1. in front of 2. opposite 3. behind
  4. between 5. among

Unit 132   p. 93

1 1. outside   2. by   3. outside   4. against
5. near   6. next to   7. outside   8. beside

Unit 133   p. 95

1 1. into/in   2. out of   3. in   4. on   5. on
6. off   7. in   8. on
2 1. on   2. out of   3. in   4. off   5. into
6. onto   7. out of

Unit 134   p. 97

1 1. up   2. down   3. down   4. from
2 1. up, to   2. toward   3. from   4. down, at
5. toward, to   6. to

Unit 135   p. 99

1 1. in front of   2. behind   3. opposite
4. between   5. close to   6. next to   7. by
8. stroll along   9. across   10. through
11. over   12. across   13. to   14. around
15. past   16. over   17. from, to   18. near
19. arrive at   20. at   21. around   22. across

Unit 136   p. 101

1 1. in/into   2. by   3. on   4. by   5. by   6. in
7. by   8. by, on   9. on
2 1. in   2. on   3. on   4. get on   5. got off

Unit 137   p. 103

1 1. at   2. in   3. in   4. on   5. in   6. in   7. on
8. at   9. on   10. in, in   11. at
12. on（winter solstice〔冬至〕為「日子」，
故用 on ） 13. on
2 1. at the Mid-Autumn Festival
2. at/on Christmas   3. on Halloween
4. on New Year's Eve
5. at Chinese New Year

Unit 138   p. 105

1 1. in   2. on   3. /   4. in   5. in   6. in   7. /
8. /   9. /   10. /   11. in   12. in   13. /   14. /
15. /   16. /（或者 at any time）, /   17. /

Unit 139   p. 107

1 1. for   2. since   3. ago   4. ago   5. for
6. for   7. since   8. ago   9. since   10. since
2 1. I have been playing the piano for fifteen
years.
2. I have studied the history of art since 2005.
3. I started my YouTube channel three years
ago.
4. I will stay in Toronto for six months.
5. I arrived four hours ago.
6. I have been selling fried chicken in the
night market since last year.

Unit 140   p. 109

1 1. during   2. for   3. During   4. during
5. for   6. during   7. while   8. for
2 1. I burned my fingers in the cooking class.
2. I had to go to the bank during my lunch
break.
3. I watched a basketball game while my wife
was taking a shower and getting ready to
go.
4. I ate a lot of ramen and pork chops during
my vacation in Tokyo.
5. I've been busy with the bank merger for
the whole week.

Unit 141   p. 111

1 1. From, to/until   2. until   3. by/before
4. from, to/until   5. before   6. by/before
7. before/after   8. before   9. until   10. after
2 1. by/before   2. before   3. from, to/until
4. until   5. After   6. after

Unit 142   p. 113

1 1. with   2. in   3. with   4. with   5. in   6. by
7. with
2 1. in pen   2. on (a) vacation
3. by Andrew Lloyd Webber
4. with two garage doors
5. with the soap   6. in a gray scarf

Unit 143   p. 115

1 1. like   2. as   3. like   4. as   5. like   6. as if
7. as if   8. as if   9. like
2 1. as   2. as   3. like   4. as   5. as if
6. had happened   7. as though   8. like
9. like   10. as if

Unit 144 p. 117

1 1. Bella will give Trevor the letter.
2. Phil will forward Dave the email.
3. John is going to buy Mindy a coat.
4. Mark bought Rita the teapot.
5. Can you read Grandpa the news?
6. I will show you the ingredients.
7. I am going to build my parents a house.

2 1. Morris is going to bring the paint to/for Gabriel.
2. Gerald is going to pay the money to Kate.
3. Suzanne is going to read a book to her son.
4. Larry will recommend a restaurant to Gail.
5. I'll buy lunch for you.

Unit 145 p. 119

1 1. about   2. at   3. at/by   4. for   5. with
6. at   7. about   8. at   9. for

2 1. amazed by the dolphin show
2. bored with our teacher's long and uninformative speech
3. satisfied with our son's English exam score
4. good at solving a Rubik's cube
5. nervous about having dinner with my girlfriend's parents

Unit 146 p. 121

1 1. from/to   2. in   3. of   4. about   5. of
6. on   7. to   8. of   9. of   10. of
11. of   12. from/to

2 1. yell at people   2. help the elderly
3. try smoking   4. take a shortcut

Unit 147 p. 123

1 1. between   2. for   3. in   4. toward   5. to
6. with   7. in   8. in

2 1. example of   2. causes of   3. demand for
4. decrease in   5. difficulty in

Unit 148 p. 125

1 1. in   2. of   3. to   4. with   5. for
6. between   7. for   8. to

2 1. (B)   2. (C)   3. (A)   4. (A)   5. (D)   6. (C)

Unit 149 p. 127

1 1. of   2. for   3. from   4. on   5. to   6. to
7. about   8. about   9. to, for   10. on   11. to

2 1. warned Marcia about the risk of buying stocks
2. borrowed a food processor from his sister
3. blame her for spoiling the children
4. complained to her husband about his overloading the washing machine
5. congratulate Bernard on winning the award
6. reminds me of my childhood

Unit 150 p. 129

1 1. in time   2. on time   3. on time   4. in time
5. on time   6. in time   7. in the end
8. at the end   9. in the end   10. in the end
11. at the end   12. at the end

2 1. by   2. in   3. for   4. in   5. In

Unit 151 p. 130

1 1. at, on, at, /   2. in   3. in, on   4. in
5. about, on, in   6. at, in, for   7. in, in
8. at, on   9. during, to   10. In   11. on, at
12. at, on, in   13. from   14. in   15. by
16. as, in, for   17. on, under, in   18. at
19. at, at, on   20. with   21. for
22. from/to, to   23. with   24. of
25. about   26. at, in, with
27. between   28. of   29. with, in
30. to, about, from   31. to, on, with   32. with
33. for

Unit 152 p. 133

1 1. Is this a seaside spa?
2. Can I soak in the hot tub in my room?
3. Have they reserved two adjacent rooms for us?
4. Has the hotel been expecting our arrival?
5. Does Connie like spas with not much sulfur in the water?
6. Did Andrew enjoy the Japanese restaurant at the resort?

2 1. I can   2. I am   3. I haven't   4. I have
5. I didn't   6. she is

3 1. Yes, I think so.   2. Yes, I hope so.
3. Yes, I'm afraid so.   4. No, I don't think so.
5. No, I don't expect so.
6. No, I'm afraid not.

Unit 153　　　　　　　　　　p. 135

1 1. are you leaving?　2. will Adrian leave early?
3. can Woody hide?　4. is Bryan coming?
5. does Rex have my hat?
6. has Susan been taking photos?
7. does Mary want to dance?
8. did Herman go to an audition?
2 1. Who does Ken like?　2. Who loves Buddy?
3. What is Randy playing on his smartphone?
4. Who called Lily?
5. What is Bruce cooking?
6. What went wrong?
7. Who is honking at Karla?
8. Who is Jack waving at?

Unit 154　　　　　　　　　　p. 137

1 1. What　2. Who　3. Which　4. What
5. Whose　6. Which　7. What　8. What
9. Which
2 1. Whose shoes　2. Which burger
3. What magazine　4. What kind of tea
5. Whose toys

Unit 155　　　　　　　　　　p. 139

1 1. Where　2. How　3. Why　4. When
5. When　6. How　7. Why　8. When
2 1. How often　2. How many　3. How long
4. How much　5. How early

Unit 156　　　　　　　　　　p. 141

1 1. Didn't you receive it?
2. Aren't you getting cold?
3. Isn't that your umbrella?
4. Aren't you paying attention to me?
5. Don't you like ballet?
6. Haven't you finished eating yet?
7. Haven't we been driving on this road too long?
2 1. Haven't you run　2. Isn't she
3. Won't you go / Aren't you going
4. Don't you love　5. Hasn't he graduated
6. Isn't this restaurant　7. Didn't you call
8. Doesn't she play / Isn't she playing / Didn't she play

Unit 157　　　　　　　　　　p. 143

1 1. are you　2. has she　3. can't she
4. isn't it　5. does he　6. has he
7. don't you　8. could she　9. aren't you
10. can he　11. hasn't she　12. is it
13. could he　14. do you　15. doesn't she
16. didn't he
2 1. can sketch　2. is　3. couldn't speak
4. talked　5. writes　6. aren't asking
7. have translated　8. doesn't cook　9. went
10. doesn't have

Unit 158　　　　　　　　　　p. 145

1 1. aren't I　2. shall we　3. will there
4. aren't I　5. won't you　6. is there　7. is it
8. didn't you
2 1. isn't it?　2. Let's clean　3. will you?
4. shall we?　5. can't you?　6. would you?
7. isn't there?　8. do they?　9. didn't you?
10. Put　11. Nothing

Unit 159　　　　　　　　　　p. 147

1 1. Are you?　2. Can't he?　3. Has she?
4. Is he?　5. Have you?　6. Does he?
7. Did she?　8. Does she?
2 1. (A)　2. (B)　3. (D)　4. (C)

Unit 160　　　　　　　　　　p. 149

1 1. where the water boilers are located?
2. how many liters this water boiler can hold?
3. what other floor lamps you have?
4. where programmable rice cookers are sold?
5. why this rice cooker can't be used to steam food?
6. when the new rice cookers arrived?
7. if/whether this is the only low-suds laundry soap you have in stock?
8. if/whether I can get this washing machine delivered tonight?
9. if/whether he could move to a small tropical island and go on with his writing?

Unit 161　　　　　　　　　　p. 151

1 1. Neither am I.　2. So do I.　3. Neither have I.
4. So am I.　5. Neither do I.　6. So have I.
7. Neither do I.　8. So did I.　9. Neither do I.

2 1. knows   2. is going to join
   3. doesn't agree   4. didn't play
   5. couldn't skydive   6. has done
   7. hasn't finished   8. doesn't like   9. is

Unit 162   p. 153

1 1. dug, (A)   2. has been dug, (P)
   3. set up, (A)   4. has been wired, (P)
   5. has arrived, (A)   6. is being poured, (P)
   7. have been working, (A)
   8. have been told, (P)
   9. was being connected, (P)
   10. are arriving, (A)
2 1. Those coffee beans were ground by the clerk.
   2. The leather shoes were polished by Father.
   3. The house is being painted by Ariel.
   4. The boar must have been found by Paul.
   5. The shop is going to be closed by us.
   6. Ian is being encouraged by the boss.
   7. A supernova has been discovered by the scientists.
   8. A cactus was planted in the garden by Freddie.

Unit 163   p. 155

1 1. The newspaper must be called.
   2. A cameraman and a reporter will be sent by the TV station.
   3. The store owner is going to be interviewed by the reporter.
   4. The store owner may have been involved with the gang in their criminal activity.
   5. The reporter should have been called earlier.
   6. The store owner doesn't like to be videotaped by the cameraman.
2 1. got torn   2. got stung   3. got spent
   4. got lost   5. got hurt   6. got elected
   7. got kidnapped   8. got caught

Unit 164   p. 157

1 1. was sent two ballet tickets by the thankful client
   2. was offered a discount tour package by the sales representative
   3. was shown the model home by the real estate agent
   4. was paid about $1,000,000 by the advertising agency

   5. was taught four nights a week by the instructor
   6. was promised a letter a day by the sailor
   7. was bought for me by Hazel
2 1. by   2. with   3. with   4. by   5. by
   6. with   7. with   8. by

Unit 165   p. 159

1 1. → It is believed that the number of school-age children will drop again this year.
      → The number of school-age children is believed to drop again this year.
   2. → It is widely known that the secret negotiations started last week.
      → The secret negotiations are widely known to have started last week.
   3. → It is thought that the sailors have been rescued.
      → The sailors are thought to have been rescued.
   4. → It is said that the pandemic completely changed how the world works.
      → The pandemic is said to have completely changed how the world works.
2 1. Sitting too long is supposed to be bad for your health.
   2. Watching TV is supposed to be bad for kids.
   3. Drinking two liters of water a day is supposed to be healthy.
   4. Quitting smoking is supposed to be simply a matter of will power.
   5. Doraemon is supposed to be the most popular cat in the world.

Unit 166   p. 161

1 1. have her shoes repaired
   2. have his shoes shined（「擦亮」的三態為 shine, shined, shined，注意不要寫成「發光」：shine, shone, shone）
   3. have your skirt dry cleaned
   4. have that dress altered
   5. had their daughter's baby shoes bronzed
   6. had her dress ripped
   7. had the heel on her left shoe broken
   8. had his briefcase stolen
2 1. Ed is having the grass in his yard cut.
   2. Dennis is having the toilet fixed.
   3. Rick just had three light bulbs replaced.
   4. Wayne will have the sheets changed later.
   5. Eleanor is having a steak fried on the stove.

6. Claudia has had all the shirts ironed.

7. Ashley could have a propane tank switched easily with this device.

Unit 167 p. 163

1 1. I wish I jogged   2. I wish I had left home

3. If only I were watching   4. If only I spoke

5. I wish I had saved   6. I wish we had come

7. If only we had brought

8. If only I had locked

9. If only I had lowered

2 1. I wish she would sing

2. I wish he wouldn't talk

3. If only the kids wouldn't swim

4. If only he would take off

Unit 168 p. 165

1 1. go, will buy   2. goes, will run

3. has, can ride   4. calls, tell her

5. has packed, will load   6. is making, will be

7. turns, will cool   8. calls, will tell

2 1. grow higher   2. doesn't rain

3. keep eating   4. will make pudding

5. go shopping   6. isn't working

Unit 169 p. 167

1 1. if   2. If   3. When   4. When   5. If

6. When   7. If   8. When   9. If

2 1. works, he takes Monday off

2. sees, she knocks on wood three times

3. does not work, we have to walk up to our 12th floor apartment

4. goes, he dresses up in his sharkskin suit

5. does not take, I give him the silent treatment

6. relaxes, she listens to jazz music

Unit 170 p. 169

1 1. were, would give   2. called, would donate

3. were held, would attend

4. would change, inherited

5. would, give, had

2 1. will need   2. won't feel   3. would ask

4. would discuss   5. will be

6. usually take   7. would find

8. job-hunts

Unit 171 p. 171

1 1. had behaved, wouldn't have embarrassed

2. had read, would have known

3. had bought, wouldn't have worried

4. had paid, wouldn't have impounded

5. had accepted, wouldn't have stayed

6. had mailed, wouldn't have paid

2 1. will find   2. will buy   3. would meet

4. would leave   5. would have known

6. would have finished

3 1. wants   2. liked   3. had inquired   4. needs

5. studied   6. had washed   7. goes

Unit 172 p. 173

1 1. Unless   2. As long as   3. Providing that

4. so long as   5. will turn   6. Suppose

7. Unless   8. will give   9. would he do

2 1. Unless you pass the driving test, you can't drive on the road.

2. Unless you read every day, you can't improve your reading comprehension.

3. As long as you apologize sincerely, I will forgive you.

4. He will come to the dinner provided that you don't mention his divorce.

5. Suppose I wrote a recommendation for you, would it help?

Unit 173 p. 175

1 1. It's time we left   2. It's time you fixed

3. It's time he picked up

4. It's time he designed

2 1. her feelings will get hurt

2. you'll get sun burned

3. Swallow the cough medicine

4. Listen to the expert

Unit 174 p. 177

1 1. (D)   2. (R)   3. (R)   4. (D)   5. (R)   6. (D)

7. (D)   8. (R)   9. (R)

2 1. said   2. told   3. told   4. said   5. said

6. said   7. said   8. tell

3 1. tell tales   2. tell a joke   3. tell a fortune

4. tell the time   5. tell the truth   6. tell a lie

Unit 175 p. 179

1 1. Kathy said she was going out to dinner.
2. Abby said she <u>had spoken</u> / <u>spoke</u> to the director.
3. Sam said he <u>had seen</u> / <u>saw</u> a car accident on his way to the store.
4. Scott said he had listened to that song thousands of times.
5. Sarah said she was in a taxi with her mom.
6. Tina said she had finished her homework long before her mom came back home.

2 1. wanted to enjoy the sea breeze
2. everyone has gone to work
3. the pizza had already arrived
4. had bought him the watch

Unit 176 p. 181

1 1. could handle   2. must get / had to get
3. is   4. was   5. should arrive
6. might drop by   7. should go
8. must cook / had to cook   9. is/was
10. would rain   11. was going to punish
12. can speak / could speak

Unit 177 p. 183

1 1. Yesterday Elmore said he would call me today.
2. Hans said I should wash my hands before meals.
3. Ann said she wanted me to go there right away.
4. Bruce said he <u>had bought</u> / <u>bought</u> the watch from a vendor in the night market.
5. Bernie said he was going to have tuna for lunch that day. /
Bernie said he is going to have tuna for lunch today.（轉述時還在今天）
6. Kayla said she would stay there until noon.
7. Charlotte said her brother had gone camping the previous day. /
Charlotte said her brother went camping yesterday.（轉述時還在今天）
8. Amy said she didn't know where Tom had been the previous week. /
Amy said she didn't know where Tom was last week.（轉述時還在這週）
9. Stevie said he would be out of town for a couple of days.
10. Bella said she would come to my place that afternoon, but she never showed up.

Unit 178 p. 185

1 1. if he/she liked ballet.
2. how he/she got enough protein and calcium.
3. what type of music he/she played.
4. how many cows he/she had.
5. if/whether he/she had ever felt nervous when flying.
6. if he/she had an affordable health insurance plan.

2 1. Pete asked his boss Annie if/whether she would like to see the file.
2. Annie asked Pete what kind of file it was.
3. Pete asked <u>where he should put the file</u> / <u>where to put the file</u>.
4. Pete asked Annie if/whether he could get a pay raise.
5. Annie asked Pete why she should give him a pay raise.
6. Pete asked if/whether he wasn't working hard enough.
7. Annie asked Pete if/whether he wanted a pay raise or a nicer office.

Unit 179 p. 187

1 1. Dan offered to do the dishes.
2. Mom ordered me to get my feet off the coffee table.
3. My neighbor warned me to stay away from that dog.
4. Tom asked/invited me to go to a karaoke with them.
5. My husband offered to help me move the sofa.
6. The painter promised to be careful up on the ladder.

2 1. I told him (that) I wanted a new job.
2. He asked me if/whether I was a chef.
3. He told me (that) he had a job opening.
4. He warned me not to touch the mushrooms.
5. He told me (that) he <u>had been</u> / <u>was</u> in the south digging truffles.
6. He said (that) maybe I could cook truffles for him.
7. I said (that) I had never cooked truffles before.
8. He told me (that) I should never overcook truffles.
9. I promised not to overcook the truffles.
10. He asked me if/whether I could start working there on Monday.

Unit 180   p. 189

1 1. (N)   2. (N)   3. (R)   4. (N)   5. (R)   6. (N)

2 1. (A)   2. (C)   3. (E)   4. (B)   5. (G)   6. (D)
    7. (F)

Unit 181   p. 191

1 1. I called the woman who/that had left a message on my answering machine.

   2. Did you see the woman who/that was sitting by me on the bus?

   3. The guy who/that talked to me while I was having my iced tea was cool.

   4. Have you seen the water bottle which/that was by the door?

   5. I tripped over the slippers which/that were in the hallway.

   6. The hat which/that is now on the floor was on the coat tree when I left home this morning.

2 1. Did you see the blue backpack ~~who~~ which/that I bought yesterday?

   2. Could you please pass me the pepper ~~who~~ which/that is on the counter?

   3. I called the history teacher who I met ~~him~~ at the party last night.

   4. I went to the new restaurant which ~~it~~ opened last Sunday.

   5. I didn't recognize the tall woman ~~which~~ who/that talked to me at the bank yesterday.

   6. Jack said the woman, ~~that~~ who he had dinner with last night, was his ex-wife.

Unit 182   p. 193

1 1. who   2. (who)   3. (that)   4. that   5. (who)
    6. who

2 1. Guam is the island we went to for our honeymoon.

   2. Sophia is the student I mentioned yesterday.

   3. The roast duck was the dish Patricia recommended in this restaurant.

   4. This is the house Janet sold in two days.

Unit 183   p. 195

1 1. (why/that)   2. whose   3. where   4. where
    5. (when)   6. where   7. (why/that)
    8. whose

2 1. I remember the day when we first met.

   2. Bangkok is the city where we go for a shopping trip every year.

   3. I know a guy whose father owns a company with two thousand employees.

   4. I don't know the reason why/that he hasn't spoken to me for a week.

   5. I need the address where I can send this parcel.

   6. The rain came at a time when the peasants needed it most.

Unit 184   p. 197

1 1. whose   2. who   3. where   4. when
    5. where   6. where   7. who

2 1. which lies in the South America

   2. who is sitting here reading a newspaper

   3. where the Emperor Penguins live

   4. whose car has a flat tire

Unit 185   p. 199

1 1. in which   2. with whom   3. in which
    4. in which   5. about whom

2 1. with which, This is Mia's favorite toy, which she can play with for hours.

   2. about whom, That woman is our new manager, who/whom I've heard a lot about.

   3. in which, This is Lulu's favorite pool, which she often swims for a long time in.

   4. for whom, That pretty woman is my wife, who/whom I make a cup of rooibos tea for every day.

15

Part 12 Modal Verbs (1) 情態動詞（1）

Unit 90

Modal Verbs: General Use (1)
情態動詞的一般用法（I）

1 情態動詞又稱為情態助動詞，通常與一般動詞搭配，表示「**可能性、意願、能力、義務、確定性、許可**」等意義。

- can
- could
- may
- might

- will
- would
- shall
- should

- ought to
- must
- need
- dare

可能性 The bus might be late.
　　　公車可能會遲到。

請求 Will you lower your voice?
　　　請你小聲一點好嗎？

能力 Can your brother draw?
　　　你弟弟會畫畫嗎？

義務 You must get up at 6 a.m.
　　　你得在早上 6 點起床。

建議 You have an oil leak from your car engine. You should fix the leak.
　　　你的車引擎漏油，應該要把漏洞修好。

請求許可 May I have some chicken nuggets?
　　　我可以吃一些雞塊嗎？

2 情態動詞的格式固定，**沒有變化形**，即使主詞為第三人稱單數也**不加 s**，沒有不定詞、分詞變化和時態變化。

✗ He mights vacation in Prague.
✓ He might vacation in Prague.
他可能去布拉格度假。

3 因為情態動詞只有一種格式，如果要描述特定情況，要用**同義詞彙或片語**代替。

✗ The sun can to produce radiation storms.
✓ The sun is able to produce radiation storms.
太陽會產生輻射風暴。

✗ Carlos may to enter the building.
✓ Carlos is allowed to enter the building.
卡洛斯獲准進入大樓。

✗ Thomas must to go on a business trip last week.
✓ Thomas had to go on a business trip last week.
湯瑪士上星期得出差。

4 所有的情態動詞後面都接「**不加 to 的不定詞**」，唯一的例外是 ought 固定用 ought to。

Nina should exercise.
= Nina ought to exercise.
妮娜應該運動。

Ducks can dive.
鴨子會潛水。

1

請勾選正確的答案。

1. Ruby would like to ☐ **be able to play** ☐ **can play** tennis.

2. Betty ☐ **had to leave** ☐ **must leave** the office early yesterday.

3. Margaret ☐ **must** ☐ **can** work late today. She doesn't have a dinner date.

4. Nicolas ☐ **will** ☐ **wills** be in San Francisco this time next year.

5. You ☐ **ought to** ☐ **should to** ride on the bikeway.

6. You ☐ **oughtn't** ☐ **shouldn't** allow your children to play on the main road.

7. ☐ **Could** ☐ **Must** you step aside please?

8. I ☐ **must to** ☐ **have to** go home to feed my dog now.

9. Adam ☐ **can do** ☐ **cans do** 25 laps around the track.

2

請以括弧內提供的「情態動詞」改寫句子。

1. He drank ten bowls of miso soup. (could)

   → *He could drink ten bowls of miso soup.*

2. Jeffery explains everything. (will)

   → ....

3. Dad quits smoking and drinking. (must)

   → ....

4. Alison files the documents. (should)

   → ....

5. We get lost without a GPS system. (might)

   → ....

6. You take off your dirty shoes and socks. (ought to)

   → ....

7. Denise speaks five languages. (can)

   → ....

Unit **91**

Modal Verbs: General Use (2)
情態動詞的一般用法（2）

YOU SHOULD KNOW!

1 肯定句中的情態動詞，應放在**主詞**和**動詞**之間。

| 主詞 | + | 情態動詞 | + | 一般動詞 |

My mom <u>will</u> **clean** the house.
我媽媽會打掃房子。

Little Johnny <u>should</u> **call** his grandfather.
小強尼應該打電話給他爺爺。

2 **否定句**的構成，是在**情態動詞**後面加 not。

| 主詞 | + | 情態動詞 | + | not | + | 一般動詞 |

I <u>can't</u> **find** my glasses.
我找不到我的眼鏡。

Penelope <u>could not</u> **find** her ballet slippers. 潘妮洛普找不到她的芭蕾舞鞋。

3 **疑問句**的構成，是在句首加上情態動詞。

| 情態動詞 | + | 主詞 | + | 一般動詞 |

肯定句 I <u>may</u> **go** for a walk.
我可以去散步。

疑問句 Mom, <u>may</u> I **go** for a walk?
媽，我可以去散步嗎？

4 不管是**否定句**或**疑問句**，情態動詞都不會和**助動詞 do/does/did** 連用。

✗ Sheila doesn't can come to the phone.

✓ Sheila can't come to the phone.
席拉無法過來接電話。

✗ Does Sheila can call me?

✓ Can Sheila call me?
席拉會打電話給我嗎？

肯定句	否定句	否定縮寫	疑問句
can	cannot	can't	Can I
could	could not	couldn't	Could I
should	should not	shouldn't	Should I
may	may not	-	May I
might	might not	mightn't*	Might I
will	will not	won't	Will I
shall	shall not	shan't*	Shall I
ought to	ought not to	↳ * 不常見 -	-
must	must not	mustn't	Must I
need	need not	needn't	Need I
dare	dare not	-	Dare I

5 情態動詞可以和 be 動詞連用。

| 情態動詞 | + | be | + | 現在分詞 |

The baby <u>must be</u> **sleeping**.
小嬰兒一定是在睡覺。

Edgar <u>might be</u> **coming** here tomorrow night. 艾德加明晚可能會來這裡。

6 情態動詞可以用於「情態動詞 + have + 過去分詞」的句型，表示「**過去可能發生或沒有發生的事件**」。

| 情態動詞 | + | have | + | 過去分詞 |

Joe hasn't arrived. He may have gotten stuck in traffic. ↳ 他可能遇上塞車，不過無法確定。
喬還沒到，他可能被塞在車陣裡了。

The service at this restaurant is so slow. They should have hired more kitchen staff. ↳ 他們沒有僱用足夠的廚師和助手。
這間餐廳的服務太慢了，他們當初該多請一些廚房人手的。

Practice

1

請勾選正確的答案。

1. We □ should go □ go should to the hot pot restaurant now.

2. □ Megan can run □ Can Megan run in the marathon?

3. Andrew really □ must go □ must be go now or he will miss the bus.

4. Carl □ may have left □ have may left home already.

5. Doug □ should not □ not should tell lies.

6. Oscar □ will not win □ will win not the game.

7. □ Do I shall □ Shall I make you a cup of tea?

8. You □ should not □ should don't have spicy food so frequently.

9. □ Could you have thrown □ Could have you thrown the memo away by accident?

2

請依圖示，從框內選出適當的動詞片語，搭配題目提供的主詞和「情態動詞」，以正確的形式填空，完成句子。

observe the lunar eclipse	play the accordion
ride his snowboard all day	have fallen off his horse
be feeding pigeons in the park	

....
.... (Karl / can)

....
.... (Audrey / will)

....
.... (Elwood / may)

....
.... (Julio / can / ?)

....
.... (Jasper / must)

Unit 92

Ability: Can, Be Able To

表示「能力」：Can、Be Able To

- 表能力
- 否定形：
  cannot /
  can't

- 可取代 can，較
  正式，較不常用
- 可代替 can，
  用於過去式

can　　　　**be able to**

1 can 可用來說明「能力」，否定形式
為 cannot 或 can't。

I can do 200 sit-ups.

我能做兩百下仰臥起坐。

How many push-ups
can you do?

你能做多少下伏地挺身？

Can you do any
bench presses?

你會做臥舉嗎？

I can't do any
running today
because my knee
hurts.

我膝蓋有傷，今天不
能跑步。

3 由於 **can** 沒有不定詞、V-ing 和過去
分詞等形態，因此遇到這些情況時，
要以 be able to 等同義用語取代，來
表示「能力」。

Marcy would like to be able to enroll her
daughter at Bunny Bear Kindergarten.
↳ 不能說 Marcy would like to can enroll . . .
瑪西希望她女兒能進入小熊幼稚園就讀。

Marcy's daughter, Elizabeth, enjoys
being able to play with blocks.
↳ 不能說 . . . enjoys canning to play . . .
瑪西的女兒伊莉莎白，很開心能夠玩積木。

Elizabeth has been able to play well with
other children since she was three years
old.
↳ 不能說 Elizabeth has could play . . .
伊莉莎白從三歲起，就能和其他小朋友一起
玩得很開心。

2 is/are able to 可以取代 can，表示「能
力」，但是較為正式，也比較不常用。

Are you able to handle your job stress?
= Can you handle your job stress?
你能夠排解自己的工作壓力嗎？

Practice

1 請用 can 或 be able to 填空，完成句子。

1. _____ you meet me at the hotel?

2. Will I _____ surf the Internet in my hotel room?

3. I would like to _____ run in a marathon.

4. If Anna _____ juggle flaming torches, she can have her own circus act.

5. I want to _____ pilot a plane one day.

6. Will you _____ to get there on time?

7. Neal _____ sing well.

8. Anita must _____ read people's minds.

2 請依圖示，從框內選出適當的動詞或動詞片語，搭配 can 或 can't 填空，完成句子。

skate

do bike tricks

swim

maintain her balance

paint with watercolors

Donny _____
_____ .

Howard _____
_____ .

Karla _____
_____ .

Paul _____
_____ .

Ian _____
_____ .

Ability: Could, Be Able To
表示「能力」：Could、Be Able To

1 could 可以用來說明「**過去具備的能力**」，這種意義之下，可以視為 **can** 的過去式。否定形式為 could not 或 couldn't。

Mozart could read music at the age of 4.

莫札特四歲時就會看譜。

Beethoven could hear his symphonies in his head.

貝多芬能在腦海裡聽見自己創作的交響樂。

2 was/were able to 可以取代 **could**，表示「**過去具備的能力**」，或「**在某種條件下可能做到的事**」。

Bach was able to compose one cantata a week for years. 有好幾年的時間，巴哈能一星期作出一首聖樂。

3 could not 和 couldn't 常用來描述「**過去不具備的能力**」，或者「**在某種條件下所不具備的能力**」。

My uncle couldn't drive, but he owned a car.

以前，我叔叔不會開車，卻擁有一輛汽車。

My uncle could not even see a car on the street in front of his house without wearing his glasses. 叔叔要是沒戴眼鏡，連住家前面馬路上的車子都看不到。

4 上述 2 的情況，若「**該行為較為困難**」，也常用 managed to 或 succeeded in，而不用 **was/were able to**。

The coach told me to stay at home, but I managed to hobble over to the field and watch the game.

教練叫我待在家裡，但是我跛著腳走到球場去看比賽。

Despite the fact that the team lost two crucial games during the regular season, they succeeded in getting into the playoffs.

雖然球隊在賽季輸了兩場重要的比賽，他們還是成功擠進了季後賽。

5 感官動詞和表達「**思想**」的動詞經常與 could 連用，說明「**過去的情況**」。

I could smell the muffins baking.

我聞到烤瑪芬的味道。

I could hear the bacon sizzling. 我能聽到煎培根滋滋作響的聲音。

I could feel Nancy pull my arm as we walked past the restaurant. 我們路過餐廳時，我能感覺到南西拉了一下我的手。

- see
- smell
- taste
- feel
- understand
- remember

6 「could have + 過去分詞」的句型用來說明某人「**在過去具備做某事的能力，但卻沒有去做**」。

Sam could have played professional baseball, but he preferred a career in business. 山姆本來可以去打職業棒球，不過他比較喜歡做生意。

The contender could have beaten the champion, but he took a nasty fall and never recovered.

那名挑戰者本來可以擊敗拳王的，不過後來一個擊倒，他就出局了。

Practice

1

請從框內選出適當的用語填空，完成句子。

could

could have

was able to

were able to

being able to

1. I _____ hear someone speaking German.

2. Even though the train was delayed, I _____ arrive on time.

3. The company _____ gone bankrupt, but it was saved by the government.

4. The boat _____ capsized, but it managed to stay afloat.

5. I love _____ backpack in New Zealand.

6. I _____ understand why he had turned down so many good offers at that time.

7. When I embraced my wife, I _____ feel her shivering from the cold weather.

2

請用括弧內提供的詞語改寫句子。

1. I saw the sunrise over the ocean from my hotel window. (could)

   → _____

   _____

2. I didn't read English newspapers before I was twelve. (couldn't)

   → _____

   _____

3. I didn't get out of the bed by myself. My mom helped me. (be able to)

   → _____

   _____

4. I walked to the bathroom while holding the IV bottle above my head. (manage to)

   → _____

   _____

5. I remember those crazy summers when we were hanging out together at the beach all the time. (could)

   → _____

   _____

Unit **94**

Permission: Can, Could, May
表示「許可」：Can、Could、May

1 can、could 和 may 都可用於「請求許可」。

can 是簡便的非正式用法，could 較 can 有禮貌，may 又比 can 和 could 更正式有禮。

正式與禮貌性 高		低
may	**could**	**can**

Can I use your bathroom?

我可以用你的廁所嗎？

Could I take an hour off?

我可以請假一小時嗎？

May I leave early today?

請問我今天可以早點離開嗎？

> might 也可以用來「請求許可」，但 might 是非常正式的用法，非常少用。
>
> Might I be excused from the ceremony?
>
> 可以容許我離開典禮嗎？

2 若要表示「許可」對方做某事，只能用 can 或 may，不能用 **could** 或 **might**。

You can use this pass anywhere in the building.

你可以持這張許可證在大樓裡通行無阻。

You may call me at home if you like.

如果你願意，可以打電話到家裡給我。

3 法律或規定上表明「不許可」的事，要用 can/cannot 或 be (not) allowed to。

You can't stay in the room after 11 a.m.

上午 11 點之後，您就不能再待在房間。

You are not allowed to leave your suitcases unattended at any time.

不論什麼時候，你都不能把行李放在這裡沒人看管。

4 如果是「過去事件」，則使用 could 和 was/were allowed to 在意義上有所差異。

1 could 用於「過去一般事件」的許可；

2 was/were allowed to 用於「過去特殊事件」下的許可。

Before they put up the fence, we could take a shortcut across their property.

在他們築起圍籬之前，我們還可以抄小路穿過他們的土地。

This morning we were allowed to look for our lost baseball in Mr. Hudson's backyard.

今天早上，我們獲准到哈德森先生家的後院，去找我們不見的棒球。

Police officer: Could I please see your ID?
Ted: Here it is, sir. 用疑問句「請求許可」則可用 could。

警員：我可以看一下你的身分證嗎？
泰德：可以。

Customs officer: May/Might I see your travel documents?
Betty: Here they are, sir. 用疑問句「請求許可」，可用 may 也可用 might。

海關官員：請出示您的旅遊文件好嗎？
貝蒂：好的。

Practice

1

請勾選正確的答案。

1. □ Can □ Be allowed to I join your club?

2. When I was in senior high school, I □ was allowed to □ may stay out late on the weekends.

3. □ May □ Can I offer you my arm for this stroll in the park?

4. She □ can □ was allowed to go camping when she was 14.

5. You □ can't □ couldn't hang your clothes outside on the clothes line because there isn't any room left.

6. You □ may □ might eat one dessert at the end of your dinner.

2

請從框內選出適當的用語填空，完成對話。

can

can't

could

couldn't

may

may not

might

are (not) allowed

was (not) able

1. Ⓐ Can I borrow some of these periodicals from the library?

   Ⓑ No, you _____ take these periodicals out of the library. You _____ read them in the library.

2. Ⓐ Can I write notes in the library books?

   Ⓑ No, you _____. You must not deface library property.

3. Ⓐ Could I please have another cup of chocolate milk?

   Ⓑ No, you _____. We have to save some for Peggy.

4. Ⓐ May I take your plate, sir?

   Ⓑ Yes, you _____. I'm finished.

5. Ⓐ Could I use your cell phone to call my mom?

   Ⓑ Of course you _____. Here you are.

6. Ⓐ Might I announce his resignation at the press conference?

   Ⓑ No, you _____. The terms of his dismissal remain to be worked out.

7. Ⓐ Can I carry this suitcase on board?

   Ⓑ No, you _____. This one is too big to put in the overhead compartment. You _____ to carry a smaller one.

8. Ⓐ Did you go to the book fair yesterday?

   Ⓑ No, I didn't. I _____ to attend the fair because it was only open to publishers on the first day.

Obligation and Necessity: Must, Have To
表示「**義務與必要**」：**Must**、**Have To**

have to 並不是情態動詞，它只是與 **must** 的意義相同。

---

1 must 與 have to 都用來說明「**個人的義務和必須做的事**」。

義務 I must **call my mom before 10 p.m. because I said I would.**
↳ 說話者說明自己的義務。

我晚上 10 點以前得打電話給我媽，因為我跟她說了我會打給她。

必要 I have to **call before 10 p.m. because the pizza shop closes then.**
↳ 特定事實所形成之必要性。

我得在晚上 10 點以前打電話，因為披薩店 10 點就會打烊了。

必要 You must **put down money before you can make an offer.**
↳ 地產專員對買家說明購屋的程序。

你在正式出價前，必須先支付訂金。

必要 We have to **put down money before we can make an offer.**
↳ 說明購屋的程序。

我們在正式出價前，必須先支付訂金。

---

2 must 只能用來說明「**現在或未來的義務**」，它本身沒有過去式。

如果要表達「**過去的義務或必要**」，則要用 had to。

現在的義務 **To get there on time, I must leave right now.**

我現在就得出發，才能準時到達。

未來的義務 **I must leave in about twenty minutes or I will be late.**

我 20 分鐘內得出發，不然會遲到。

過去的義務 **Last night I felt sick and** had to **leave the party before it was over.**

昨晚我覺得不舒服，不得不在派對結束前就離開。

---

3 由於 must 沒有不定詞、V-ing 和分詞形式，因此在要使用這類動詞形式時，要以**其他同義用語取代**，例如 have to。

✕ **Did** you must **leave the party and go to the after-hours club?**

✓ **Did** you have to **leave the party and go to the after-hours club?**

你一定要提早離開派對趕去通宵俱樂部嗎？

✕ **She hates** musting **go home early.**

✓ **She hates** having to **go home early.**

她討厭得早點回家。

✕ **She hates** musting **go home early.**

✓ **She hates** having to **go home early.**

她討厭得早點回家。

✕ **She** musted **check out every club in town.**

✓ **She** had to **check out every club in town.**

她得到城裡的每一間俱樂部都看看。

---

4 have to 不是情態動詞，是一般動詞，因此它的**疑問句**和**否定句**是用 do/does/did 來構成。

When do **you** have to **finish the report?**

你得在哪一天完成報告？

Roger doesn't have to **work so hard on that report.**

羅傑不需要太努力做那份報告。

Did you have to **give your boss a draft of the report yesterday?**

昨天你得先交一份報告的初稿給老闆嗎？

Practice

1 請用 must 或 have to 的正確形式填空，完成句子。

1. You _____ use a pencil when filling in the answers on a machine-readable answer sheet.

2. You _____ deliver the samples now as per the contract.

3. Did you _____ stay in the office because of your meeting with your clients?

4. She's mad at _____ do the same thing every day.

5. I _____ read two hundred pages last night for today's class discussion.

6. _____ I drink this cough syrup?

7. Do I _____ wash the dishes right now?

2 請從框內選出適當的動詞，搭配 must 填空，完成對話。

Two friends, Charlotte and Jane, are visiting the consulate to prepare for their trip. Charlotte talks to an immigration officer.

have

take

show

Officer: You ❶ _____ a visa to enter the country.

Charlotte: I'm just staying for five days.

Officer: Even a tourist needs a visa. You ❷ _____ your passport and go to window 12.

Charlotte: What else do I need to do?

Officer: You ❸ _____ proof that you have had the appropriate vaccinations and paid the visa application fee.

3 請從框內選出適當的動詞，搭配 have to 填空，完成對話。

Charlotte explains to Jane what she just learned from the visa officer.

apply

take

process

Jane: What did the immigration officer say?

Charlotte: He said we ❶ _____ for tourist visas.

Jane: How does that work?

Charlotte: He said we ❷ _____ our documents to window 12.

Jane: Can we do that now?

Charlotte: He said we ❸ _____ our paperwork at least ten days before the trip.

Unit **96**

Obligation and Necessity: Have To, Have Got To
表示「義務與必要」：Have To、Have Got To

1 have to 和 have got to 都可以用來說明「義務或必要」，其中 have got to 是非正式英式英語的用法。

非正式美式 Do you have to call tonight?
你今晚得打電話嗎？

非正式英式 Have you got to call tonight?
你今晚得打電話嗎？

非正式美式 I have to talk to Tommy now.
我現在得和湯米談一談。

非正式英式 I have got to talk to Tommy now.
我現在得和湯米談一談。

2 have got to 只能用於「單一事件」。如果這種義務或必要是「重複在發生的事件」，就要用 have to，不能用 **have got to**。

這種情況下經常搭配頻率副詞如 always 或 often 來強調次數。

Does Cathy often have to rush to get to her office?
凱西經常得趕著去上班嗎？

Cathy always has to hurry to get to work on time.
凱西總是得趕著準時上班。

英式 Has Cathy got to rush to get to her office today?
凱西今天要趕到辦公室嗎？

英式 Cathy has got to hurry to get to work on time today.
凱西今天得趕著準時上班。

3 have got to 只用於**現在式**，沒有過去式。如果要說明「**過去的義務或事件**」，要用 had to，不能用 had got to。

✗ Calvin had got to work in his office last Saturday afternoon.
✓ Calvin had to work in his office last Saturday afternoon.
上個星期六下午，凱文得進辦公室上班。

✗ Jack had got to pay a $100 ticket for parking illegally.
✓ Jack had to pay a $100 ticket for parking illegally.
傑克必須繳交一百元違規停車的罰款。

4 have to 有未來式 will have to，用來表示「**未來的義務或必要**」。

muffins

I will have to make twenty muffins for the party on Saturday.
我得為星期六的派對做二十個瑪芬。

You will have to find a job after you graduate. 你畢業之後，得找一份工作。
He will have to drive fifty minutes to his girlfriend's house.
他得開五十分鐘的車，才能到女友的住處。

Practice

1

請從框內選出適當的動詞，搭配 have got to 填空，完成對話。

Charlotte and Jane rush to the immigration window.

hurry

eat

give

Charlotte: The office closes soon. We ❶_____.

Jane: I'm hungry. I ❷_____ something.
We missed lunch.

Charlotte: We don't have time. We ❸_____ our
documents to the clerk at window 12 now.

Jane: OK. Let's go. We can eat later.

2

請勾選正確的答案。

1. You always □ have to □ have got to sort your recyclable garbage.

2. I □ had to □ have got to pack these gift boxes right now. The
courier will be here in any minute.

3. Sonia □ had to □ had got to cook dinner for her parents, so she
didn't join us for the dinner party.

4. □ Do you always have to □ Have you always got to say such negative
things about my parents?

5. I □ had to □ will have to fly to New York for a seminar on
international finance next month.

6. □ Does Nancy have to □ Has Nancy often got to wash her dog in the
bathroom instead of outside in the backyard?

7. I □ will have to □ have got to see the manager now. It's an
emergency.

8. □ Would you have to □ Will you have to edit her book after she
finishes writing it?

9. I □ had got to □ had to call a locksmith because I locked myself out
when I took the garbage out.

Unit **97**

Obligation and Choices: Mustn't, Don't Have To, Haven't Got To, Don't Need To, Needn't, Didn't Need To

表示「義務與選擇」：Mustn't、Don't Have To、Haven't Got To、Don't Need To、Needn't、Didn't Need To

1 mustn't 和 don't have to 的意義不同，差別在於一是**義務**、一是**選擇**。

mustn't 表示「**有義務不做某事**」；
don't have to 表示「**選擇不做某事**」。

You mustn't touch the freshly painted walls. 你不可以去碰剛漆好的牆壁。

You don't have to help me paint the house if you don't want to.

如果你不想，你可以不必幫我油漆房子。

2 除了 don't have to，haven't got to、don't need to 和 needn't 都是表示「**可以選擇不做某事**」。

haven't got to 是**英式非正式用語**。

You don't need to be here next weekend.
你下週末不用過來。

You don't have to come with us.
你不必和我們一起來。

You needn't skip your meeting to join us.
你不必為了陪我們而不去參加會議。

3 「**允許別人可以不用做某事**」時，用 needn't 是最禮貌的說法，不過目前已經少有人用 needn't，也被視為過時的說法。

You needn't trouble yourself over this trifle. 你不必為這件芝麻小事操心。

4 didn't need to 也是表示「**沒有必要做某事**」，但這種用法並沒有明確指出「事情是否已經做了」，除非句子裡有另外說明。

I didn't need to clean the guest room.
↳ 沒有必要打掃，但卻沒說到底做了沒。
我那時其實不必打掃客房的。

I didn't need to change the towels and sheets, but I did.
↳ 沒必要換，但後面的句子說明了「事情已經做了」。
我那時沒必要換毛巾和床單，可是我換了。

如果 didn't need to 的句子裡，沒有明確指出事情到底做了沒，那麼「**沒有做**」的可能性是比較高的。

I didn't need to cook extra food because we weren't sure if my husband's parents were coming for dinner.
↳ 我們不確定他們會不會來，所以我沒多準備食物。
我應該不用多準備食物，因為那時我們不確定我公婆會不會來吃晚餐。

5 美式英語 didn't need to 可以與 **needn't have done something** 意思一樣，表示某人已經做了一件沒必要做的事；口語中，可以藉由加重 need 的音調來表示這個意思。

You didn't need to prepare all that extra food. I said my parents would call if they were coming to dinner.

你實在沒有必要多準備那些食物，我已經說過如果我爸媽要來，他們會先打電話。

6 但如果用「needn't have + 過去分詞」，則表示「**雖然某件事沒必要，但卻已經做了**」，這個用語稍微過時，但仍有人在用。

I needn't have avoided the office since my co-workers did not have any work for me.
↳ 我那時沒必要刻意遠離辦公室，但是我卻做了。
我根本沒必要刻意躲開辦公室，同事又不會派給我任務。

Practice

1

請勾選正確的答案。

1. You ☐ **mustn't** ☐ **don't have to** cross the yellow line on the train platform.

2. I ☐ **mustn't** ☐ **don't have to** pick up my daughter after her archery class.

3. The nurse says they ☐ **mustn't** ☐ **haven't** got any physical therapy appointments this afternoon.

4. You ☐ **mustn't** ☐ **needn't** work this weekend if your project is already done.

5. Janet ☐ **mustn't** ☐ **don't have to** drink any alcohol because of her medication.

6. The committee finished selecting textbooks so they ☐ **mustn't** ☐ **didn't have to** schedule another meeting.

7. The sign says, "No Littering," so we ☐ **have to** ☐ **don't have to** throw our trash in the garbage can.

8. Today is Monday. The sign says, "Visitors Free on Mondays," so we ☐ **have to** ☐ **don't have to** pay.

9. I'm the teacher, and if I say you ☐ **mustn't** ☐ **don't have to** turn in the assignment this week, then you can give it to me next week.

10. The boss says you ☐ **must** ☐ **have to** stop surfing the internet and get to work.

11. The boss's wife says you ☐ **mustn't** ☐ **don't have to** listen to the boss.

2

請以「didn't need to」或「needn't have + 過去分詞」的句型填空，完成句子。

1. I _____ (bring) my passport with me when I went to exchange some money so I kept it locked up.

2. Rudy _____ (go back) to get his keys because his mom was at home the whole time.

3. We _____ (buy) extra water and food. The typhoon turned and went far to the south of us.

4. You _____ (call) the landlady about the power. She left a message on my cell phone that said the whole block had lost electricity.

5. You _____ (get up) so early. Today is a holiday. Go back to bed.

6. Last night Sheila _____ (work) late on her part of the project. She's almost done with it and will finish it in the morning.

Unit **98**

Obligation and Advice:
Should, Ought To, Shall

表示「**義務與建議**」：
Should、Ought To、Shall

1 should 和 ought to 都用來「**說明義務**」或「**提供意見**」。但 should 後面接「**不加 to 的不定詞**」，ought 後面則一定要加 to。

Fred should pick up the crayons on the carpet.

= Fred ought to pick up the crayons on the carpet.

佛瑞德應該把地毯上的蠟筆撿起來。

✗ You should to do your homework now.

✓ You should do your homework now.

你現在應該做家庭作業了。

✗ You ought do your homework now.

✓ You ought to do your homework now.

你現在應該做家庭作業了。

You should stop jumping on the couch.

你不應該在沙發上跳來跳去。

Mom says you ought to stop jumping on the couch now or you'll get into trouble.

媽媽說你應該馬上停下來在沙發上跳來跳去，不然你就要倒大楣了。

2 「should have + 過去分詞」用來表示「**過去該做而未做的事**」。這種情況下也可用「ought to have + 過去分詞」。

I should have called her. Now she's even madder at me. ↳ 我沒打電話，這是個錯誤。

我應該打電話給她的，現在她氣我氣得更厲害了。

I ought to have gone to see her. Now she won't even speak to me.
↳ 我沒去找她，這實在是個天大的錯誤。

我應該去找她的，現在她甚至連話都不跟我說了。

3 「shouldn't have + 過去分詞」則用來表示「**過去不該做卻做了的事**」。

You shouldn't have hit your sister on the head. She has been crying for twenty minutes because of you.
↳ 你不該打，但你打了。

你不該打妹妹的頭，她被你一打已經哭了二十分鐘了。

You shouldn't have embellished your résumé. Now your application has been rejected.
↳ 你不該過度美化，但你美化了。

你不該過度美化你的履歷的，現在你的應徵被駁回了。

4 shall 通常只搭配**第一人稱代名詞**來「**徵求對方的建議**」，一般對話比較少用。

What shall I do? 我該怎麼做？

Shall we go? 我們要去嗎？

Practice

1 請依括弧提示，用 should、shall 或 ought to 回應問句，來給予建議、說明義務或詢問意見。

1. Do you think it is a good idea for me to go to the auction? (should)

→ *I think you should go to the auction.*

2. Do you think it is a good idea for me to bid on the small statue? (ought to)

→ _____

3. Do you think it is a good idea for me to offer $2,000 for the statue? (should)

→ _____

4. Do you think it is a good idea for me to use an online auction company? (ought to)

→ _____

5. You can give the statue to your mother. (shall / ?)

→ _____

2 請用 should have 或 shouldn't have 搭配過去分詞的句型，回應句子。

1. I didn't bring in the laundry before it started to rain. Now it's all wet.

→ *You should have brought in the laundry before it started to rain.*

2. I didn't simmer the sauce for five more minutes. Now it doesn't taste right.

→ _____

_____

3. Angus poured too much soy sauce on the fried noodles. Now they are too salty.

→ _____

_____

4. I've thrown away the receipt. Now I want to return the electric steamer.

→ _____

_____

3 請將括弧內的動詞以「ought to have + 過去分詞」的句型填空，完成句子。

1. I _____ (tell) the truth. Now the wrong man has been punished by mistake.

2. You _____ (know) that she was depressed. Now she has left home and we don't know where to find her.

Unit **99**

Obligation and Advice:
Had Better, Be Supposed To
表示「義務與建議」：
Had Better、Be Supposed To

1 「had better + 不加 to 的不定詞」這個句型，常用來表達「**強烈的建議**」，口氣比 should 或 ought to 還重。had better 經常縮寫為'd better。

Connie <u>had better</u> **tell** her mother she got divorced.
康妮最好跟她媽媽說她已經離婚了。

You <u>had better</u> **be** careful what you tell the boss about me. 你跟老闆談到我的時候，說話最好小心一點。

You<u>'d better</u> **put** your wet umbrella in a plastic bag before you go into the store.
你最好把濕答答的雨傘放進塑膠套裡，再進到店裡。

2 had better 不是**過去式**的用法，它說明的是「**現在或未來的情況**」。沒有 have better 這種用法。

I hear your phone ringing. You had better **answer** it.
我聽到你的電話在響，你應該去接電話。

Tax time is almost over. You had better **finish** your tax return soon.
報稅時間快要截止了，你最好趕緊完成報稅。

3 had better 的**否定形式**為 had better not，表示「**強烈建議不要做某事**」。

You had better not **borrow** Mom's scooter. 你最好別跟媽媽借摩托車。
You had better not **arrive** late.
你最好別遲到。

4 「**預期他人應該要做某事**」時，常用 be supposed to 這個句型。小至每個月理髮，大如當兵等重要事項，都可以用這個說法，是說明「**義務**」很基本的用語。

According to the terms of the contract, our company is supposed to **provide** engineering support for two years.
根據合約內容，我們公司應該要提供兩年的工程支援。

Mark is supposed to **pick** you up from work today.
馬克今天應該要去接你下班。

5 說明「**限制或禁止做某事**」時，可用 be not supposed to。

You're not supposed to **be** in your sister's room. 你不應該進你姐姐房間。
We're not supposed to **go** out without telling Mom. 我們不應該沒告訴媽媽就出門。

6 如果使用 was/were supposed to，則表示「**該發生卻沒有發生的事**」。

The vendor was supposed to **deliver** the prototype today, but it's not finished.
賣家今天原本要把樣本送來給我，但是到現在還沒完成。

We were supposed to **change** planes in Tokyo, but our flight has been rerouted because of bad weather, and now we are in Seoul. 我們本來應該在東京轉機，可是班機因為天候不佳改變航線，結果現在我們來到了首爾。

7 be supposed to 也可以用來表達「**對某件事的看法**」。

It's supposed to **be** a good art exhibit. My friend at work said so.
這應該會是不錯的藝術展，我在工作上認識的朋友說的。

Practice

1

請勾選正確的答案。

1. You □ **had better** □ **have better** not open the lid. The pot is extremely hot now.

2. I □ **hadn't better** □ **had better not** wake him. He worked late last night.

3. You'd better □ **leave** □ **to leave** now, or I'll call the police.

4. □ **Are you supposed to** □ **Had you better** work on weekends?

5. We □ **are supposed not to** □ **are not supposed to** spend too much time on social media.

6. The soup □ **wasn't supposed to** □ **had better not** taste sweet. Did she add any sugar to it?

7. It □ **is supposed to** □ **was supposed to** be a good hot spring hotel, but the owners haven't maintained it very well.

2

請依括弧提示，用 had better 或 be supposed to 回答問句，來給予建議或說明義務。

1. Do you think I should clean the house before the guests arrive? (had better)

   → *I think you had better clean the house before the guests arrive.*

2. Should I take a number and wait for my turn? (be supposed to)

   → ....

3. Should I invite my motorcycle club to the party? (had better not)

   → ....

4. Should I cut in the line? (be not supposed to)

   → ....

5. Do you think I should vacuum the rug? (had better)

   → ....

6. Should I fill out my deposit ticket while I am waiting? (be supposed to)

   → ....

7. Should I let the dog into the house? (had better not)

   → ....

8. Should I just hand the passbook and the cash to the clerk? (be supposed to)

   → ....

Possibility: May, Might, Could
表示「可能性」：May、Might、Could

---

1 may、might 和 could 都是用來說明「**現在與未來可能發生的事**」，may 的可能性高於 might，而 could 的可能性最低。

可能性	高		低
	may	**might**	**could**

Roger may get us tickets.
↳ 羅傑去買票，有這個可能性。

羅傑可能會幫我們買票。

Jane might come with us.
↳ 珍或許會和我們一起去。

珍可能會跟我們一起去。

Roger could have one last extra ticket for your sister.
↳ 雖然不太可能，不過羅傑或許有多出一張票。

羅傑說不定會多出一張票可以給你妹妹。

---

2 may 的**否定形式**是 may not，沒有縮寫；might 的**否定形式**為 might not，縮寫是 mightn't，不過很少用；而 **could** 的否定形式無法用來表達「**可能性**」。

There may not be any seats left.
↳ 很可能已經沒有空餘的位子了。

座位可能都沒有剩了。

There might not be any parking spaces in the lot.　↳ 很可能已經沒有空的車位了。

停車場或許沒有任何車位了。

✗ There could not be a place to sit in the balcony.

✓ There could be a place to sit in the balcony.　↳ 只能使用 could 的肯定形式來表達「可能性」

露台或許會有位子可以坐。

---

3 說明可能性時，也可以使用**現在進行式**，表示「**現在可能正在發生的事**」。

may/might/could	+	be	+	V-ing

Bobby may be looking for a parking space right now.

巴比現在可能正在找停車位。

William might be circling the block and looking for a place to park his car as we speak. 在我們說話的同時，威廉或許正繞著街道在尋找停車位。

Ron could be hunting for a place to park his car by the university.

榮恩此刻說不定正在大學旁邊找停車位。

---

4 如果要說明「**過去可能發生的事**」，則要用：

may/might/could	+	have	+	過去分詞

Victoria may have bent the rules a little bit. 薇多莉亞可能已經有點違反了規定。
Patti might have driven her car through the garden.

派蒂或許已經開車穿過花園了。

Wendy could have chipped your aunt's teapot.

溫蒂可能把你阿姨的茶壺敲破了一個缺口。

---

5 但是某件事如果是「**過去可能發生，實際上卻沒發生的事**」，則會使用：

could/might	+	have	+	過去分詞

may 不會用在這種用法裡。

That bee might have stung you but I whacked it.

那隻蜜蜂本來可能會螫你，不過我已經把牠揮走了。

Your new scarf could have shrunk if you had used hot water to wash it.

如果你當時用熱水清洗，你的新圍巾可能已經縮水了。

Practice

1 請用括弧裡提示的「情態動詞」改寫句子。

1. It is possible that Bonnie will go out with us tomorrow night. (may)

   → *Bonnie may go out with us tomorrow night.*

2. Perhaps the plane will be delayed because of the fog. (might)

   → ....

3. It is possible that the movie star has arrived by now. (could)

   → ....

4. The police think perhaps Carl has stolen a Ming dynasty vase. (may)

   → ....

   ....

5. It is possible that the chocolate-flavored pastry has sold out. (might)

   → ....

   ....

6. It is possible you have sprained your ankle. (could)

   → ....

2 請依圖示，用括弧內提供的詞語，搭配 could have 或 may have 填空，完成句子。

Bob .... (get up) in time, but he smashed the alarm and went on sleeping.

He .... (present) the report well at the meeting, but he stayed up late last night writing the report and didn't sleep well.

He .... (spend) too much time driving to our party, because he isn't a good driver.

Unit **101**

Possibility: Can, Should, Ought To
表示「可能性」：
Can、Should、Ought To

1 can 用來說明「**理論上的可能性**」，在此用法下，can 的意義和 **sometimes** 相似。

Any one of you can win the race.
↳ 你們當中的每一個人都可能是勝利者。

你們任何一個人都有可能贏得比賽。

The habit of sitting for too long can be dangerous. 久坐的習慣可能傷害身體。
↳ 久坐的習慣有時候就是有害的。

2 can 不能說明「**現在或未來可能發生的事**」，這種情況要用 may、might 或 could。

✗ The winner can be announced tonight.
✓ The winner may be announced tonight.
今晚可能就會宣布優勝者。

✗ The water is deep. You can drown.
✓ The water is deep. You could drown.
水很深，你可能會溺水。

3 may 也可用來說明「**理論上的可能性**」，此時，和 can 有程度上的差異。

You may win. 你可能會贏。 ↳ 說不定你會贏。
You can win. 你可能會贏。 ↳ 有時候你會贏。

4 can 不能說明「**過去可能發生的事**」，這種情況要用「could + have + 過去分詞」。

We could have lost the game, but we pulled through in the last five minutes.

我們本來可能會輸掉比賽的，但是我們撐過了最後五分鐘。

5 should 和 ought to 可以用來說明「**現在或未來可能發生的事**」。

I'd better get ready to leave. Jimmy should be picking me up soon.
↳ 吉米可能很快就會抵達。

我最好趕緊準備離開，吉米應該很快會過來接我。

My cousin Jessica ought to be graduating soon. I need to call and congratulate her.
↳ 潔西卡可能不久後就要畢業了。

我表妹潔西卡應該就快畢業了，我得打個電話恭喜她。

6 「should + have + 過去分詞」和「ought to + have + 過去分詞」常用來說明「**預期可能會發生，但不確定是否已經發生的事**」。

Bruce should have received word from the school about his son's registration.
↳ 學校應該已經通知布魯斯了，不過還不確定。

布魯斯應該已經收到兒子學校的註冊通知才對。

Mary ought to have filed the Power of Attorney form by now.
↳ 她可能已經提出申請，不過還不確定。

瑪麗現在應該已經提出授權書的申請了。

7 「should + have + 過去分詞」和「ought to + have + 過去分詞」也可以說明「**預期可能會發生，實際上卻沒有發生的事**」。

We should have gone home an hour ago, but we wanted to stay for dessert.

我們一個小時前就應該回家了，但是我們想留下來吃甜點。

You ought to have read the instructions before trying to assemble the gas grill.

你應該在組合瓦斯烤架之前先看說明書的。

Practice

1 請從框內選出適當的動詞，搭配 can 填空，完成句子。

sell
connect
make
scan
locate

1. Many printers ____*can scan*____ documents.

2. Many notebook computers _____ to wireless networks.

3. Many cars with GPS systems _____ street addresses.

4. Many vending machines _____ both beverages and snacks.

5. Many smartphones _____ digital video recordings.

2

請勾選正確的答案。

1. The package ☐ should be ☐ should have been here now.

2. You ☐ can ☐ could have missed the exam if you hadn't found your examination permit in time.

3. The letter ☐ ought to arrive ☐ ought to have arrived there by now.

4. She ☐ should have received ☐ should receive my email about that job opportunity by now.

5. Don't eat too many salty crackers. You ☐ can ☐ may get thirsty.

6. He ☐ ought to contact ☐ ought to have contacted them as soon as he can.

7. She ☐ ought to have heard ☐ ought to hear from them soon.

8. They ☐ should know ☐ should have known the results in an hour or two.

9. You ☐ can ☐ could succeed if you work hard.

Unit **102**

Deduction: Must, Can't
表示「推論」：Must、Can't

1 must 用來表示「**肯定的推測**」，有**想必、一定是、八成**的意思。

You are holding roofing shingles, a hammer, and nails. It must be time for me to help you fix the leak in your roof.
↳ 我確定現在該幫你了。

你手上拿著修屋頂用的瓦片、槌子和釘子，我該幫你修屋頂的裂縫了吧。

She must be very tired after her long trip to Tibet.

在去西藏的長途旅行之後，她應該會很累。

2 can't 用來表示「**某件事應該不可能發生**」，**mustn't** 不能用來表示推斷。

Oh, no! That can't be true.
喔，天哪！那不可能是真的。

I saw him this morning. He can't be in New York.

我今天早上才看到他，他不可能在紐約呀。

3 表示推斷的句型也有**現在進行式**。

| must | + | be | + | V-ing |
| can't | + | be | + | V-ing |

可以表示「**想必正在發生的事**」或「**想必沒有在發生的事**」。

She must be eating right now. You'd better call her later.

她想必正在吃飯，你最好晚點再打給她。

She can't be out dancing at some party because she has a big test tomorrow.

她現在不可能在派對上跳舞，因為她明天有一個大考。

4 當我們要「**對過去的事件做推論**」，要使用：

| must | + | have | + | 過去分詞 |
| couldn't | + | have | + | 過去分詞 |

I can't believe you cooked us such a nice dinner. You must have spent all day cooking.

我不敢相信你為我們做了一頓這麼豐盛的晚餐，你一定花了一整天準備吧。

This is such a unique and beautiful sweater. You couldn't have bought it from a store. You must have knitted it yourself.

這件毛衣很特別也很好看，不可能是在店裡買的，這一定是你自己織的。

5 表示「**對過去的事件做推論**」時：

| 美式 | must | + | have | + | 過去分詞 |
| 英式 | couldn't | + | have | + | 過去分詞 |

美式 The remodeling of your house is wonderful. You couldn't have done it all by yourselves.

英式 The remodeling of your house is wonderful. You can't have done it all by yourselves.

你的房子整修得太棒了，不可能全都是你自己做的。

6 表示推論的句子也有**疑問句**，如果要詢問「**過去某件事情發生的必然性**」，可以用：

| could | + | have | + | 過去分詞 |

Could they have finished fixing the roof already? 他們有可能已經完成屋頂的修繕了嗎？
Could they have left work without telling me they were going? 他們有沒有可能已經結束工作離開，卻沒告訴我？

7 如果是「**一般推論的疑問句**」，則用 can。

We put a whole new roof on your house. Where can that water be coming from?

我們幫你的房子換了全新的屋頂，那麼水究竟是從哪裡來的？

1

請勾選正確的答案。

1. The squirrel has disappeared. It ☐ must ☐ can't have crawled into a hole.

2. I hear a beautiful voice coming from Joey's room, but he doesn't know how to sing. It ☐ can't ☐ must be him.

3. The barbershop is closed today, so you ☐ must ☐ can't get a haircut.

4. You slept late this morning. You ☐ can't ☐ must have been tired.

5. I saw some migratory birds going south. They ☐ must ☐ can't have come from a colder climate.

6. That weird-looking guy is wearing a seal skin coat and is carrying a harpoon. He ☐ mustn't ☐ couldn't have bought that harpoon around here.

7. Somebody said Mary ate your lobster. She ☐ couldn't ☐ must have eaten the lobster because she is allergic to seafood.

8. How ☐ can ☐ can't it be possible to cross the river at this time of year?

9. ☐ Could ☐ Must they have found the document and given it to the police?

2

請從框內選出適當的詞語，以正確的形式填空，完成句子。

talk with

make a fortune

drink in the bar

buy this villa

You couldn't have _____ with your salary. It's too expensive.

Susan can't be _____ Matt. He's on the plane to London now.

Sandra must have _____. How else is she able to buy such jewelry?

Murray must be _____ right now. He goes there every time when he loses a job.

33

Unit **103**

Requests: Can, Could, May, Will, Would

表示「要求」：
Can、Could、May、Will、Would

1 can、could 和 may 都可以用於「**請求許可**」。can 是最不正式的用法，could 比 can 正式，may 是三者中最正式的用語。

正式與禮貌性 高　　　　　　低
may　　could　　can

Can I change the channel on the TV?
我可以轉台嗎？

Can I eat the last piece of fruit?
我可以吃最後一塊水果嗎？

Could we watch a variety show instead of this movie? 我們可不可以看綜藝節目，不要看這部電影？

Could I finish the cake?
我可以把蛋糕吃完嗎？

May I please sit in this armchair?
請問我可以坐這張扶手椅嗎？

May I make myself a cup of your special tea? 請問我可以泡一杯你那種很特別的茶嗎？

2 如果要「**要求得到某物**」，可以用：

| can/could/may | + | I/we | + | have |

Can I have another piece of cake?
我可以再吃一塊蛋糕嗎？

Could I have your cell phone number, please? 可以給我你的手機號碼嗎？

May I have your attention, please?
請注意一下這裡好嗎？

3 can you 和 could you 可用來「**請求對方做某事**」。could 的語氣比 can 禮貌而婉轉。

4 will you 和 would you 也可以用來「**請求對方做某事**」。would 的語氣比 will 禮貌而婉轉。

Will you help us move this sofa?
你要幫我們搬這張沙發嗎？

Will you walk the dog and feed the cat?
你會幫忙遛狗和餵貓嗎？

Would you be so kind as to help us for a few minutes? 可以麻煩你好心幫忙我們幾分鐘嗎？

5 「would you mind + 過去式」可以用來「**詢問對方是否介意某事**」。此時要注意回答如果是肯定句，表示「介意、反對某事」，如果是否定句，才是「不介意、同意某事」。

Would you mind if I turned down the music?
我把音樂關小聲一點你不介意吧？

No, I would not.
(= No, that would be fine.)
↳ would not 表示「不介意」、「可以關小一點」。
好啊。

Would you mind if I drove?
我開車你介意嗎？

No, I would not.
(= No, that would be nice.)
↳ would not 表示「你可以開車」。
不介意啊。

6 「I would like you to + 過去式」是一種禮貌性「**請求對方做某事**」的用法，可以縮寫為「I'd like you to . . .」。

Things have not worked out well for you at this company. I'd like you to consider a career change. 你在這間公司的表現並不是太好，我希望你考慮一下轉換職業跑道。

Can you help me to move this box? It's pretty heavy.
你可不可以幫忙搬這個箱子？它實在很重。

Could you give me a hand with this box?
可以麻煩你幫我搬這個箱子嗎？

Practice

1

請用括號內的「情態動詞」將句子改寫成問句，但不能改變語意。

1. I want to have a cup of coffee. (can)

   → *Can I have a cup of coffee?*

2. I want you to answer the phone for me. (would / please)

   → _____

3. I want you to turn off the air conditioner. (will)

   → _____

4. I want to use the bench press when you are finished. (may)

   → _____

5. I want to take a nap on the sofa if you are not going to watch TV. (could)

   → _____

6. I want you to go jogging with me tomorrow morning at 5:30. (can)

   → _____

2

請從圖示中選出適當的用語，以正確的形式填空，完成句子。

open the gift

borrow this book

pass me a tissue

get off the phone

turn the light on

a copy of the application form

fix the fence

1. Can I _____ on your bookshelf? I've always wanted to read it.

2. Would you _____, please? I'm expecting an important call.

3. Can I have _____? I'd like to apply for the job.

4. May I _____ now? I really want to know what's in it.

5. Will you _____? I feel like blowing my nose.

6. Would you mind if I _____? I'm afraid of the dark.

7. I'd like you _____ today. The kids next door keep sneaking into our garden and picking flowers.

Unit 104

Offers: Will, Shall, Can, Could, Would
表示「提供幫助或物品」：
Will、Shall、Can、Could、Would

1 I will 可以用來表示「願意或提議幫對方做某事」。

I will cook dinner for you.
我會幫你做晚餐。
Don't worry. I'll take care of it.
別擔心，我會處理的。

I will help you set the table for afternoon tea. 我會幫你把下午茶的餐具擺好。

2 will you 可用於「提供物品」或「邀請對方做某事」。

Will you join us for our outing to the beach? 你要和我們一起去海灘玩嗎？
Will you please take the last piece of French toast?
請你把最後一片法式土司吃了吧？

3 shall I 可用來表示「提議」，多半是對方已經預期由你來做某事，相當於「**Do you want me to . . . ?**」。

Shall I give the kids their baths tonight?
今天晚上由我幫孩子們洗澡嗎？
Shall I wash the dishes since you cooked such a lovely dinner? 既然你做了這麼一頓豐盛的晚餐，應該讓我來洗碗吧？

4 can/could 表示「有做某事的能力」，也常用於「提議幫忙做某事」。

I can take care of your baby for an hour if you have a doctor's appointment.
如果你已經預約了看醫生的話，我可以幫你照顧你的小寶寶一個鐘頭。
I could keep your kids overnight if you are going to be out of town. 如果你要出城，我可以幫你照顧孩子們一晚。

5 can/could 表示「請求許可」，有時也有「提議幫忙」的意味。這種用法是禮貌性提議幫忙做事，而不是要等別人許可。

Can I read the kids a book while you cook dinner? 你煮晚餐的時候，我可以唸書給孩子們聽嗎？
You look a bit unhappy. Could I give you a glass of orange juice? 你看起來心情不是很好，要我幫你倒杯柳橙汁嗎？

6 要有禮貌地「提供對方某物」，可用 would like、would prefer 和 would rather。

Would you prefer some hard rock?
你要聽一些重搖滾樂嗎？
Would you rather I played some R&B?
要我為你放一些節奏藍調的音樂嗎？

Would you like to listen to some heavy metal music?
你想聽一些重金屬樂嗎？

No, thanks.
不了，謝謝。

Practice

1 請用括號內的「情態動詞」將句子改寫成問句，但不能改變語意。

1. I want you to sew this button back on my pajamas. (will)

   → *Will you sew this button back on my pajamas?*

2. I want to carry that big heavy suitcase for you. (shall)

   →

3. I want to help you change that light bulb. (can)

   →

4. I want to have your daughter's hand in marriage. (may)

   →

5. I want to know if you would like to go out to a French restaurant for dinner this evening. (would)

   →

6. I want you to try a glass of white wine with the meal. (will)

   →

2 比較各組用語，請勾選屬於「提供幫助或物品」或「邀請」的用法。

1. ☐ Shall I accept the offer?
   ☐ Shall I pay the phone bill at the convenience store?

2. ☐ Can I take out the garbage you put by the door?
   ☐ Can I have another cup of green tea?

3. ☐ Will you please have another cookie?
   ☐ Will you clean the screens on our windows?

4. ☐ I could fry an egg for your breakfast.
   ☐ I could eat two tea eggs and some rice soup.

5. ☐ I would like to hear your excuse.
   ☐ Would you like to hear my explanation?

6. ☐ I can walk the dog for you tonight.
   ☐ I can run faster than your dog.

Unit **105**

Suggestions: Shall, Let's, Why Don't We, How About, What About, Can, Could

表示「建議」：
Shall、Let's、Why Don't We、How About、What About、Can、Could

1 shall we 可以用於「尋求建議」和「提出建議」。

What shall we do about our phone bill?
我們的電話帳單該怎麼辦？
Shall we try a new long distance phone service?
我們要試試新的長途電話服務嗎？
Shall we look into one of these data plans? 我們要從這些資費方案中選一個嗎？

2 let's 可用來「提出建議」，後面要接「不加 to 的不定詞」。

Let's call in sick and take the day off.
我們打電話請一天病假吧。

3 why don't we 可用來「提出建議」，後面要接「不加 to 的不定詞」。

Why don't we quit our jobs and backpack around Australia?
我們何不辭了工作，背著包包環遊澳洲？
Why don't we fry some shrimp cakes tonight? 我們今晚炸一些蝦餅來吃怎麼樣？

4 how about 和 what about 可用來「提出建議」，後面要加名詞或動名詞。

How about a swim in the lake?
去湖邊游泳如何？

What about finding a quiet island with white sand beaches?
何不找一個海邊布滿白沙灘的平靜島嶼？
How about quitting this crazy rat race and living in the mountains?
我們何不拋開這種瘋狂競爭的生活，到山中居住？

5 can/could 用來「提出建議」的時候，主要是在提出一些「可能的行為或想法」。

We can pick berries and make our own jam. 我們可以撿一些莓果自己做果醬。
We could open a bed and breakfast near the top of the mountain.
我們可以在靠近山頂的地方開一間民宿。

Practice

1

請勾選正確的答案。

1. Where □ shall we □ let's go shopping for some second-hand clothes?

2. I don't have any money. □ Can □ Let's spend the afternoon in the library.

3. □ Why don't we □ How about go to the wholesale fashion market?

4. □ Shall we □ Let's buy some cute T-shirts and try to sell them?

5. □ How about □ Shall we selling them at the night market near the MRT station?

6. □ We can □ Why don't we double the price we paid.

7. We □ let's □ could sell them to teenagers and make some money.

8. Then □ we could □ how about go shopping.

2 請依據題意，從圖中選出適當的用語，以正確的形式填空，完成句子。

take a coffee break

visit the wine factory

go bicycling

make dumplings

join the health club

wait for five more minutes

1. How about _____ on the second day of our tour?

2. How about _____? If Jack still doesn't come home, then we'll quit waiting and go buy some dog treats.

3. We've got some ground pork in the fridge. Why don't we _____ ourselves?

4. Why don't we _____ as soon as we get our new bicycles?

5. Shall we _____ before going on to the next issue?

6. Shall we _____? They are having a special discount on six-month memberships.

Unit **106**

Habits: Used To
表示「習慣」：Used To

1 used to 用來談論「**過去的習慣**」和「**過去經常從事的活動**」，而這些習慣或活動「**已經結束且不會再發生**」。

Peggy used to walk to school when she was in junior high school, but now she is a senior high school student at another school and has to take a bus.
↳ 現在不走路上學了。
珮琪以前讀國中時走路上學，不過不過她現在在另一所學校上高中，得搭公車上學。

Dean used to collect seashells on vacation, but now he takes motorcycle trips when he has time off.
↳ 現在不蒐集貝殼了。
過去迪恩度假時會蒐集貝殼，但是現在他休假時會騎著摩托車旅遊。

2 used to 也可以用來說明「**過去的狀態和情況**」。

Chuck used to be a student, but he graduated last spring and got a job.
查克以前是學生，不過他去年春天畢業了，也找到了工作。

Barbara used to have a boyfriend, but she dumped him last month.
芭芭拉以前有一位男朋友，不過她上個月把他給甩了。

3 used to 只能用於**過去式**。
如要說明**現在的習慣和情況**，要使用**現在簡單式**。

Rosemary is a vice president now.
蘿絲瑪麗現在是副總裁。
Pam likes to drive to work now that she has a car. 潘喜歡開車上班，因為她現在有車子。

4 used to 的**否定式**為 didn't use to
（注意不是 didn't used to）。

Norman didn't use to commute to the city. 諾曼以前不常通勤到市中心。

5 used to 的**疑問句型**是：
「did . . . use to . . . ?」，用來「**詢問過去的習慣**」。

Did you use to go ice skating with Tom?
你以前常和湯姆一起去溜冰嗎？
Where did you use to go ice-skating?
你以前常去哪裡溜冰？

6 used to 和 be used to 的意義完全不同。

1 used to 是「**過去的習慣**」，後面接「不加 **to** 的不定詞」；

2 be used to 則是「**逐漸習慣於做某事**」，後面要接**動名詞**。

Andrew used to ride his unicycle all the time. 安德魯過去經常騎著他的單輪腳踏車。
Helen is used to riding a unicycle.
海倫已經習慣騎單輪腳踏車。

a unicycle

1

請勾選正確的答案。

1. Linda ☐ used ☐ used to knit, but now she crochets.

2. Naomi used to ☐ spend ☐ spending a lot of money on clothes.

3. Carol used to ☐ work ☐ worked in a clothing store.

4. Amy ☐ use to ☐ used to play computer games in the morning, but now she has to go to work at a mall.

5. Neal ☐ used to go ☐ used to going to bed early.

6. Irene ☐ loves to ☐ used to jog these days.

2

請用括弧內的詞語改寫句子。

1. She drank a cup of black tea when reading a book. (used to)

   → *She used to drink a cup of black tea when reading a book.*

2. He sips a glass of wine before going to bed. (be used to)

   → ....

3. Kristine watched horror movies. (used to)

   → ....

4. Did Karl stay in his office overnight to work? (use to)

   → ....

5. Sam was naive, but now he is a mature young man. (used to)

   → ....

6. Where did you go bowling? (use to)

   → ....

7. I write a journal every day. (be used to)

   → ....

8. Do you read a newspaper before going to work? (be used to)

   → ....

Unit 107

Habits: Will, Would
表示「習慣」：Will、Would

1 will 也可以用來說明「**目前經常從事的行為**」。

He prefers to drive. He will drive for ten hours to visit his parents instead of flying.

他比較喜歡開車，他會開十小時的車去探望父母，卻不搭飛機去。

2 would 可以用來說明「**過去經常從事的行為**」。

在以上這兩種用法中，will 和 would 都不必以重音強調。

He would always drive down to visit his parents.

他以前總是開車南下去探望父母。

He would often stand in a line for three hours to get a concert ticket.

他以前會排隊三個小時，只為了買一張演唱會門票。

3 以**重音**強調 will 和 would 時，原句便轉而帶有「**批評**」的意味。

You know she will lose it.
She is so disorganized.

你明知道她會弄丟的，
她就是這麼一個做事沒有條理的人。

He would always have some lame excuse. He was so lazy.

他老是會有一些爛藉口，他就是這麼懶散。

4 would 和 used to 都用來說明「**過去的習慣**」。

Terry used to give up his seat on the bus to the elderly.

泰瑞過去總是會在公車上讓位給老人家。

Terry would always offer his seat to pregnant women and little kids.

過去泰瑞都會讓位給孕婦和小孩。

5 但是 **would** 不能說明「**過去的狀態**」，這種情況只能用 used to。

✗ My father would like to take the bus to work.

✓ My father used to like to take the bus to work.

以前我爸爸喜歡搭公車上班。

Practice

1

請勾選正確的答案。

1. She ☐ will ☐ would jog every day if she can.

2. When David was a boy, he ☐ would ☐ will read comic books for hours.

3. Jack ☐ would ☐ used to shave his head, but now he has started to let his hair grow long.

4. Don't tell her our plan. She ☐ will ☐ would let everybody know.

2

請從框內選出適當的詞語，用 will 的句型來描述圖中人物「目前」的習慣。

often sneak onto the bed

always go to the beach

always spread a lot of peanut butter

always sing loudly

Polly .... and sleep by her owner.

They .... on Saturdays.

Lisa .... when taking a shower.

He .... on his bread.

3

請從框內選出適當的詞語，用 would 的句型來描述圖中人物「過去」的習慣。

often sit by Grandpa

often chat with friends

always doze off

always eat her breakfast

She .... on Facebook Messenger all day.

Little Sam .... in the park for the whole afternoon.

Claire .... while driving to work.

He .... in front of the TV.

Unit **108**

Other Uses of "Will," "Won't," and "Wouldn't"

Will、Won't、Wouldn't 的其他用法

won't、wouldn't 表示「拒絕」

1 won't 可以表達「拒絕」，並且是「目前拒絕做某事」。

Mommy, Julie won't let me play with her doll house.

媽咪，茱莉不讓我玩她的娃娃屋。

Daddy, Lydia won't come out of the bathroom and she is crying.

爹地，莉蒂雅關在廁所哭，不肯出來。

The door on the toy sports car won't open. 玩具賽車的車門打不開。

2 wouldn't 也可以表達「拒絕」，並且是「過去拒絕做某事」。

Katrina wouldn't let me wear her pink jumper. 凱翠娜不讓我穿她的粉紅色連身裙。

My car door wouldn't open this morning.

我的車門今天早上打不開。

Joy wouldn't talk to me for a whole week.

整整一個星期，喬伊都不肯跟我說話。

will 表示「強調承諾」

3 will 可以用於「強調承諾」。

I will remember our anniversary this year. I promise.

我這次一定會記得我們的週年紀念，我保證。

I won't forget your mother's birthday. I promise.

我不會忘記你媽媽的生日，我保證。

will 表示「威脅」

4 will 可以用於「威脅」。

You'll be in big trouble if you forget my dad's birthday.

要是你忘了我爸爸的生日，那你可就麻煩大了。

You'll fail the exam if you don't study hard. 你不用功，考試就會不及格。

You'll have dark circles around your eyes if you don't go to bed early.

你不早點睡，就會有黑眼圈。

1 請用 won't 或 wouldn't 改寫句子。

1. Kathy refuses to change her opinion.

   → _Kathy won't change her opinion._

2. Kenny refuses to come out of his room.

   → ....

3. Yesterday I invited Lionel to the party, but he refused to go.

   → ....

4. I suggested Yvonne get a new suit for the interview, but she refused to buy one.

   → ....

   ....

5. The washing machine refuses to work properly.

   → ....

2 請用 will 或 won't 改寫句子。

1. If you don't stay out of my room, I am going to tell Mom.

   → _If you don't stay out of my room, I will tell Mom._

2. If you let me use your computer, I am going to be careful with it.

   → ....

3. If you tell Dad what I did, I am not going to forget and you'll regret it.

   → ....

4. I took your favorite doll. Unless you stop kicking my sheep, I am not going to tell you where your doll is.

   → ....

   ....

5. If you tell me where Mom hid the cookies, I am going to buy you snacks next time.

   → ....

"Would Rather" and "May/Might As Well"
Would Rather 與 May/Might As Well 的用法

would rather

1 would rather 用來表示某人的「**偏好**」，後面要接「**不加 to 的不定詞**」。

Albert would rather cut the grass.
艾伯特寧願去除草。
Would you rather give the baby a bath or take out the garbage?
你是要幫孩子洗澡，還是要倒垃圾？

2 would rather 的**否定句型**是 would rather not。

Martha would rather not compost fresh food waste. 瑪莎寧願不用廚餘做堆肥。
I would rather not watch this stupid movie. 我寧可不要看這齣爛電影。

3 如果要**比較兩件事**，可以用「would rather . . . than . . .」，動詞都要用「不加 to 的不定詞」。

Rita would rather clean the kitchen than read the kids a goodnight story.
麗塔寧願清理廚房，也不想唸故事哄孩子們睡覺。
I would rather walk to school than take a bus with no air conditioning. 我寧可走路去上學，也不要搭沒有冷氣的公車。

4 「would rather + somebody + did something」用來表示「**寧願由某人做某事**」，did something 要用過去式動詞。

Richie doesn't want to do it. He would rather Valerie did it.
瑞奇不想做這件事，他寧願讓薇拉莉去做。
I would rather you didn't turn off the air conditioner.
我寧可你不要把冷氣機關掉。
Pam would rather Jessica called earlier in the evening.
潘希望潔西卡晚上早點打電話。

may/might as well

5 may/might as well 表示「**沒有強烈理由不做某事**」，後面會接「**不加 to 的不定詞**」。

Louis is going to be late. We may as well grab a bite to eat while we are waiting for him. 路易斯會遲到，我們等他的同時可以先吃點東西。
Rob won't be here for another 30 minutes. We may as well get a cup of coffee while we are waiting for him.
羅伯再過三十分鐘才會到，我們等他的時候可以順便喝杯咖啡。

Practice

1 請從框內選出適當的動詞，搭配 would rather 或 would rather not 填空，完成對話。

drink

hunt

continue

jump

1. Ⓐ Do you want to drink some tea?

   Ⓑ I _____*would rather drink*_____ coffee.

2. Ⓐ Let's try base jumping off a tall building. What do you say?

   Ⓑ I _____ off a tall building.

3. Ⓐ I want to try bear hunting. Do you want to try it?

   Ⓑ I _____ bears.

4. Ⓐ Ivan wants to meet with you before continuing to work on the project. Do you want him to continue without you?

   Ⓑ I _____ he _____ without me.

2 請用「would rather + somebody + did something」的句型續寫句子。

1. Liz doesn't want to do the dishes. She would like Lisa to do the dishes.

   → _*She would rather Lisa did the dishes.*_

2. Joe doesn't want Mary to revise too much of his paper.

   → _____

3. I want you to go to the play with me. I don't want to go alone.

   → _____

4. I don't want you to cook chicken for dinner every day.

   → _____

3 請從框內選出適當的動詞，依括弧提示，搭配 may as well 或 might as well 填空，完成句子。

ride

wash

order

go

read

have

1. Since there's nothing interesting on TV tonight, I _*may as well go*_ to bed early. (may as well)

2. Since the refrigerator is empty, we _____ pizza. (may as well)

3. If nobody wants to do anything tonight, I _____ my book. (may as well)

4. If Tommy is driving to school, we _____ with him. (might as well)

5. When we finish swimming, we _____ a snack at the concession stand. (might as well)

6. If you're not using the washing machine, I _____ my clothes. (might as well)

Unit **110**

Important Uses of "Should"
Should 的重要用法

1 should 經常出現在表示「**建議**」或「**要求**」的句子中。

當**主要子句**裡使用了下列動詞，那麼**附屬子句**就使用 should（英式）或原形動詞（美式）。

- suggest
- ask
- insist
- propose
- request
- recommend

Jasmine suggests **(that)** I take / I should take the car to the repair shop.
↳ that 可以省略。

潔絲敏建議我把車送去修車廠。

Ray requests **(that)** you call / you should call him when you finish playing chess.

雷要你下完棋之後打電話給他。

The National Theater requires **(that)** we pay / we should pay in advance for the season tickets.

國家戲劇院要我們先購買季票。

2 important、essential、vital 這類的形容詞，也很常用這種搭配 should（英式）或原形動詞（美式）的句型。

Marjorie says it is important **(that) you** emphasize / **you** should emphasize **your circuit design experience during the interview.**

瑪喬莉說，在面試時強調你有電路設計的經驗是很重要的。

Donald said it was essential **(that)** I bring / I should bring **my graphics and photography portfolio to the presentation.**

唐納德說，把我的繪圖和攝影集帶去發表會是很必要的。

此時不管**主要子句**是現在式或過去式，**附屬子句**都用 should 或原形動詞。

現在時態 **Buddy** suggests **(that) we** visit / **we** should visit **the National Concert Hall on Sunday.**

巴迪建議我們星期天去看看國家音樂廳。

過去時態 **Cornelia** insisted **(that)** I pick up / I should pick up **her father before going to get her.**

康妮莉亞堅持要我去找她之前，一定要先去接她父親。

1 請用「that . . . should」的句型，改寫句子。

1. The nurse asked me to consult the doctor about the bump on my leg.
   → The nurse suggested *that I (should) consult the doctor about the bump on my leg* .

2. The butcher said it would be better to fry the meat quickly with high heat.
   → The butcher recommended _____
   _____ .

3. The flight attendant told me to walk around by the lavatory.
   → The flight attendant suggested _____
   _____ .

4. The teacher told the child, "You must finish your homework every night."
   → The teacher told the child, "It is important _____
   _____ ."

5. While packing for vacation, the wife told the husband because of his sensitive skin, he should pack the sunscreen.
   → While packing for vacation, the wife told the husband because of his sensitive skin, it was vital _____ .

6. The man behind the two teenagers in the movie theater said, "Would you please watch the movie and not talk?"
   → The man behind the two teenagers in the movie theater said, "It is important _____ ."

2 請將下列使用 should 的句型，改寫為「不使用 should 的句型」。

1. They say it is important that you should drive without talking on your phone.
   → _____
   _____

2. The mayor ordered that free food should be distributed to the poor.
   → _____
   _____

Part 14 Adjectives 形容詞

Unit 111

Form, Position, and Order of Adjectives
形容詞的形式、位置與順序

1 形容詞的形式只有一種，不會隨任何情況改變。不管修飾單數或複數名詞，格式都一樣。

a healthy boy 一位健康的男孩

two healthy boys 兩位健康的男孩

an anxious child 一位焦慮的孩子

anxious children 焦慮的孩子們

2 名詞也常用來修飾**名詞**，當作形容詞用，此時當形容詞用的名詞多用「**單數形**」。

✗ a fifteen-minutes run

✓ a fifteen-minute run 十五分鐘的跑步

✗ two summers breaks

✓ two summer breaks 兩個暑假

3 形容詞通常位於**名詞的前面**。

a busy schedule 忙碌的行程

a heavy burden 沉重的負擔

4 形容詞也可以放在 **be 動詞**和連綴動詞、感官動詞的後面。

- be
- look
- appear
- seem
- feel
- taste
- smell
- sound

Craig is busy. 克雷格很忙。

The job looks hard.
這件工作看起來很難。

The assignments are difficult.
這些任務都很困難。

5 有些形容詞「只能」放在 **be 動詞或連綴動詞後面**，不能放在名詞前面。遇到這種情況，如果要修飾名詞，則會採用同義的其他形容詞形式。

✗ The baby is an asleep baby.

✓ The baby is asleep.
小寶寶熟睡著。

Let a sleeping dog sleep.
〔喻〕別惹麻煩。

位於 be 動詞或連綴動詞後	位於名詞前
asleep	sleeping
alive	living
afraid	frightened
ill/sick	sick
well	healthy

6 有一種情況下，形容詞可以放在**名詞的後面**，就是談論「**度量**」的時候。

The boy is ten years old. 這位男孩十歲。

The girl is 130 cm tall.
這位女孩身高一百三十公分。

7 多個形容詞連用時，「**詮釋意見的形容詞**」通常會放在「**描述事實的形容詞**」之前。

a controversial new book
一本極具爭議的新書

an attractive red blouse
一件迷人的紅色上衣

8 多個形容詞連用時，請依照下列原則排列順序。

尺寸 → 形狀 → 年齡 → 顏色 → 來源 → 材料 → 目的

the Egyptian cotton dress 埃及製的棉洋裝
↳ 來源 + 材料

a plastic watering can 一個塑膠的澆水壺
↳ 材料 + 目的

my old green running shoes
↳ 年齡 + 顏色 + 目的
我那老舊的綠色跑步鞋

1

請將括弧內的形容詞，搭配各組詞語，重組出一個有意義的句子。

1. (old) / the / sat / man / on the bench

   → _The old man sat on the bench._

2. (delicious) / tea / this / tasted

   → ....

3. (tall) / is / woman / 160 cm / the

   → ....

4. (blue) / coat / is / the / mine / large

   → ....

5. (hot) / we / weather / have had / three weeks of

   → ....

6. (sleeping) / shelter / on the second floor / the / has / quarters

   → ....

2

請將右列錯誤的句子改寫為正確的句子。

1. The rope is long 45 cm.

   → ....

2. We had a two-hours walk after dinner.

   → ....

3. It was a crystal lovely lamp.

   → ....

4. Did you see my blue silk Japanese dress?

   → ....

5. I'm going to visit my ill Grandpa tomorrow.

   → ....

6. Is your bird still living?

   → ....

7. I fell sleeping.

   → ....

8. We have a schedule tight.

   → ....

Unit 112

Comparative and Superlative Adjectives: Forms

形容詞比較級與最高級的形式

Form 形式

單音節形容詞 + er/est
thick → thicker → thickest
short → shorter → shortest

字尾「單母音 + 單子音」的單音節形容詞 → 重複字尾 + er/est
thin → thinner → thinnest
big → bigger → biggest

字尾 e 的單音節形容詞 + r/st
close → closer → closest
wide → wider → widest

字尾 y 的雙音節形容詞 → 去 y + ier/iest
funny → funnier → funniest
naughty → naughtier → naughtiest

字尾非 y 的雙音節形容詞 → more/most
modern → more modern → most modern
serious → more serious → most serious

三音節以上的形容詞 → more/most
expensive   comfortable
→ more expensive   → more comfortable
→ most expensive   → most comfortable

more/most 是具有「**正面意義**」的比較級和最高級，如果要表示**負面意義**「較不」、「最不」，則改用 less/least。

• less expensive
• least expensive

---

1 左表構成形容詞比較級與最高級的原則，也有例外。有些**字尾非 y 的雙音節形容詞**，卻是加 (e)r/(e)st 構成比較級和最高級。

narrow → narrower → narrowest
cruel → crueler/crueller → cruelest/cruellest
gentle → gentler → gentlest
remote → remoter → remotest
subtle → subtler → subtlest

---

2 有些**雙音節的形容詞**，有兩種比較級和最高級形式。

- common   - handsome   - simple
- obscure   - clever   - stupid
- mature   - quiet

common → commoner → commonest
common → more common → most common
obscure → obscurer → obscurest
obscure → more obscure → most obscure

---

3 有些形容詞的比較級和最高級是**不規則變化**，請逐一牢記。

good → better → best
bad → worse → worst
little → less → least
many → more → most
much → more → most

---

4 有些**形容詞**有兩種不同的比較級和最高級，且**意義上有差異**。

far → farther → farthest ↳ 距離上的遠
far → further → furthest ↳ 程度上的進一步
old → older → oldest ↳ 可形容人或物
old → elder → eldest ↳ 英式：只能形容人／只能用在名詞前

Practice

1

請將括弧內的形容詞以「比較級」或「最高級」填空，完成句子。

1. These shoes are too small. Do you have a pair in a ＿＿＿＿＿＿ (big) size?

2. Who is the ＿＿＿＿＿＿＿＿ (young) child in our school?

3. I think bubble milk tea is the ＿＿＿＿＿＿＿ (delicious) drink.

4. The weather is OK. It is cloudy. It could be ＿＿＿＿＿＿ (sunny), but at least it's not raining.

5. How many kilometers do we have to drive? How much ＿＿＿＿＿＿ (far) do we have to go to get there?

6. The flight from Taipei to Tokyo is ＿＿＿＿＿ (long) than the flight from Taipei to Hong Kong.

2

將左欄圖片中的名詞，與右欄相對應的描述結合，並將括弧內的形容詞改為「最高級」，寫出完整的敘述句。

1 **Mount Everest**

2 **The Louvre**

3 **The Mariana Trench**

4 **Shakespeare**

5 **Solar energy**

6 **Cirque du Soleil**

is the (high) mountain in the world.

is one of the (famous) museums in the world.

is the (innovative) contemporary circus.

is considered to be one of the (great) poets and dramatists.

is the (deep) place in the ocean.

is one of the (important) sources of energy.

1. *Mount Everest is the highest mountain in the world.*

2. ＿＿＿＿＿＿＿＿＿＿＿＿＿＿＿＿＿＿

3. ＿＿＿＿＿＿＿＿＿＿＿＿＿＿＿＿＿＿

4. ＿＿＿＿＿＿＿＿＿＿＿＿＿＿＿＿＿＿

5. ＿＿＿＿＿＿＿＿＿＿＿＿＿＿＿＿＿＿

6. ＿＿＿＿＿＿＿＿＿＿＿＿＿＿＿＿＿＿

Part 14 Adjectives 形容詞

Unit 113

Comparative and Superlative Adjectives: Use
形容詞比較級與最高級的用法

1 形容詞比較級用於**比較兩件事物**，通常會用「比較級 + than」的句型。

Sandy is smarter than **Judy.**
珊蒂比茱蒂聰明。

Sharon is more energetic than **Harriet**. 雪倫比哈里特更有活力。

2 形容詞比較級也常用「比較級 + and + 比較級」的句型，來表示「**逐漸增加或減少**」、「**愈來愈……**」。

Computers are getting faster and faster. 電腦的速度變得愈來愈快。

Hard drives are getting more and more compact. 硬碟的體積變得愈來愈小。

3 可以結合兩個「the + 比較級」的子句，來表達「**兩件事物互相影響、改變的關係**」。

The more cheese on the pizza, the better it will be.
披薩上的起司愈多愈好吃。

The better Internet phones become, the more money traditional phone companies will lose.
網路電話發展的愈好，傳統電話公司損失的金錢就愈多。

4 比較級的前面，可以用 (very) much、a lot、a bit、a little bit 等來描述其程度。

very much brighter 明亮非常多
a lot paler 蒼白很多
a little bit shallower 比較淺一點

5 比較三個以上的人或事物，則要使用形容詞的最高級。最高級前面要加 the。

- the happiest 最開心的
- the most pragmatic 最實際的

This is the ripest **one of the five mangoes on the table.** 桌子上的五個芒果，就這一個最熟了。

Kirk is the quietest **child in the family.**
科克是家裡最安靜的孩子。

The office on the right is the most spacious.
右邊那間辦公室最寬敞。

6 形容詞最高級的前面，可以用 by far（顯然）或 easily（顯然）來強調其「**獨特性**」。

by far the most realistic 顯然最實際的
easily the cleverest 顯然最聰明的

7 若要表示「**兩個事物一樣（或不一樣）**」，會用「(not) as + 形容詞原級 + as」的句型。

The appetizer was as good as **the main meal.**
開胃菜就和主菜一樣美味。

The tea is as strong as **the coffee at this café.**
這間咖啡廳的茶就和咖啡一樣濃。

The park didn't have as many **visitors today** as **it did yesterday.**
今天公園裡不像昨天人那麼多。

It isn't as hot **now** as **it was this morning.**
今天早上不像平常那麼熱。

8 在「as . . . as」的句型中，口語常用 me 或 him 等受詞代名詞，在正式用法中通常會使用「主詞代名詞 + 動詞」，如 I 或 he。

You aren't as cool as me. 你沒有我酷。
↳ 口語

You couldn't represent the citizens of our district as well as I could.
↳ 正式
你無法像我一樣代表本區的全體市民。

Practice

1

請勾選正確的答案。

1. Tonya is □ short □ shorter than Lesley.

2. Helen is the □ happy □ happiest child I've ever seen.

3. Adam is □ honester □ more honest than Max.

4. Alvin is the □ more careful □ most careful child in his class.

5. This is the □ worse □ worst milk tea I've ever had.

6. Too bad this dress isn't □ cheaper □ more cheap.

7. The summer is getting □ hotter and hotter □ hottest.

8. The colder the air conditioning is, the □ more □ most I like it.

9. I am not as emotional as □ she □ she is.

2

請將括弧內的形容詞，以正確的「原級」、「比較級」或「最高級」填空，並視需要加上 than、the 或「as . . . as」，完成句子。

1. I'll let you use the phone first. Your call is a lot _____ (important) mine.

2. In general, the larger a diamond is, _____ (expensive) it is.

3. Lemons may be _____ (sour) of all fruit.

4. Today is not _____ (hot) as yesterday.

5. We're getting _____ (close) to sending people to Mars.

6. This is by far _____ (boring) movie I've ever seen.

7. This corporate profile is too general. Can you make it a little _____ (specific)?

3

請從框內選出適當的形容詞，以「as . . . as」的句型填空，完成句子。

hip

neat

smart

high

frugal

fast

1. If you get new sunglasses, then you can be _____ me.

2. I got a higher test score, so you're not _____ me.

3. I can't afford these prices, so if you want to be _____ me, then we can go shopping at the night market.

4. You were not _____ me. I ran two laps in the time it took you to run one.

5. If you cleaned up your room as often as I clean my room, then your room would be _____ mine.

6. The mountain called K2 in Pakistan is almost _____ Mount Everest.

Unit 114

Adverbs of Manner
狀態副詞／方式副詞

1 狀態副詞／方式副詞用於描述「某事發生的方式」。

The press conference was run professionally. 那場記者會進行得很專業。

Jeff remembers the accident distinctly.

傑夫清楚記得那次的意外。

Pan is doing the research passionately.

潘積極投入這次的研究。

2 狀態副詞通常由形容詞加 ly 衍生而來。

- high → highly
- sincere → sincerely
- mischievous → mischievously

professional + ly = professionally

Walter is a professional manager.

華特是一名專業的經理。

Walter manages the department professionally.

華特十分專業地管理部門。

confident + ly = confidently

Anthony is a confident guy.

安東尼是個有自信的人。

Anthony talks about the future confidently.

安東尼信心滿滿地高談未來。

confidential + ly = confidentially

It was a confidential letter.

這是一封機密信函。

Please treat this letter confidentially.

請將這封信的內容保密。

3 狀態副詞／方式副詞可以放在**動詞**的**前面或後面**，也可以放在**句首**。

Natalie whispered into the phone angrily.

= Natalie angrily whispered into the phone.

= Angrily, Natalie whispered into the phone.

娜塔莉憤怒地對著電話低語。

4 有些以 **ly** 結尾的詞彙，實際上是**形容詞**，不是**副詞**。這類的形容詞沒有對應的副詞，因此如果要修飾動詞，會用「in a ... way」的句型。

- friendly
- lovely
- lonely
- silly
- ugly

Sally smiled in a friendly way as we drove off.

我們駕車離開時，莎莉友好地微笑著。

5 副詞也有比較級和最高級，構成方式和形容詞一樣。

Daryl runs faster than Chad.

德瑞跑得比查德快。

As Maria talked longer, I began to know the whole story. 瑪麗亞說得滔滔不絕，我開始瞭解事件的始末。

The later Valerie arrives, the longer we will have to wait.

薇拉莉愈晚抵達，我們就得等愈久。

Of the girls in our class, Cornelia runs the fastest.

我們班上的女生，就屬可娜麗雅跑得最快。

I am hammering as hard as I can on these two pipes, but they are still stuck together.

我盡量用力敲打兩支管子，不過它們還是黏在一起了。

例外

good 是一個例外，它的副詞是 well。

- He is a good supervisor.

  他是一位很好的管理者。

- He supervises the department well.

  他把部門管理得很好。

Practice

1

請勾選正確的答案。

1. Margery is a ☐ graceful ☐ gracefully dancer.

2. Gabriel manages the lab ☐ efficient ☐ efficiently.

3. That is an ☐ absurd ☐ absurdly story.

4. Clara is an ☐ inspiring ☐ inspiringly speaker.

5. You're acting ☐ silly ☐ in a silly way.

6. Wendell handled the press conference ☐ impressive ☐ impressively.

7. Florence answered the question ☐ tentative ☐ tentatively.

8. She talked to her mother ☐ ugly ☐ in an ugly way.

9. Sarah finished her work ☐ quickly ☐ in a quickly way.

2

請將括弧內的副詞以正確的形式填空，可視需要加上 more、most、than、the 和 as 等字。

1. Penelope jumps _____ (high) as Lisa.

2. The house was _____ (beautifully) decorated.

3. Our team played _____ (well) the other team.

4. Don arrived _____ (late) of all the people.

5. I want to move _____ (far) possible away from this city.

6. Vivian needs to _____ (carefully) prepare her reports.

7. No one can solve this problem _____ (intelligently) than he can.

8. Buffy called me back _____ (soon) I expected.

9. The rain was pouring _____ (heavy) all night.

10. Larry dealt with the murder case _____ (emotionlessly).

3

請將括弧內的形容詞以「in a . . . way」的句型填空，完成句子。

1

Huck licked the boy _____ _____ (friendly).

2

The little girl is smiling _____ (lovely).

Unit **115**

Adverbs of Time and Place
時間副詞與地方副詞

1 地方副詞用來描述「**事件發生的地點**」，通常位於**動詞或受詞的後面**。

- here
- there
- upstairs
- downstairs
- behind the shed

Linus rode his bike to the laboratory.
↳ to the laboratory 是地方副詞片語，放在「動詞 + 受詞」後面。
李納斯騎腳踏車到實驗室。

Bonnie signed here. 邦妮在這裡簽了名。

2 時間副詞用來描述「**事件發生的時間**」，通常位於**動詞後面**或「**動詞 + 受詞**」後面。

- now
- today
- immediately
- next month

Larry rode his bike home after the concert.
↳ after the concert 是時間副詞片語。
音樂會結束後，勞瑞騎著他的腳踏車回家。

Stella withdrew from the competition yesterday. 史黛拉昨天退出了比賽。

3 有些時間副詞通常放在**動詞或助動詞的前面**。

Natasha just laughed at her boyfriend.
娜塔莎剛才嘲笑她男友。

Jerome still couldn't believe what he had seen. 傑洛姆還是不敢相信他所看到的。

4 當句中同時出現了**狀態動詞**、**地方副詞**、**頻率副詞片語**和**時間副詞**時，語序為：
狀態動詞 → 地方副詞 → 頻率副詞 → 時間副詞。

Max calculates effortlessly in his head.
　　　　　　　↳ 狀態副詞 + 地方副詞
麥克斯心算起來毫不費力。

Donald stops at the diner every morning.
　　　　　　↳ 地方副詞 + 頻率副詞
唐諾每天早上都會光顧那個餐車。

Della sneaks quietly up the back stairs at night.　　↳ 狀態副詞 + 地方副詞 + 時間副詞
黛拉夜裡會悄悄地從後面的樓梯溜上去。

5 狀態副詞、地方副詞、頻率副詞片語和時間副詞都不會放在**動詞和受詞的中間**。

✗ Archie watched silently the football game.
✓ Archie watched the football game silently.
亞契靜靜地觀看美式足球賽。

✗ Frances cheered loudly Jimmy.
✓ Frances cheered Jimmy loudly.
法蘭西絲大聲地為吉米加油。

✗ Joyce played yesterday video games.
✓ Joyce played video games yesterday.
喬伊絲昨天在玩電視遊樂器。

6 狀態副詞、地方副詞、頻率副詞片語和時間副詞都可放在**句首**，產生「**強調**」的效果。

Longingly, Martina stared at the map of New Zealand.
瑪蒂娜充滿渴望，直盯著紐西蘭的地圖。

At the Sydney airport, Holly finally felt a twinge of excitement.
在雪梨的機場，荷莉總算感到一陣興奮。

In just a couple of hours, Billie would finally arrive in her ancestral home.
就在幾小時後，比莉終將抵達祖先的故鄉。

Practice

1 請將括弧內的詞語以正確的語序填空，完成句子。

1. Ariel devoured _____ (hungrily / the food).

2. The Executive Vice President _____ (works / in this office).

3. The attorney entered our office _____ (at 2:30 in the afternoon / casually).

4. The tech support team reacted _____ (quickly / last week / in the office).

5. The contender punched _____ (last night / hard / at the champion).

6. We _____ (the fight / excitedly / watched), forgetting that we should call the police.

7. An earthquake occurred _____ (this afternoon / in the south).

8. He threw a book _____ (angrily / at his brother).

2 請將下列錯誤的句子改寫為正確的句子。

1. Trent put here the box.

   → _____

2. Sally poured some milk into her coffee just.

   → _____

3. Sonia left at 10 a.m. the library.

   → _____

4. I will buy some books tomorrow at the bookstore.

   → _____

5. Mom won't still let me go to the party.

   → _____

6. Jacky jumped off quickly the tree.

   → _____

Unit **116**

Adverbs of Frequency
頻率副詞

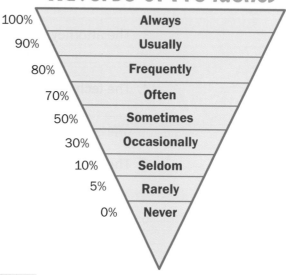

頻率副詞
Adverbs of Frequency

100%	**Always**
90%	**Usually**
80%	**Frequently**
70%	**Often**
50%	**Sometimes**
30%	**Occasionally**
10%	**Seldom**
5%	**Rarely**
0%	**Never**

1 頻率副詞用來表示「**事件發生的頻率**」，通常放在**主要動詞的前面**，或者 **be** 動詞和助動詞的後面。

- always
- normally
- usually
- frequently
- often
- sometimes
- occasionally
- rarely
- seldom
- hardly ever
- never
- ever

Clifford always puts **condensed milk in his tea.** 克里佛總是在茶裡加奶精。

Winnie is normally **a kind and gentle soul.**
溫妮平常是個善良溫柔的人。

Frank can usually work **all day without stopping.**
法蘭克通常可以工作一整天不休息。

These socks have never been worn.
↳ 即使較長的助動詞組 have been worn，頻率副詞 never 還是放在第一個助動詞的後面。

這些襪子還沒穿過。

2 部分的頻率副詞可以放在**句首**或**句尾**。

- sometimes
- usually
- normally
- frequently
- often
- occasionally

Do you eat hot and spicy curry often?

你常吃口味又重又辣的咖哩嗎？

Sometimes **I buy foreign products in that luxurious supermarket.**

有時候我會在那家高級超市購買外國的產品。

3 頻率副詞片語如 every morning、once a day 等，通常會放在**句尾**，不過有時候也會放在**句首**。

Cecilia practices tai chi in the park every morning.

西西莉雅每天早上在公園裡練習太極拳。

Bart takes a calcium supplement tablet once a day. 巴特每天吃一個鈣片。

Every night **Joyce has to take a sleeping pill before she goes to bed.**

喬伊絲每晚睡前都要吃一顆安眠藥。

4 一些「**明確指出多久**」的頻率副詞，會放在**動詞後面**，也就是**句尾**的位置。

We do file transfers daily.
我們每天交換檔案。

The website is updated monthly.
這個網站每月都會更新。

- daily
- weekly
- monthly
- twice a week

Practice

1

請將括弧內的「頻率副詞」放入句中正確的位置，改寫句子。

1. Trisha gets up at 6:30 in the morning. (usually)

   → *Trisha usually gets up at 6:30 in the morning.*

2. Ester is late for work. (never)

   → ....

3. Vanessa will bring a box of donuts for her coworkers. (sometimes)

   → ....

4. Does Brigit take time off work? (often)

   → ....

5. Felix goes to a client's office. (once a week)

   → ....

6. Irvin writes up his sales report. (daily)

   → ....

2

請依圖示，從第一個框內選出適當的「動詞片語」，第二個框內選出適當的「頻率副詞」，以正確形式搭配填空，完成句子。

have a sandwich for breakfast

has his car maintained

go biking

go to a yoga class

have Thai food

every three months

every weekend

every day

once a week

monthly

Mon.	Tue.	Wed.	Thu.	Fri.	Sat.	Sun.
					🚲	🚲

1. My family ....

Mon.	Tue.	Wed.	Thu.	Fri.	Sat.	Sun.
🥪	🥪	🥪	🥪	🥪	🥪	🥪

2. I ....

Mon.	Tue.	Wed.	Thu.	Fri.	Sat.	Sun.
				🧘		

3. Kim ....

Jan.	Feb.	Mar.	Apr.	May	Jun.	Jul.	Aug.	Sep.	Oct.	Nov.	Dec.
🍲	🍲	🍲	🍲	🍲	🍲	🍲	🍲	🍲	🍲	🍲	🍲

4. We ....

Jan.	Feb.	Mar.	Apr.	May	Jun.	Jul.	Aug.	Sep.	Oct.	Nov.	Dec.
🚗			🚗			🚗			🚗		

5. James ....

Adverbs of Probability
可能性副詞

1 可能性副詞用來表示「**事件發生的可能性**」，通常放在主要動詞的前面，或者 **be** 動詞和助動詞的後面。

❶ 可能性副詞 + 主要動詞

❷ be 動詞／助動詞 + 可能性副詞

- certainly
- obviously
- definitely
- probably

Probability

Daniel definitely understands **the textile business.**

丹尼爾一定對紡織業很了解。

Conrad is obviously **ready to sign the contract.**

顯然康瑞德已經準備好要簽合約了。

Josh is probably talking **on the cell phone in the stairwell.**

喬許可能正在樓梯間講手機。

Colleen can probably arrange **for the first shipment on Monday.**

可琳或許能在星期一安排第一批貨運。

Byron will certainly get **caught smoking in the bathroom.**

拜倫在廁所抽菸一定會被抓到。

Isaac certainly knows **his way around the back alleys of this town.**

艾薩克想必對城裡的小巷弄熟悉得很。

perhaps		surely	definitely
possibly	maybe	probably	certainly

可能性低　　　　　　　　　　　　　可能性高

2 在「**否定句**」裡，可能性副詞通常會放在 won't、isn't、not 這些詞彙的**前面**。

The bread definitely won't **rise if you forget to add yeast.**

如果沒有加酵母，麵包就發不起來。

The price is obviously not **cheap, but the quality is excellent.**

價格顯然並不便宜，但是品質極佳。

The engagement cake probably won't **be ready until tomorrow.**

訂婚蛋糕可能要到明天才會好。

3 perhaps 和 maybe 也是可能性副詞，perhaps 比 maybe 來得正式。這兩個副詞只能放在**句首**。

Perhaps **we should provide cinnamon rolls during the coffee break.**

我們或許應該在休息時間提供肉桂捲。

Maybe **I'll call Derek and see if he can swing by with some cookies.**

說不定我可以打電話給德瑞克，看他能不能帶點餅乾過來。

Practice

1

請勾選正確的答案。

1. Kristy ☐ **knows definitely** ☐ **definitely knows** the subway system in Tokyo since she's been there over ten times.

2. Johnny ☐ **certainly won't** ☐ **won't certainly** believe you because he has learned his lesson.

3. The stone is ☐ **not obviously** ☐ **obviously not** naturally shaped.

4. ☐ **Stanley will perhaps** ☐ **Perhaps Stanley will** visit Busan next month.

5. Sonia ☐ **probably is** ☐ **is probably** watching a Wimbledon match in the Center Court.

6. ☐ **Maybe Jill** ☐ **Jill maybe** has gone to the Villa Breeze Spa.

2

請將括弧內的「頻率副詞」放入句中正確的位置，改寫句子。

1. Beryl will run in the 100 meter race. (probably)

   → *Beryl will probably run in the 100 meter race.*

2. Amy swims faster than anybody I know. (certainly)

   →

3. Luke is in the running for a medal. (definitely)

   →

4. Jenna won't continue dancing after her injury. (obviously)

   →

5. Kathleen isn't the best teacher, but she is well loved. (certainly)

   →

6. Mort is not going to get promoted this year. (probably)

   →

7. Shirley can fill in for you while you're gone. (maybe)

   →

8. Rod will play his guitar in a concert for the earthquake survivors. (perhaps)

   →

Adverbs of Degree
程度副詞

1 程度副詞強調「**事件到什麼程度**」，
通常用來修飾**形容詞和其他副詞**，因
此，**程度副詞會放在它們修飾的形容
詞或副詞前面**。

- fairly
- pretty
- almost
- quite
- very
- simply
- rather
- really
- extremely

She was dressed fairly well.
她衣服穿得非常好看。 ↳ 修飾副詞

The scent was quite good.
這個味道很好聞。 ↳ 修飾形容詞

2 以「**強調的程度**」來說，very、
fairly、quite、rather、pretty 這幾個
字的語氣強弱如下：

強			弱
very	**rather/pretty**	**quite**	**fairly**

Jerry is a fairly good runner.
傑瑞是個相當不錯的跑者。
Darla is quite hungry. She says let's eat
as soon as we can.
黛拉滿餓的，她說我們盡量早點吃飯。
I had a rather long visit with Aunt Edna.
我去艾德娜阿姨那裡待了很久。
Richard is pretty boring, isn't he?
↳ pretty 和 rather 的語氣差不多，但 pretty 較不正式。
李察這個人滿無趣的，是吧？
This restaurant has very large portions.
這個餐廳的食物份量很多。

3 quite 若遇到 a/an，要放在 a/an 前面，
其他程度副詞都是放在 a/an 後面。

Tanya is quite a good singer.
譚雅是位很不錯的歌手。
Portia is a fairly good fiddler.
波莎是個很不錯的小提琴手。

4 有些程度副詞也可以修飾**動詞**，如
quite、rather、almost、simply 等，
可以放在**主要動詞的前面**，或 **be 動詞
和助動詞的後面**。

Brad rather enjoyed himself tonight.
布萊德今晚玩得很盡興。
Carrie is quite pleased with herself these
days. 這些日子凱莉對自己的表現頗為滿意。

5 如果要修飾**形容詞比較級**，只能用
rather。

Today's weather is rather colder than
yesterday's. 今天的天氣比昨天冷多了。
Today our street is rather noisier than
usual. 今天我們街上比平常更吵了。

6 如果要修飾具有「**絕對**」意義的**形容詞或
副詞**，可用 quite，此時 quite 表「**完全**」。

The parrot is quite dead.
這隻鸚鵡已經死了。
No, it's not. That parrot is quite alive. It's
just sleeping soundly. Please don't wake it
up.
不，牠沒有死，那隻鸚鵡還活著，牠只是睡
得很熟，請別把牠吵醒。
Your son behaved quite well today.
你兒子今天表現得很好。

1

請勾選正確的答案。

1. Polly is ☐ quite ☐ fairly a helpful person.

2. Samuel is a ☐ fairly ☐ quite friendly neighbor.

3. Tim ☐ pretty ☐ quite enjoyed the art exhibit.

4. Warren is ☐ fairly ☐ rather enjoying the party tonight.

5. Aaron is ☐ rather ☐ quite more sincere than I expected.

6. Clive was ☐ fairly ☐ quite a perfect gentleman.

7. The top of the mountain is ☐ extremely cold ☐ cold extremely.

8. Today our class is ☐ rather ☐ very quieter than usual.

9. You are ☐ rather ☐ quite right.

10. Let's hurry. We're ☐ almost there ☐ there almost.

11. She is ☐ rather ☐ quite more professional than I expected.

12. Pam ☐ is quite ☐ quite is good at tennis.

2

請將括弧內的「程度副詞」放入句中正確的位置，改寫句子。

1. Antone is a famous chef. (quite)

   → ....

2. Meg was satisfied with the result. (rather)

   → ....

3. I feel depressed. (fairly)

   → ....

4. Louis drove faster than usual. (rather)

   → ....

5. Tim pushed the "Start" button. (simply)

   → ....

6. Larry is a smart person. (pretty)

   → ....

7. Mom's roast beef is delicious. (really)

   → ....

Unit **119**

Adverbs "Still," "Yet," and "Already"
副詞 Still、Yet、Already 的用法

1 still 是時間副詞，描述「**目前的時間**」、「**較預期晚的時間**」或「**特定的時間**」。
still 可以放在**主要動詞的前面**，或者 **be** 動詞和助動詞的後面。

目前的情況
My sister still drives to work for an hour one way every day.

我姐姐還是每天開一小時的車去上班。

某特定時間
Stephanie says it is still Tuesday in California, but it is Wednesday in Taipei right now.

史黛芬妮說現在加州還是星期二，不過台北已經星期三了。

較預期晚的時間
Chris can still get it done before the end of the day, but he has other things he needs to do first.

克里斯還是可以當天完成工作，只不過他有別的事需要先做。

2 still 可以在**否定句**裡表達「**驚訝**」、「**不耐**」的情緒。此時 still 會放在 won't、haven't 等否定詞彙的**前面**。

The lab tests still haven't been completed.
實驗室的測試還有沒完成。

3 yet 是時間副詞，描述「**目前的時間**」、「**較預期晚的時間**」或「**特定的時間**」。
yet 只用於**疑問句**和**否定句**，通常放在**句尾**。

Have you left your office yet?
你已經離開辦公室了嗎？

When I last checked, the committee had not finished that project yet. 我最後一次查看時，委員會還沒有完成他們的專案。

4 yet 的**否定簡答句**經常用 not yet。

Alan popped in to see if I was ready to go to the gym, but I said, "Not yet."

艾倫跑進來看我是不是準備好要去健身房了，但是我說：「還沒有。」

Betsy said, "Not yet." I said, "OK. When will you be ready?" 貝西說：「還沒。」我說：「好吧！那什麼時候會好？」

5 already 是時間副詞，描述「**目前的時間**」、「**較預期早的時間**」或「**特定的時間**」。
already 可以放在**主要動詞的前面**，或者 **be** 動詞和助動詞的後面。

The Curry Restaurant chain has already opened two more locations.

這家咖哩連鎖餐廳已經多開了兩家分店。

The company has already filed the legal papers for its initial public stock offering.

公司已經繳交法律文件申請股票上市。

When I finished visiting all the clients, it was already 2:00 and I had missed lunch.

我拜訪完所有的顧客時已經 2 點了，我還沒吃午餐。

6 already 也可放在**句尾**，來「**加強語氣**」。

It's only March, and Darryl has sold his annual quota already. 現在才 3 月，德瑞爾就已經把他的年度配額量賣完了。

How did he finish it already?
他是如何現在就已經完成的？

They said they would end by noon, but when I checked they had not wrapped up their meeting yet.

他們說中午會結束，不過我進去看時，發現他們還沒開完會。

1

請勾選正確的答案。

1. Clive: Have you picked up little Johnny yet?
   Jenny: ☐ **Not yet** ☐ **Yet not**.

2. Lydia ☐ **knits still** ☐ **still knits** her grandmother a sweater every winter.

3. It ☐ **is still** ☐ **still is** raining outside. It has been raining for two days.

4. We ☐ **can still** ☐ **still can** catch the train if we take a cab.

5. ☐ **Already I have weeded** ☐ **I have already weeded** the garden twice this week.

6. I ☐ **have already warmed up** ☐ **have warmed up already** for twenty minutes. Now I'm going to swim for an hour.

7. I ☐ **cooked already** ☐ **already cooked** two vegetarian dishes. Now I'm going to fry some chicken.

8. Julia hasn't passed the driving test ☐ **still** ☐ **yet**.

9. Have you sold your textbooks ☐ **yet** ☐ **still**?

10. I ☐ **haven't gone to bed yet** ☐ **haven't yet gone to bed**.

2

請用 still、yet 或 already 填空，完成句子。

1. I have _____ called him.

2. He hasn't finished his science report _____.

3. I can _____ remember my trip to Japan five years ago.

4. I _____ look at the photos I took at that time.

5. I have not had an opportunity to go back to Japan _____.

6. Murray has _____ realized his dream of working in Japan.

7. Murray went to Japan two years ago and is _____ there.

8. I thought it was _____ early, but it is actually almost 12 o'clock.

9. It is _____ midnight. You'd better call tomorrow.

10. He has gone to the airport _____.

11. The shoes are _____ on sale. You're lucky.

Part 15 Adverbs 副詞

Unit 120

Adverbs "Too" and "Enough"
副詞 Too 與 Enough 的用法

1 too 和 enough 都可修飾**形容詞和副詞**，但 too 要放在形容詞或副詞**前面**；enough 要放在形容詞或副詞**後面**。

Jacob is too pushy. 雅各實在太過積極了。
Fritz is not persistent enough.
弗里茲不夠有毅力。

2 too much、too many 和 enough 如果修飾**名詞**，則一律放在名詞的**前面**。

Toby gets too many messages.
托比收到太多訊息了。
Sebastian gets too much spam.
賽巴斯丁收到太多垃圾郵件。
Adele has enough cash **for the whole trip.**
愛黛兒的現金足夠走完整趟旅程。

3 too much、too many 和 enough 也可以單獨使用，當作**代名詞**。

Did you get enough? 你得到的夠嗎？
You gave me too much. 你給我太多了。
I already have too many. 我已經擁有太多了。

4 too 具有**負面意義**，若要表達**正面意義**，要用 very。

Gregory is very tall, **but his feet don't stick out of the bed.** 葛瑞戈里很高，不過他的腳還不會伸出床鋪外面。

Chester is too tall, **and his head and feet both stick out of the bed.** 切斯特太高了，他的頭和腳都已經超過床沿了。

5 too 和 enough 的片語後面，可以接 for *somebody*。

I can't take all the leftover food home because it is too much for *me*.
我沒辦法把剩菜都帶走，那些對我來說太多了。
My knapsack isn't big enough for *me* **to carry all this food.**
我的背包不夠大，沒辦法裝下所有這些食物。

6 too 和 enough 的片語後面，可以接「加 to 的不定詞」。
1 「too . . . to . . .」
意指「**太⋯⋯以致於不能⋯⋯**」；
2 「. . . enough to . . .」
意指「**夠⋯⋯而可以⋯⋯**」。

Wally is too young to marry **Selma.**
威利年紀太輕，還不能娶賽瑪。
Wayne isn't old enough to retire **from his job.** 偉恩還不到可以退休的年紀。

7 too 和 enough 的片語後面，可以先接 for somebody，再接「加 to 的不定詞」。

It is too early for us to plan **the wedding.**
現在就計畫婚禮，對我們來說還太早。
Hiram and Stephanie have not been dating long enough for her parents to start **thinking about wedding plans.**
希來姆和史黛芬妮交往的時間，還沒有久到請她父母開始考慮婚禮的計畫。

8 too 前面可用 much、a lot、far、a little、a bit 或 rather 來修飾，但 **enough** 不行。

I think we improvised a bit too much **when we were assembling the grill.**
我想我們在組裝烤肉架的時候多做了一些步驟。
The instructions were much too complicated.
說明書實在太複雜了。
Unfortunately, there are far too many **leftover nuts and bolts.**
不巧的是還剩下了太多的螺帽和螺絲釘。

Practice

1

請勾選正確的答案。

1. Elizabeth is ☐ **too** ☐ **enough** late, and she will miss dinner.

2. Faye says the oven is hot ☐ **too** ☐ **enough** now to put in the roast.

3. Lorrie has ☐ **too many** ☐ **too much** shoes in her closet.

4. Jill has ☐ **too many** ☐ **too much** clothing in her dresser.

5. Martin needs more socks because he doesn't have ☐ **enough** ☐ **too**.

6. Sidney wants to move because his apartment is ☐ **enough small for him** ☐ **too small for him**.

7. Geraldine says it is ☐ **too early to look** ☐ **enough early to look** for a new job.

8. Malcolm says his salary is ☐ **much enough high** ☐ **much too high** for him to leave the company.

9. Dinah has ☐ **coins enough** ☐ **enough coins** for the tolls on the highway.

2

請依圖示，從框內選出適當的用語填空，完成對話。

too

too many

much

enough

Ⓐ I've prepared ❶ _____enough_____ fruit for your diet today.

Ⓑ Those are ❷ _____ for me. I only need one apple today.

Ⓐ Maybe you'll be interested in some blueberries. They are a little sweet and sour, but not ❸ _____ sweet and sour.

Ⓑ Thanks, but I had ❹ _____ blueberries yesterday. I think I'll have some orange juice now.

Ⓐ I know there isn't ❺ _____ orange juice left, but I'd like to have a glass, please.

Unit **121**

Adverbs "So," "Such," "Anymore/Longer," and "No Longer"

副詞 So、Such、Anymore/Longer、No Longer 的用法

so/such

1 such 通常放在**名詞的前面**，該名詞可以帶有**形容詞**，也可以沒有。
名詞前面如果有 a/an，則 such 要位於 a/an **之前**。

I've never seen such a big motorcycle.
我從沒看過這麼大的摩托車！

I felt happy to have achieved such an accomplishment.
對於達到如此的成就我覺得很開心！

2 so 則是修飾**形容詞或副詞**，不直接修飾**名詞**。

Derek is so agile. 德瑞克是如此敏捷！

Don't be so selfish. 別這麼自私！

Brian prepared for yesterday's department meeting so thoroughly that his boss was very impressed.
布萊恩為了昨天的部門會議做了十足的準備，他的老闆很滿意。

3 so 可以搭配 many 和 much 來表達**數量**，但 **such** 沒有這種用法。

There were so many customers in the meeting room that I had to stand.
會議室裡的顧客太多了，我不得不站著。

Gary has so much money that he doesn't know what to do with it.
蓋瑞有太多錢，不知道該如何用。

4 such 可以搭配 a lot (of) 來表達**數量**，so 則不行。

We have such a lot of cheese. Maybe we should have pizza every night for a week.
我們有這麼多的起司，也許這個星期的每天晚上我們都應該吃披薩。

Stuart has such a lot of work. I am going to help him.
史都華有這麼多工作得做，我要去幫他的忙。

5 so 和 such 都可以搭配 that 子句，來表示「**事情的結果**」，但句型不同。
❶ so + 形容詞 + that 子句
❷ such + 名詞 + that 子句

The meeting went so long that I missed lunch. 會議開得太久，害我錯過了午餐。
It was such a successful presentation that everybody wanted to shake the speaker's hand. 那場發表會實在太成功了，大家都想去和演講者握手致意。

anymore / any longer / no longer

6 「not . . . anymore」和「not . . . any longer」用來表示「**情況已經改變**」、「**事情已不再如此**」，通常放在**句尾**。

Candice is not single anymore.
康蒂絲已經不再是單身了。

Edna does not work for our airline any longer. 艾德娜已經不在我們航空公司上班了。

7 no longer 也表示「**情況已經改變**」、「**事情已不再如此**」。no longer 會放在**主要動詞前面**，或 **be 動詞和助動詞後面**。

Jasper no longer volunteers at the hospital.
賈士柏沒有在醫院當義工了。
Tracey is no longer delivering newspapers.
崔西現在已經沒有送報紙了。
My parents can no longer afford my tuition.
我的父母再也負擔不起我的學費了。

8 no more 的意義和「**not . . . anymore/longer**」以及 **no longer** 很類似，但沒有 no anymore 這樣的用法。

✗ The mother told the babysitter no anymore dessert for the twins.

✓ The mother told the babysitter no more dessert for the twins.

這位母親對保姆說，不要再給雙胞胎吃點心了。

Practice

1

請用 so 或 such 填空，完成句子。

1. After the party, the house was ＿＿＿＿＿ a mess.

2. Why has Sue had ＿＿＿＿＿ many headaches since she became pregnant?

3. Why are you walking ＿＿＿＿＿ slowly?

4. Annabelle is ＿＿＿＿＿ kind and generous.

5. It was ＿＿＿＿＿ a good performance that the band gave two encores.

6. Bruce is ＿＿＿＿＿ a tough kid that we never have to worry about him.

7. The scenery was ＿＿＿＿＿ amazing that no one wanted to stop taking pictures.

8. There are ＿＿＿＿＿ many phone calls this morning. I could hardly concentrate on my work.

2

請從括弧內選出適當的「副詞片語」，插入句子中改寫句子。

1. Victoria doesn't wear glasses. (anymore / no longer)

   → *Victoria doesn't wear glasses anymore.*

2. Matthew watches auto racing on TV. (no longer / any longer)

   → ＿＿＿＿＿＿＿＿＿＿＿＿＿＿＿＿＿＿＿＿＿

3. Laurie doesn't read comic books. (anymore / no longer)

   → ＿＿＿＿＿＿＿＿＿＿＿＿＿＿＿＿＿＿＿＿＿

4. Sandy is very tired. She can't drive today. (no more / any longer)

   → ＿＿＿＿＿＿＿＿＿＿＿＿＿＿＿＿＿＿＿＿＿

5. Andy will play in the Asian Cup. (no longer / any longer)

   → ＿＿＿＿＿＿＿＿＿＿＿＿＿＿＿＿＿＿＿＿＿

Unit **122**

Linking Words of Time: When, As, While, As Soon As, Before, After, Until

表示「時間」的連接語：

When、As、While、As Soon As、Before、After、Until

1 如果要說明「**兩件同時發生的事情**」，常用 when、as 和 while 來連接**兩個子句**。其中 when/as/while 的子句裡，會用進行式來表示「**持續時間較長的動作**」。

When I am swimming, I don't use goggles.
我游泳的時候不戴泳鏡。

As I am swimming up and down the lane, I count my laps. 我在水道來回游泳時，計算了自己游了幾趟。

As I am swimming up and down the lane, I feel something like a runner's high. 當我在水道中游泳時，感覺到一陣運動的快感。

When I start out, I swim slowly, but later I swim hard and fast.
↳ 要注意的是，while 不能用於「短暫的動作」；when 才可以。

當我開始游時，我游得很慢，不過接著我加快速度賣力地游。

2 說明「**兩件同時發生的事情**」時，可以用 just as 來描述「**持續時間較短的動作**」。

My adrenaline peaks just as I hit the water. 就在我揮手拍打水面時，我的腎上腺素急速分泌。

3 如果要說明「**直到某個時候**」，會用 until 和 till。

Susan worked in the garden until sunset.
蘇珊在花園裡工作直到日落。

Al studied at the library till midnight.
艾爾在圖書館裡唸書直到午夜。

4 如果要說明「**兩件接連發生的事情**」，可以用 when、as soon as、before 和 after 來連接**兩個子句**。

After I got my haircut, I called home to check on the kids. 當我剪完頭髮後，便打電話回家確認孩子有沒有事。

The nanny said she would serve dinner as soon as I got home. 保姆說我一到家，她就會把晚餐端上桌。

I said I might not get home before the kids had dinner.
我說孩子們吃晚餐前，我可能沒辦法回到家。

As it turned out, I was delayed and didn't get home until after the kids had a bath.
結果我耽擱了，一直到孩子們洗完澡才回到家。

5 when 的用法十分靈活，在某些情況下，when 的意義常相當於 while、as、before 或 after。

When/While/As Lena was washing the dishes, she heard a crash in the living room. 莉娜洗碗的時候，聽到客廳傳來一陣巨大的聲響。

A different real estate agent had sold the house when/before we had a chance to look at it. 我們還沒有來得及去參觀那棟房子時，房子已經被另一名房屋仲介售出了。

When/After Arthur had finished mowing the lawn and trimming the bushes, the property looked great. 在亞瑟除過草、修剪過樹叢之後，整個建築景觀看起來棒極了。

6 when、as soon as、before 所引導的子句，可以用現在簡單式來表達「**未來**」意義。

I have told the housekeeper we'll talk about the weekend schedule as soon as I get home. 我告訴管家等我回到家，我們再討論週末的安排。

Practice

1

請勾選正確的答案。

1. □ **When** □ **Just as** I was flying between Kaohsiung and Sydney, I read the whole book.

2. □ **While** □ **When** Jessica finished mopping the kitchen floor, she cleaned the bathroom.

3. I will call my uncle □ **as soon as** □ **while** I get home.

4. The basketball coach waited □ **until** □ **when** all the players had finished running □ **before** □ **until** beginning skill drills.

5. Mark usually takes a shower □ **as soon as** □ **before** he gets up.

6. I drank a cup of tea □ **while** □ **until** I was reading the newspaper.

2

請用括弧內的「連接詞」合併句子。

1. I counted the steps. I was walking home from the MRT station. (when)
   → _I counted the steps when I was walking home from the MRT station._

2. You have food in your mouth. Do not speak. (when)
   → _____

3. I was making a cup of cappuccino. I got grains of instant coffee all over the table. (while)
   → _____

4. Mom was humming a lullaby. The baby fell asleep. (while)
   → _____

5. The light went out. We were playing cards. (as)
   → _____

6. I lost eight pounds. I quit eating hamburgers and French fries. (after)
   → _____

7. Dad checked on the electricity, gas, and windows. We set off for our vacation. (before)
   → _____

8. I ran to my computer and checked the email. I got home. (as soon as)
   → _____

Unit 123

Linking Words of Contrast:
Although, Even Though, Though, However,
In Spite Of, Despite, While, Whereas
表示「對比」的連接語：Although、Even
Though、Though、However、In Spite
Of、Despite、While、Whereas

1 連接詞 although 和 even though 都用來連結「**相反的概念**」，意指「**雖然**」。兩者都要連接主句和子句。

even though 的語氣比 although 來得強烈。

Although we were on the ninth floor, we didn't have a view because of the fog.

雖然我們身在九樓，但是卻看不到什麼景觀，因為都被霧遮住了。

We went up to the rooftop garden,
even though we knew it was rainy and overcast. 雖然我們知道天氣陰雨，但還是上去了屋頂花園。

Even though you are late for work, I will let it go this time.

雖然你上班遲到，不過這次我就算了。

2 連接詞 though 的意義和 **although** 一樣，但 though 多用於**非正式用語**中。

Though it was cold, we enjoyed our picnic in the park.

天氣雖然很冷，我們還是
很享受在公園裡野餐。

Though you've explained the plan thoroughly, I still don't understand.

雖然你已經鉅細靡遺地解釋了這個計畫，我還是不懂。

3 however 是副詞，也可以用來連接兩個「**對比的概念**」。

An old car requires constant maintenance. However, keeping an old car is cheaper than buying a new car.

一輛舊車得持續保養，但是養一部舊車比買一部新車便宜多了。

比較 though 如果放在**句尾**，意義就等同於 **however**。

• The cost of the building is high, but it is quite spacious though.

這棟大樓的價格很高，不過空間卻也很寬敞。

4 in spite of 和 despite 也用於表示「**對比的概念**」，但兩者都是介系詞（片語），後面要接**名詞**，而不是接子句。

In spite of Clint's negative reaction, we went ahead with the plan.

儘管科林特反對，我們還是繼續進行計畫。

Despite Blake's connections, he couldn't get an interview. 雖然布雷克有人脈關係，卻還是沒得到面試的機會。

5 如果要連接**主句和子句**，要用 in spite of the fact that 或 despite the fact that，兩個句型中的 that 都**可以省略**。

In spite of the fact (that) only half the sales reps showed up, the event was a success. 儘管只有一半的業務員現身，整場活動依然非常成功。

Despite the fact (that) there was no advance preparation, somehow the whole thing worked out fine.

雖然沒有預先準備，但整件事進展順利。

6 although 的意義和用法與 **in spite of the fact** 相當（後面接**名詞**），但用法不同於 **in spite of**（後面接子句）。

In spite of the fact that Dina and Gordon could have walked home, they took a taxi.
= Although Dina and Gordon could have walked home, they took a taxi.

雖然蒂娜和高登可以走路回家，但他們還是搭了計程車。

7 連接詞 while 和 whereas 也可以用來連接「對比的概念」。

I like to go fishing whereas my sister Jane likes to go mountain climbing.
= I like to go fishing while my sister Jane likes to go mountain climbing.

我喜歡釣魚，而我姐姐珍喜歡爬山。

Practice

1 請用括弧內的「連接詞」，合併句子。

1. Kathy likes toy dinosaurs, but she doesn't like dinosaur movies. (although)
   → ....

2. The plot was silly, but we enjoyed the movie. (despite)
   → ....

3. The movie was a little long, but it was great. (though)
   → ....

4. We planned to have dinner in the Italian restaurant before the movie, but we didn't have time. (though)
   → ....

   ....

5. The movie received bad reviews, but we went to see it anyway. (in spite of)
   → ....

6. Hank planned to stay up for the late movie, but he fell asleep before it started. (even though)
   → ....

7. Alan looks very conservative, but his wife is totally wild and artistic. (while)
   → ....

8. Jerry likes to get up at dawn, but his wife likes to sleep until noon. (whereas)
   → ....

Unit 124

Linking Words of Reason: Because, Because Of, As, Since, Due To

表示「原因」的連接語：Because、Because Of、As、Since、Due To

1 because 表「原因」，後面要接子句，這種子句因為修飾整個主要子句，因此屬於副詞子句。because 子句可以位於句首，也可以位於句尾。

Because my brother was addicted to online games, Dad refused to buy him a new computer. 我哥哥因為沉迷網路遊戲，老爸不願意幫他買新電腦。

My mother fed the children some soup because they were hungry. 我媽媽餵孩子們喝了點湯，因為他們肚子餓了。

The kids slept at my mother's house because it was late when we returned.

孩子們睡在我媽媽家，因為我們回去時已經太晚了。

2 because of 表示「原因」，屬於介系詞片語，後面要接名詞，不能接子句。

We like downhill skiing because of the thrill. 我們喜歡下坡滑雪，因為很刺激。

We don't go skiing often because of the cost.

我們不常去滑雪，因為很花錢。

3 as 可以表示「原因」，as 子句可以位於句首，也可以位於句尾，意義等同 because。

As I had no idea what they were talking about, I just kept my mouth shut and nodded every now and then. 因為我根本不知道他們在說些什麼，只好閉上嘴，不時點點頭。

4 since 可以表示「原因」，since 子句可以位於句首，也可以位於句尾，意義等同 because。

Since you know about the topic, why not give a short presentation on it and share your point of view?

既然你對這個議題已經完全瞭解，何不做個簡短的報告，跟大家分享你的觀點呢？

I was stunned when they asked me to stand up and say something since it seemed to them that I knew everything about the topic. 他們好像以為我對這個主題瞭如指掌，所以當他們要我站起來發言時，我整個人傻眼。

5 due to 是介系詞片語，可表示「原因」，後面要接名詞而不接子句。根據傳統語法，「due to + 名詞」片語只能當做形容詞，置於 be 動詞後面，但現在也可以用作副詞，意思相當於 owing to、because of、as a result of。

All the flights to Hong Kong were cancelled due to the nasty weather.

所有飛香港的航班，都因天候不佳而取消了。

6 due to 後面如果要接子句，要用 due to the fact that。

Due to the fact that vitamin C has a great effect on anti-oxidization, it has been widely applied in skin care products. 維他命 C 具有優異的抗氧化效用，已被廣泛運用於肌膚保養品之中。

Everybody assumed that I already knew all about the topic as I didn't ask any questions. 由於我沒發問，大家都假定我對這個主題已經完全瞭解。

1

請勾選正確的答案。

1. Arnold was tired ☐ **because** ☐ **because of** he stayed up late the previous night.

2. ☐ **Since** ☐ **Due to** Jim was delayed, everybody had to wait.

3. Gabriel didn't buy the house ☐ **since** ☐ **because of** the price.

4. I changed designers ☐ **due to** ☐ **due to the fact that** the first one was so irresponsible.

5. ☐ **As** ☐ **Due to** I know he has a large house mortgage, I won't invite him on our trip to New Zealand.

6. ☐ **So** ☐ **Because** you don't want my opinion, I won't say anything from now on.

2

請用括弧內提供的「連接語」取代原句的粗體連接語，改寫句子。

1. **Because** he is miserly, I won't ask him for help. (because of)
   → *Because of his miserliness, I won't ask him for help.*

2. **Because** it was raining, we had to stay home. (because of)
   → _____

3. **Because of** his generosity, we survived the hard times. (because)
   → _____

4. They decided to close the front gate after sunset **due to** security concerns. (since)
   → _____
   _____

5. **Due to the fact that** cherries are rich in vitamins, they are good for our health. (due to)
   → _____
   _____

6. He can't play tennis as well as before **because of** his ankle injury. (as)
   → _____

7. **Since** he didn't play fair in the final, he was deprived of the title two days after the match. (as)
   → _____
   _____

Unit **125**

Linking Words of Result: So, As A Result,
Therefore, So . . . That, Such . . . That

表示「**結果**」的連接語：So、As A Result、
Therefore、So . . . That、Such . . . That

1 連接詞 so 常用來表示「**結果**」，後面
會接子句。so 引導的表示結果的子句
要放在**主句後面**，常用逗號跟主要子句分開。

I had already eaten, so I said that I wasn't
hungry.　　　↳ 以逗號分開

我已經吃過了，所以我說我不餓。

Bonnie was tapping her foot in time to
the music, so I asked her if she wanted
to dance.

邦妮隨著音樂節奏用腳打拍子，所以我問她
想不想跳舞。

2 as a result 也用來表示「**結果**」，是
一個副詞片語，在句中可有多種位置。

I hadn't eaten any dessert for two
months. As a result, I lost five pounds.
　　　　　　　↳ 位於句首

= I hadn't eaten any dessert for two
months. I lost five pounds as a result.

我已經兩個月沒吃甜食了，　↳ 位於句尾
所以瘦了五磅。

✗ There were no jobs in my hometown
as a result I moved to the city.

✓ There were no jobs in my hometown
and as a result I moved to the city.
　↳ 因為 as a result 是副詞片語，不是連接詞，所以
　　不能用來連接兩個子句，這裡搭配了 and 使用。

我家鄉沒有工作可做，所以就搬到城市來。

3 therefore 可以用來表示「**結果**」，屬
於比較**正式**的用法。therefore 本身是
副詞，在句子中可以有多種位置。

I didn't have any friends or relatives in
the city, and therefore I had to get my
own place to live.

↳ 因為 therefore 是副詞，不是連接詞，所以不能
　用來連接兩個子句，這裡搭配了 and 使用。

我在城市裡沒有朋友，也沒有親戚，所以得
自己找地方住。

The apple pie was delicious. Therefore,
I asked for a second piece.　↳ 位於句首

= The apple pie was delicious. I, therefore,
asked for a second piece.　　↳ 位於句中

那塊蘋果派非常美味，結果我又點了第二塊。

I didn't have enough money to buy a
house, and I therefore decided to rent
an apartment. ↳ therefore 可以直接接動詞，
　　　　　　　　但這種用法較不普遍。

我的錢不夠買一棟房子，所以我決定租一間
公寓。

4 「so . . . that」片語可以表示「**結果**」，
意思是「**太……以致於**」。so 後面要接**形
容詞**，也就是「so + 形容詞 + that 子句」。

The tea was so good (that)
I drank several cups.　↳ that 可以省略。

茶太好喝了，所以我喝了
好幾杯。

5 「such . . . that」片語也表示「**結果**」，
意思是「**太……以致於**」。such 後
面要接**名詞**，也就是「such + 名詞 +
that 子句」。

It was such a good price (that) I bought
five boxes of the tea.　↳ that 可以省略。

因為價格太划算，於是我買了五盒茶。

Practice

1

請勾選正確的答案。

1. ☐ As ☐ So Vera felt exhausted, she closed her eyes for a couple of minutes.

2. Joey was in a comfortable armchair, and ☐ as a result ☐ since he fell fast asleep.

3. There was a traffic jam on the highway, ☐ so ☐ because we took side streets.

4. The traffic on the route Monica took was slow. ☐ As a result ☐ since, she was late.

5. Linda is ☐ so ☐ such a good cook that even a simple meal at her house is a gourmet feast.

6. Yesterday was ☐ so ☐ such hot that I stayed indoors all day.

2

請依據範例，將括弧內的「副詞片語」分別以兩種位置改寫句子。

1. Grandma was sick. We had to put off our trip. (as a result)

   → *Grandma was sick. As a result, we had to put off our trip.*

   → *Grandma was sick. We had to put off our trip as a result.*

2. We didn't have vegetables at home. We went out for dinner. (therefore)

   → ....

   → ....

3. I left home late this morning. I was caught in the traffic. (as a result)

   → ....

   → ....

3

請將下列使用 so 的句子以 such 改寫；反之，使用 such 的句子以 so 改寫。

1. Those peaches were so sweet that I ate three of them.

   → ....

   ....

2. It was such splendid scenery that we took hundreds of pictures.

   → ....

   ....

3. The show was so amazing that the audience applauded the performers for three minutes.

   → ....

   ....

Part 16 Linking Words 連接語

Unit 126

Linking Words of Purpose: To, In order To, So As To, For, So That
表示「目的」的連接語：To、In Order To、So As To、For、So That

1 「加 to 的不定詞」常用來表示「目的」。

Let's stop at this convenience store to buy a bottle of water.
我們在這間便利商店停下來買瓶水吧。

Dave uses Skype to communicate with his son who is studying abroad.
戴夫使用 Skype 來和在國外求學的兒子聯絡。

2 in order to 和 so as to 也用來表示「目的」，兩者後面都是加不定詞。

Can I use your truck in order to move some furniture and boxes?
我可以借用你的卡車搬些家具和箱子嗎？

We vacuum pack the rice so as to prevent it from being spoiled.
我們用真空包裝白米是為了防止腐壞。

3 in order to 和 so as to 的否定句型是 in order not to 和 so as not to，表示「目的是不要……」。

✗ Did you call in sick not to miss your son's gymnastics meet?

✓ Did you call in sick in order not to miss your son's gymnastics meet?
你打電話請病假，是為了不想錯過兒子的體操比賽嗎？

I sneaked into the room so as not to wake you up.
我躡手躡腳溜進房間，因為不想吵醒你。

4 如果要接子句，可以用 in order that 的句型。

Steve leaves a light on every night in order that he won't trip over something when he uses the bathroom at night.
史帝夫每晚都留一盞燈，以便半夜上廁所時不會絆到東西。

5 for 也是常用來表「目的」的介系詞，後面要接名詞或動名詞。

Use these noodles for dinner.
用這些麵條來煮晚餐吧。

Eve is going to Seoul for plastic surgery.
伊芙要去首爾做整型手術。

This razor is good for shaving legs.
這把剃刀用來刮腿毛很好用。

Mick uses his room for storing samples.
米克把他的房間用來存放樣品。

6 so that 可以說明「目的」，後面要接子句，子句裡常使用 can、can't、will、won't 等助動詞。that 可以省略。

Conrad always breaks a big bill before taking a cab so (that) he can pay the driver the exact fare.
康瑞德會在搭計程車前先把大鈔換成零錢，這樣就可以給計程車駕駛剛好的車費。

Ellen takes the bus so (that) she won't have to spend money on cabs. 愛倫選擇搭公車，就不必把錢花在計程車費上。

7 so that 也可以搭配 could、couldn't、would、wouldn't，說明「**過去的目的**」。

Nicole called her friend Jay so (that) he could help translate a letter from Poland.
妮可打電話給她的朋友傑，請他幫忙翻譯來自波蘭的信。

Liz hired a limo to pick up Greg at the airport so (that) he wouldn't have to take the bus.
莉茲租了禮車去接機場接葛瑞格，他就不必搭巴士了。

Practice

1 請用括弧提示的「連接語」，將兩個句子合併。

1. William brought his own bag. He needs to carry his groceries. (to)
   → <u>William brought his own bag to carry his groceries.</u>

2. The dog wants to go for a walk. The dog needs to go to the bathroom. (so as to)
   → _____

3. Lauren got to the store early. She wanted to avoid the rush. (in order to)
   → _____

4. Kevin often eats dinner out. He wants to avoid messing up his kitchen. (so as not to)
   → _____

5. Paulina bought some shrimp. She will have shrimp for lunch. (for)
   → _____

6. Lawrence has a knife with a serrated edge. The knife is good for cutting bread. (for)
   → _____

7. Nadia will give you some money. You can buy a new dress. (so that)
   → _____

8. Tamara closed the window. That way it wouldn't get too cold. (so that)
   → _____

Unit **127**

Linking Words of Purpose: In Case
表示「目的」的連接語：In Case

1 in case（以防）可以用來表示「**目的**」，說明「**做某事的目的是什麼**」。
in case 的後面會接子句，當表示「**未來的目的**」時，會用現在簡單式。

Bring a bottle of water in case **you** get **thirsty.**

帶一瓶水免得你口渴。

Please give me your business card in case **I** need **to contact you.**

請給我一張名片，好讓我能跟你聯絡。

2 in case 和 if 不同，if 說的是「**假設**」，in case 則是「**明確要做準備**」。in case 用來談論預防措施，意思是「以防、免得」。

Save a seat for Randy in case **he comes.**
↳ 確定要為藍迪過來而找好位子。
幫藍迪留個位子，他要是來了就有得坐。

We will find a seat for Randy if **he comes.**
↳ 如果藍迪過來，才會幫他找位子。
如果藍迪過來，我們會幫他找個位子。

3 in case 如果用來說明「**過去做某件事的目的**」，則會用過去簡單式。

I ordered a lunch box for Rhonda in case **she** forgot **to buy one.**

我替蘭達點了一個便當，以防她忘了買。

I invited all the parents in case **they** wanted **to come.** 我邀請了所有的家長，這樣他們想來就可以來。

4 in case 後面所接的事件，如果**發生的機率不太確定**，則會在子句中使用 should。

Reserve a later connecting flight in case **your first flight is delayed.**
↳ 認為飛機延誤的可能性不小
轉接的班機訂晚一點，以免你的頭一班飛機延誤。

Reserve a later connecting flight in case **your first flight** should **be delayed.**
↳ 不太確定飛機會不會延誤
轉接的班機訂晚一點，以防你的頭一班飛機延誤。

比較

in case of 和 in case 不同。in case of 是指「**萬一**」、「**如果某事發生的話**」，後面會接**名詞**。

• **In case of emergency, dial 119.**
萬一發生緊急事件的話，就撥 119。

Practice

1

請用 if 或 in case 填空，完成句子。

1. Bring your coat _____ it gets cold.
2. Let's make more sandwiches _____ Joey comes for lunch.
3. Write down your mailing address _____ I need to forward any mail.
4. I called to reserve another table _____ your sister's family comes.
5. Go back to your office _____ you haven't finished your report.
6. I will pack our swimsuits _____ the hotel has a pool.

2

請分別自 A 欄和 B 欄選出語意搭配的子句，以 in case 連結，造出句子。

A ▶

take your purse with you	lock your cell phone keypad
give me your phone number	give Mary a call
call him later	back up your files every day

B ▶

you accidentally make a call

I need to reach you

she's forgotten about her promise to buy some frozen pizzas for tonight

your computer crashes

you want to buy anything while walking the dog

he hasn't arrived at the office

1. *Take your purse with you in case you want to buy anything while walking the dog.*
2. _____
3. _____
4. _____
5. _____
6. _____

Unit 28

Prepositions of Place:
Basic Meanings of "In," "At," and "On"
表示「地點」的介系詞：
In、At、On 的基本意義

in **the vehicle**
在裡面

on **the vehicle**
上方；有接觸到

at **the end**
在一個點上

---

1 in 表示「在一個三度空間裡」。

Put the book in **your backpack.**
把書放進你的背包裡。
We will be in **the garden.**
我們會在花園裡。

2 on 表示「在一個平面上」。

Please pick up your socks on **the floor.**
請把你地板上的襪子撿起來。
Sign your name on **the lease, and give them the deposit.**
請你在租約上簽名，再把保證金交給他們。

3 at 表示「在一個點上」。

Let's meet at **the train station.**
我們約在火車站見面吧。
I was standing at **the main entrance to the museum.**
我當時就站在博物館的主要入口前。

4 in 也可以表示「在一個特定的範圍內」。

Your name is mentioned in **the email message.**
電子郵件的訊息裡有提到你的名字。
I think that city is somewhere in **Brazil.**
我想那座城市位在巴西的某個地方。

5 on 也可表示「在一條線上」。

A squirrel is standing on **the fence.**
有一隻松鼠站在籬笆上。

It's risky to stand on **the edge of a cliff.**
站在懸崖邊緣是很危險的。

1

請用 in、at 或 on 填空，完成句子。

1. Tina is waiting ⎯⎯⎯ the ticket window.

2. Your keys are ⎯⎯⎯ the kitchen table.

3. Get off the highway ⎯⎯⎯ the Cedar Point exit.

4. I put your watch ⎯⎯⎯ the drawer. Did you see it?

5. Can you put this dictionary ⎯⎯⎯ the top shelf for me?

6. Jeffery left his suitcase ⎯⎯⎯ the sofa again.

2

請依圖示，用 in、at 或 on 填空，完成句子。

1 Lulu was told to sit ⎯⎯⎯ the dike and wait.

2 Migu is looking at the goldfish ⎯⎯⎯ the aquarium.

3 Sunny and Moony wait ⎯⎯⎯ the front door every evening.

4 The little boy is hanging the laundry ⎯⎯⎯ the clothesline.

5 Muddy is ⎯⎯⎯ the door ringing the bell. He wants to get inside.

Unit **129**

Prepositions of Place:
"In," "At," and "On" With Different Locations
表示「地點」的介系詞：
In、At、On 說明各種地點的用法

1 in、at、on 常用來說明「**實際地點**」。

Yvonne's office is in the Hancock Building. 伊芳的辦公室就在漢考克大樓裡。

The elevator in the Guangzhou CTF Finance Center is the fastest in the world.
廣州周大福金融中心的電梯是全世界速度最快的。

We ate lunch in/at the food court in the basement of the Taipei 101 building.
我們在台北 101 樓下的美食街吃午餐。

2 如果特別強調「**在一棟建築物內進行活動**」，也就是強調「**建築物的功能**」的話，常用 at。

Henry is getting money at the bank.
亨利正在銀行領錢。

Trudy is studying at/in college.
楚蒂正在大學唸書。

Terrence is paying his overdue bill at the phone company office on Central Avenue. 泰倫斯正在位於中央大道的電話公司繳交過期的帳單。

6 說明「在某條河川、海岸」，會用 on。

We cruised on the Yangtze River and enjoyed the scenery along its banks.
我們航行於長江之上，欣賞沿岸風光。

3 說明「**在某個城市、城鎮內**」，要用 in。

The brewery is in Sapporo.
啤酒廠就位於札幌市。

Reporters from many countries gathered in New York to broadcast the World Series. 許多國家的記者進駐紐約，轉播美國職棒總冠軍賽。

4 但如果只是「**旅途中經過某個城市或城鎮**」，則要用 at。

The bus will stop at the park after we have lunch.
等我們吃完午餐，巴士會在公園停下來。

We will stop at Tokyo, Yokohama, and Kamakura on this trip. 我們這次的行程將會參觀東京、橫濱和鎌倉。

5 in、at、on 經常拿來說明「**地址**」，既定用法如下：

國家、洲名、城市 → in
I lived in Australia for three years.
我在澳洲住了三年。

街道 → on
We live on Wentworth Street, near the corner of Forest Avenue. 我們住在溫沃斯街，接近佛瑞斯特大道的轉角。

含門牌號碼的地址 → at
I live at 421 Judson Avenue.
我住在賈德森大道 421 號。

樓層 → on
Our apartment is on the third floor.
我們的公寓在三樓。

We stayed on the East Coast for two weeks.
我們在東岸停留了兩週。

Practice

1

請用 in、at 或 on 填空，完成句子。

1. Fred is _____ the garage.

2. There is a historic house _____ my neighborhood.

3. The house is _____ Old River Road.

4. We live _____ the town of West Milton.

5. The meeting will be held _____ our office.

6. There are two large conference rooms _____ our office building.

7. My grandmother lives _____ 201 East 74th Street.

8. I went to the bookstore _____ Angel Avenue last night.

2

請依圖示，用 in、at 或 on 填空，完成句子。

1 Three old boats are floating _____ the river.

2 Lisa studied the Patent Act _____ graduate school.

3 The train will stop _____ Union Station.

4 The 2022 FIFA World Cup will take place _____ Qatar.

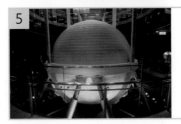
5 A tuned mass damper _____ the Taipei 101 building is a technique to control seismic vibration.

Part **17** **Prepositions of Place and Movement**
表示地點與移動方向的介系詞

Unit **130**

Prepositions of Place:
Over, Under, Above, Below, Underneath
表示「地點」的介系詞：Over、Under、
Above、Below、Underneath

over **the boat**
正上方；未接觸到

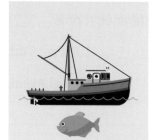

under **the boat**
正下方；未接觸到

above **the boat**
上方（不必正上方）

below **the boat**
下方（不必正下方）

1 over 表示「**某物的位置高於另一物**」，
通常是垂直的相對關係，也就是
「**正上方**」。

Turn on the light that
is over the table.
把桌子上方的燈打開。

2 under 表「**某物的位置低於另一物**」，
通常是垂直的相對關係，也就是
「**正下方**」。

Clean up the food on the floor under the
table. 把桌子底下地板上的食物清理乾淨。
I saw a mouse under the sofa this
afternoon!
我今天下午在沙發底下發現一隻老鼠！

3 over 也可以表示「**覆蓋**」；
under 也可以表示「**被覆蓋**」。

Pour the sauce over the vegetables.
把醬汁倒到蔬菜上。

The rice should be under the omelet.
白飯應該被蓋在歐姆蛋下面。

4 above 表「**某物的位置高於另一物**」，
但不在同一垂直線上，也就是「**非正
上方**」。

The birds glided above the lake and trees.
鳥兒飛過湖泊和樹木上空。

5 below 表示「**某物的位置低於另一
物**」，但不在同一垂直線上，也就是
「**非正下方**」。

Bob was standing below the birds.
鮑伯就站在鳥兒下方。
From the top of the Taipei 101 building,
we could see the city below.
我們可以從台北 101 的頂樓眺望整座城市。

6 underneath 的意義和用法等同於
under。

He's hiding underneath/under the
blanket. 他躲在毯子下面。

Practice

1

請勾選正確的答案。

1. The ball rolled ☐ under ☐ below the sofa.

2. The mobile dangled ☐ over ☐ under the baby's crib.

3. Be sure to sweep the dirt ☐ under ☐ below the floor mat.

4. Aren't those snow-capped mountains ☐ above ☐ over the village beautiful?

5. You can spread out the jigsaw puzzle pieces ☐ above ☐ over the whole table.

6. Who is that guy talking and laughing ☐ above ☐ below our tree house?

2

請依圖示，從框內選出適當的「介系詞」填空，完成句子。

| over | under | below | above |

1

Pour some tarragon sauce _____ the grilled salmon and garnish it with vegetables before you serve the dish.

2

A meerkat is an animal that lives _____ the ground.

3

The moon hangs quietly _____ our city.

4

A lionfish swam _____ the diver.

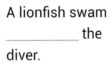

5

Jenny is snorkeling _____ the surface of the ocean.

6

Susan kept her money _____ the mattress.

Unit **131**

Prepositions of Place: In Front Of, Behind, Between, Among, Opposite

表示「地點」的介系詞：In Front Of、Behind、Between、Among、Opposite

in front of
the box

behind
the box

1 in front of 指「在某物／人的前面」。

Ernie is standing in front of **the elementary school.**

爾尼正站在小學的前面。

Do not stand in front of **the car when it's being started.**

車子發動的時候，不要站在車子前面。

between **the boxes**

2 behind 意指「在某物／人的後面」。

The children are playing behind **the bus shelter.** 孩子們正在公車亭後面玩耍。

I was scared by a stray dog coming out from behind **the tree.** 我被樹後面跑出來的一隻流浪狗給嚇到了。

among **the boxes**

3 between 意指「在兩個物品／人物的中間」。

Sonny's motorcycle is between **the tree and the fire hydrant.**

桑尼的摩托車就停在樹木和消防栓之間。

Who is that girl sitting between **Johnny and Annie?**

坐在強尼和安妮中間的那個女生是誰？

opposite

5 opposite 表示「在對面」。

The lion and the hyenas stood opposite **each other, ready to fight for the dead antelope.**

獅子和土狼群為了爭奪一頭死掉的羚羊而對峙，準備打鬥。

4 among 意指「在三個以上之物品／人物的中間」。

Peter is the best singer among **his classmates.** 彼得是全班最會唱歌的人。

Practice

1 請依圖示，勾選正確的答案。

There is a woman ☐ opposite ☐ in front of the gate.

Lily was ☐ between ☐ among the students who raised their hands to answer the teacher's question.

The puppies are kissing their mother, who is sitting ☐ among ☐ between them.

Do you recognize the boy ☐ behind ☐ opposite the chain link fence?

2 請從框內選出適當的「介系詞」填空，完成句子。

between
among
behind
in front of
opposite

1. May I stand _____ you? You're taller than me. I can't see the singer on the stage.

2. Can we buy some sugar cane juice from the drink vendor on the _____ side of the street?

3. Who's there hiding _____ the curtain?

4. Do you have to travel _____ the clinic and your house every day?

5. Our teacher let us discuss it _____ ourselves before explaining in detail.

Unit

Prepositions of Place: Near, Next To, By, Beside, Against, Inside, Outside

inside
the box

outside
the box

near
the box

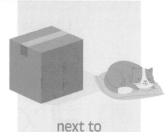

next to
the box

by/beside
the box

against
the box

1 near 表示「在附近」。

The university is near the town of Amherst. 這所大學離安赫斯特鎮很近。
The kids are playing near the lake.
孩子們在湖泊附近玩耍。

2 next to 表示「比鄰著」。

The dormitory is next to the Sports Center. 宿舍就在體育中心旁邊。
Would you mind if I sat next to you?
你介不介意我坐在你旁邊？

3 by 和 beside 的意義相同，都指「在旁邊」。

The Science Center is by the front gate.
= The Science Center is beside the front gate. 科學中心與前門相鄰。
The engineering building is by the Performing Arts Center.
= The engineering building is beside the Performing Arts Center.
工程大樓在表演藝術中心隔壁。

4 against 表示「靠著；倚著」。

A woman is leaning against the wall.
有名女子倚靠在牆上。

5 inside 表「在裡面」，意義與 in 相同。

The extra blankets are inside the chest.
= The extra blankets are in the chest.
多餘的毯子都放在衣櫃裡。
Are you sure the thieves are still inside the house? 你確定小偷還在屋內嗎？

6 outside 表示「在外面」。

The maid stood outside her room for 30 minutes.
女僕在自己的房間外站了 30 分鐘。
Can you let my dog in? I don't want to leave him outside the house.
可以讓我的狗狗進去嗎？我不想留牠在屋外。

Practice

1 請依圖示，勾選正確的答案。

1

Jason parked his scooter ☐ outside ☐ inside the house.

2

Matilda left her scooter ☐ by ☐ on the wall.

3

Those new scooters are standing ☐ outside ☐ against the rental shop.

4

There is an old bicycle ☐ along ☐ against the wall.

5

Sam parked his scooter ☐ inside ☐ near the forest.

6

The sisters are sitting ☐ against ☐ next to each other.

7

The laundry is hanging ☐ outside ☐ near the house.

8

A man is standing ☐ beside ☐ inside the car.

Prepositions of Movement:
In, Into, Out Of, On, Onto, Off
表示「移動方向」的介系詞：
In、Into、Out Of、On、Onto、Off

on the box
在上面

in the box
在裡面

on/onto the box
到上面

off the box
脫離

in/into the box
進入

out of the box
出來

---

1 in 表示「在裡面」。

My car is in the repair shop.
我的車在修車廠。

2 in 和 into 都可表示「進入某處」。

Put the trash in the garbage can.
= Put the trash into the garbage can.
把垃圾丟到垃圾桶裡。

Larry put his hands into his pockets to avoid the cold wind.
賴瑞把手放進口袋裡，免得被冷風吹。

3 out of 表示「從某處出來」。

Take your clothes out of the washer.
把你的衣服從洗衣機拿出來。

4 on 表示「在上面」。

The bananas are on the counter.
香蕉就在櫃台上。

5 on 和 onto 都可表示「到某處上面」。

Put the tea kettle on the stove.
= Put the tea kettle onto the stove.
把茶壺放到火爐上。
Please step on the scale.
= Please step onto the scale.
請站到體重計上面。

6 off 表示「脫離某處」。

Take your feet off the coffee table.
把你的腳從咖啡桌上移開。
Gary, get off the wall right now.
蓋瑞，現在立刻從牆上下來。

Practice

1 請從框內選出適當的「介系詞」填空，完成句子。有些空格的答案不只一個。

in

on

into

out of

off

1. Tom dove _____ the swimming pool.

2. Sandy took the cake _____ the oven.

3. The villains were hiding _____ their secret cave.

4. The jewel thief put the fake ring _____ the counter.

5. Put the plates _____ the table.

6. Take your hat _____ the bust of Beethoven.

7. The sugar is _____ the cabinet.

8. Victoria was sitting _____ Bobby's motorcycle.

2 請依圖示，勾選正確的答案。

Jennifer squeezed some lotion □ on □ into the back of her hand.

Molly is taking her bicycle □ off □ out of the car.

The mother and daughter put the cookies □ in □ onto the oven.

Lily, get your paws □ off □ out me.

I poured some milk □ into □ on the coffee.

Simon sprinkled some parsley □ in □ onto the dish and served it.

A goldfish jumped □ onto □ out of the tank.

Unit **134**

Prepositions of Movement:
Up, Down, From, To, Toward
表示「移動方向」的介系詞：
Up、Down、From、To、Toward

up **the stairs**

down **the stairs**

1 up 意指「往上」。

My big cat is <u>up</u> that tree.
我的大貓上到了那棵樹上。
Father went <u>up</u> the hill for rare herbs.
父親上山去採集稀有草藥了。

2 down 意指「往下」。

I fell <u>down</u> the stairs and broke my leg.
我跌下樓梯，摔斷了腿。
George went <u>down</u> the mine to look for his daughter.
喬治走下礦坑去找他女兒。

3 from 表示「出發點」、「從某處來」。

My family came <u>from</u> the countryside.
我的家人來自鄉村。
We drove <u>from</u> the suburbs to the mall downtown.
我們從郊區開車前往市區的購物中心。

4 to 表示「到某處」、「目的地」。

My parents moved <u>to</u> the city when I was ten years old.
我父母在我十歲的時候搬到這座城市。
I drive <u>to</u> work every day.
我每天開車去上班。

5 toward 或 towards 表「往某處移動」。

Let's walk <u>toward</u> the park so I can see something green.
我們往公園走，讓我看看綠色植物吧。
I've been thinking about moving the couch <u>toward(s)</u> the windows.
我一直想把沙發搬到靠窗一點的地方。

6 表示「到達一個城鎮、城市或國家」，可以用 get to 或 arrive in。

When will we <u>get to</u> Dubai?
= When will we <u>arrive in</u> Dubai?
我們什麼時候會抵達杜拜？
Jennifer <u>got to</u> Bangkok yesterday morning.
= Jennifer <u>arrived in</u> Bangkok yesterday morning.
珍妮佛昨天早上抵達曼谷。

7 如果是「抵達一個比較小的地方」，則會用 get to 或 arrive at。

We <u>got to</u> the Prado Museum in Madrid at 1:00.
= We <u>arrived at</u> the Prado Museum in Madrid at 1:00.
我們一點的時候抵達馬德里的普拉多美術館。
When will the directors <u>arrive at</u> the office for the board of directors?
董事們何時會抵達公司召開董事會？

Practice

1 請依圖示，勾選正確的答案。

The firefighter climbed ☐ **up**
☐ **down** the ladder to the rooftop.

Tears keep falling ☐ **from** ☐ **down**
her face.

Larry walked ☐ **up** ☐ **down** the
hill to the lake.

The guest wanted to make a phone
call ☐ **toward** ☐ **from** the hotel
room.

2 請從框內選出適當的「介系詞」填空，完成句子。

up

down

from

toward

to

at

1. We walked slowly _____ the hill and got _____ the top
   at around 2:30 p.m.

2. We saw a bird resting in a tree, so we moved slowly _____ the
   tree to get a closer look.

3. We tried not to disturb the bird. However, it flew away _____
   the tree when it saw us.

4. We headed _____ the hill in the afternoon and arrived
   _____ a restaurant at the foot of the hill by night.

5. The head waiter walked _____ us and took us _____
   our table.

6. After we had a good meal, we sipped some coffee and then drove
   back _____ our apartment.

Unit **135**

Prepositions of Movement: Along, Across, Over, Through, Past, Around

表示「移動方向」的介系詞：Along、Across、Over、Through、Past、Around

along the path   across the path

over the bridge

past the tree   around the tree

1 along 表示「沿著」。

Drive along the shoreline and look for a place to picnic.

沿著海岸線開，找個可以野餐的地方。

Walk along the main road, and you'll see a blue building. That is the gallery.

沿著大路走，你會看到一棟藍色的建築，那裡就是畫廊。

2 across 表示「橫越」。

She is swimming across the river.

她游泳橫越了這條河。

3 over 也有「穿越」的意思。

Let's walk over the bridge and look around on the other side of the stream.

我們走過橋到溪的對岸看看吧。

比較

但 across 和 over 有差別，over 通常是「穿越一個高起的物體」。

- I saw him walking across the street.
  我看到他穿越了馬路。

✗ Michelle drove across the mountains to see her cousins in the valley.

✓ Michelle drove over the mountains to see her cousins in the valley.
  蜜雪兒開車越過山脈，去拜訪住在山谷裡的表親。

4 through 也表示「穿越」。

Walk through the woods, and you'll see our village.

穿過樹林後，你就可以看到我們的村莊了。

5 past 表示「經過」或「超過」。

As we walked past the bakery, we could smell cinnamon rolls in the oven.

在我們走過麵包店時，可以聞到烤箱裡肉桂捲的香味。

Let's speed up and get past that slow truck ahead of us.

我們加速超越我們前面那輛開得很慢的卡車吧。

6 around 或 round 表示「環繞」。

We walked around the fountain and watched the water shoot up from different directions.

我們繞著噴泉走，看著水柱從各種角度噴出。

We sat round the table, talked, and laughed. 我們圍桌談笑。

around 和 round 還有「到處」的意思。
另外美式英語常用 around，比較少用 round。

Practice

1

請勾選正確的答案（包含 **Units 128-135** 所介紹的「介系詞」）。

1. I will meet you ☐ in front of ☐ from the main entrance to the zoo.

2. I'm going to sneak a cigarette ☐ towards ☐ behind the store.

3. Set up the chess pieces on the ☐ opposite ☐ around sides of the board.

4. Park ☐ up ☐ between the lines, or you will get a ticket.

5. The pub is so ☐ close to ☐ next to here that we should pop in for some pizzas and beer.

6. Pull up a chair ☐ next to ☐ through your brother and join us for dinner.

7. There is an umbrella rack ☐ by ☐ between the front door.

8. Let's ☐ stroll along ☐ arrive at the promenade and see the sights.

9. You can save a few steps cutting ☐ near ☐ across the parking lot.

10. Since it's raining, let's walk ☐ through ☐ opposite the mall to the car.

11. The elevated highway goes right ☐ over ☐ get to the old meat packing district.

12. This street will take us ☐ between ☐ across town.

13. Why don't we go up ☐ to ☐ along the men's department on the seventh floor?

14. I will be walking ☐ around ☐ in the second floor of the history museum.

15. We just walked ☐ past ☐ at a guy sleeping face down on the sidewalk.

16. Step ☐ over ☐ between the construction material, and don't fall into the hole.

17. Take the bus ☐ from ☐ up downtown ☐ over ☐ to the university.

18. When we get ☐ near ☐ behind San Jose, you will see Silicon Valley.

19. Tell me when we will ☐ near ☐ arrive at Harrods Department Store.

20. I will be ☐ at ☐ between home all night.

21. Can we go ☐ around ☐ over the traffic circle again?

22. Walk ☐ across ☐ around the pedestrian walkway and turn right.

Unit **136**

Transport: Get In, Get Out Of, Get On, Get Off, By, On, In

表示「交通方式」的詞彙：Get In、Get Out Of、Get On、Get Off、By、On、In

1 「位於轎車內」要用 in。

Mike left the flyers in his car.

麥克把傳單留在車上了。

2 「上車」要用 get in 或 get into；「下車」要用 get out of。

Jerry got in(to) his car and sped off.

傑瑞上了車後加速離開。

Tommy, get out of the car now.

湯米，現在就下車。

3 搭乘大眾交通工具、飛機、船舶，都用 on。

Joan's suitcase is already on the train.

瓊的行李箱已經在火車上了。

This is a non-smoking flight. Please do not smoke on this plane.

本班機為禁菸航班，請勿在機上吸菸。

All the cargoes have been put on the ship. 所有的貨物都放到船上了。

4 「上大眾交通工具、飛機、船舶」，都用 get on 或 get onto；

「下大眾交通工具、飛機、船舶」，都用 get off。

I saw the man get on(to) the train with a suspicious box. 我看到那個男子提著一個可疑的箱子上了火車。

Patsy got off the plane and walked across the tarmac.

派西下了飛機後就步行穿過停機坪。

5 「上下機車或單車」也用 get on(to) 或 get off。

Nancy hesitantly got on(to) the back of Stan's motorcycle.

南西有些遲疑地坐上史丹的摩托車後座。

Nick got off the bike and went into the post office. 尼克下了腳踏車，走進郵局。

6 如果是表示「**交通方式**」，會用「by + 交通工具」，並且不能加 **the**。

In the old days, people traveled by horse and wagon. 過去人們是搭乘馬車旅行的。

When people started to travel by car, the automobile was called the horseless carriage.

人們剛開始乘坐汽車時，這種交通工具被稱為「無馬馬車」。

7 唯獨「**走路**」的固定片語是 on foot。

It's too close to take a cab. Let's go on foot.

太近了，不需要搭計程車，我們走路去吧。

8 如果交通工具前面有**冠詞 a**、**an**、**the**，或**所有格 my**、**his**、**her** 等，則不能用 **by**，要用「in . . . car」或「on . . . 其他交通工具」。

Willa offered to drive us to the pet store in her car. 薇拉說要開車載我們去寵物店。

Alice said she would never ride on a motorcycle again.

艾麗絲說她以後絕不再坐摩托車了。

Fritz wants to travel around Europe on his bicycle. 費利茲想要騎自行車漫遊歐洲。

Practice

1

請從框內選出適當的「介系詞」填空，完成句子。

in
into
on
by

1. Tell your brother to get ＿＿＿＿＿＿ the car. We're leaving.

2. My car is being repaired, so I came ＿＿＿＿＿＿ subway.

3. The best way to learn your way around a new place is ＿＿＿＿＿＿ foot.

4. I don't want to go ＿＿＿＿＿＿ train.

5. I would rather go ＿＿＿＿＿＿ plane.

6. Don't take your car. Both of us can ride ＿＿＿＿＿＿ Sue's van.

7. Which shipping method is cheaper, ＿＿＿＿＿＿ train or truck?

8. I usually get to work ＿＿＿＿＿＿ taxi, but sometimes I go ＿＿＿＿＿＿ foot.

9. Stanley left his suitcase ＿＿＿＿＿＿ a subway train.

2

請依圖示，勾選正確的答案。

The little boy is sleeping □ in □ on a car.

The boy is getting □ into □ on the bus.

We will be having our lunch □ on □ in the plane.

The woman asked her son to □ get on □ get off the boat. They were going for a ride.

The woman □ got out □ got off the train at the wrong station. She had no idea what to do.

Part 18 Prepositions of Time
表示時間的介系詞

Unit 137

Prepositions of Time: In, At, On (1)
表示「時間」的介系詞：In, At, On（1）

1 「較長的一段時間」多半用 in，如**年分、月分、世紀**。

in January 在 1 月

in 2021 在 2021 年

in the ten years from 2011 to 2021
在 2011 年到 2021 年間的 10 年

in the twentieth century 在二十世紀

2 說明「**季節**」要用 in。

in spring 在春天

in summer 在夏天

in autumn / in the fall 在秋天
↳ fall 前要加 the

in winter 在冬天

3 說明「**星期**」、「**週末**」，要用 on。

on Monday 在星期一

on Friday 在星期五

on Sundays 在每個星期日

on the weekend 在週末

on weekends 在每個週末

4 說明「**日期**」，要用 on。

on November 22nd 在 11 月 22 日

on the first of December 在 12 月 1 日

on December 22nd, 2023
在 2023 年 12 月 22 日

5 表示「**一天中的一個時段**」，要用 in。

in the morning 在上午

in the afternoon 在下午

in the evening 在傍晚

例外

at **night** 和 at **midnight**
是例外的慣用語。

6 表示「**一天中的一個確切時間**」，要用 at。

at three o'clock 在 3 點

at noon 在正午

at 5:32 在 5 點 32 分

at dinner time 在晚餐時間

at 10 p.m. 在晚上 10 點

7 表示「**國定假日**」，通常用 at。但是如果有提到 day、eve 等表示「**假日當天**」的用語，則要用 on。

at Thanksgiving 在感恩節

at Easter 在復活節

on Memorial Day 在陣亡將士紀念日

on Halloween 在萬聖節

on Christmas Day 在聖誕節

on New Year's Eve 在除夕

at/on Christmas 在聖誕假期間
↳ Christmas 用 at 或 on 都可以。

102

Practice

1

請以 in、at 或 on 填空，完成句子。

1. I will call you ＿＿＿＿＿ 1:00.
2. Shall we go to watch the fireworks ＿＿＿＿＿ the evening?
3. We go to a tropical island on vacation ＿＿＿＿＿ winters.
4. I have a lunch appointment ＿＿＿＿＿ Friday.
5. Movable type printing was invented by Bi Sheng ＿＿＿＿＿ approximately 1040.
6. Printing was applied extensively across the world ＿＿＿＿＿ the eighteenth century.
7. Irving was born ＿＿＿＿＿ August 19th.
8. A stranger called ＿＿＿＿＿ midnight yesterday.
9. Do you usually go bowling ＿＿＿＿＿ the weekend?
10. Rice is planted ＿＿＿＿＿ spring and harvested ＿＿＿＿＿ summer or autumn.
11. Meet me ＿＿＿＿＿ lunch time.
12. The night is the longest ＿＿＿＿＿ winter solstice.
13. Traditionally, Chinese families gather for their annual reunion dinner ＿＿＿＿＿ Chinese New Year's Eve.

2

請從圖中選出與敘述相對應的節日，並搭配正確的「介系詞」填空。

 Halloween

 Chinese New Year

 Christmas

 New Year's Eve

 the Mid-Autumn Festival

1. We eat moon cakes and look at the full moon ＿＿＿＿＿.

2. Families and friends will get together and exchange cards ＿＿＿＿＿.
   Also, doors and windows will be decorated with lights and mistletoes.

3. Children in ghost costumes will go from house to house playing "trick or treat" ＿＿＿＿＿.

4. People shoot off fireworks ＿＿＿＿＿ all over the world.

5. Every family thoroughly cleans the house to sweep away ill luck ＿＿＿＿＿.
   People also call or visit their friends to wish them a happy and wealthy new year.

Prepositions of Time: In, At, On (2)
表示「時間」的介系詞：In, At, On（2）

1 如果 morning、evening 等字的前面還有提到「**星期**」，則要用 on。

on Tuesday **morning** 在星期二早上

on Thursday **afternoon** 在星期四下午

on Saturday **evening** 在星期六傍晚

2 如果 morning、evening 等字的前面還有提到「**昨天、明天**」等，則完全**不加介系詞**。

tomorrow **morning** 在明天早上

yesterday **afternoon** 在昨天下午

✗ Mona has agreed to help you on tomorrow afternoon.

✓ Mona has agreed to help you tomorrow afternoon.

夢娜已經答應明天下午要幫你。

3 時間的前面如果有 next、some 等限定詞，不需要再加任何**介系詞**。

some **day** 總有一天

last **night** 在昨天晚上

next **summer** 在明年夏天

- next
- last
- every
- each
- some
- any
- one

✗ Kate will arrive on next Friday.

✓ Kate will arrive next Friday.

　凱特將於下星期五抵達。

✗ Gerald goes to see Sheryl at every weekend.

✓ Gerald goes to see Sheryl every weekend.

　傑瑞德每週末都去看雪柔。

4 「in + 一段時間」用來表示「**多久之後**」。

in **five minutes** 過五分鐘

in **two months** 兩個月後

Joanna will have finished getting her hair done in an hour.

↳ 從現在起的一小時之後

瓊安娜再過一小時就做完頭髮了。

Charlotte has to finish writing her master's thesis in one month.

↳ 從現在起的一個月之後

夏綠蒂得在一個月內寫完她的碩士論文。

You can have the car in two hours.

↳ 你要等兩小時。

再過兩小時你就能拿到這輛車。

You will get your score reports in three weeks.

↳ 需要三星期才能收到成績單。

三星期後你們就會收到成績單。

5 in 也可和「所有格 + time」的用語搭配，一樣表示「**多久以後**」。但這種所有格結構不簡潔。in a week 比 in a week's time 簡潔且自然。

You will hear from Megan again in a week's time.

一週內你就會再收到梅根的消息。

You will see Trisha in about two weeks' time.

大約兩星期後，你就會見到翠莎了。

6 what time 通常不加 **at**。at what time 雖非錯誤，但已經是過時的用法，**when** 前面不能用 **at**。

What time are we meeting?

我們幾點碰面？

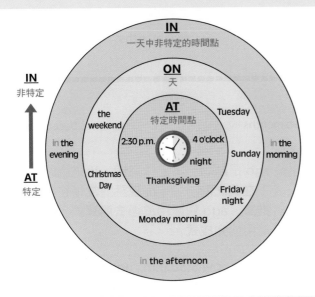

Practice **1** 請以 in、at 或 on 填空，完成句子。如果不需要介系詞，請在空格內劃上「/」。

1. Are we going to meet _____ the afternoon?

2. Let's meet _____ Monday night instead.

3. I will go on a tour to Jakarta _____ next Wednesday.

4. He will finish his homework _____ twenty minutes.

5. You will lose five pounds _____ a month if you follow this diet carefully.

6. If you are ready now, then you can get there _____ ten minutes.

7. She visits her grandma _____ every weekend.

8. Where were you _____ yesterday morning? I kept calling you, but you never answered.

9. I'm going to the bookstore _____ this afternoon. Do you want me to buy any books for you?

10. When did you hear the noise _____ last night?

11. Do you think you can finish the project _____ two weeks?

12. Since I have to find the illustrations from the picture bank, I might be able to finish this book _____ two months.

13. My parents went to the farmers' market twice _____ last week.

14. The spokesman for the Ministry of Foreign Affairs is having a press conference _____ tomorrow night.

15. Will you join the company outing _____ next weekend?

16. You can meet me _____ any time _____ tomorrow afternoon.

17. I saw him in the laundromat _____ one day.

Unit **139**

Prepositions of Time: For, Since, Before (Compared With the Adverb "Ago")
表示「時間」的介系詞：For、Since、Before（與副詞 Ago 比較）

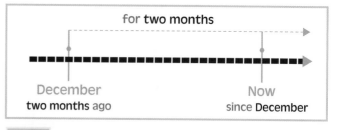

1 for 用來說明一個事件「持續了多久」。for 後面會接「一段時間」，可以用於**過去**、**現在**或**未來**時態。

We waited in line for two hours.
我們排隊等了兩小時了。

Most of the time we wait here for about two hours.
多數的時候，我們在這裡要等兩小時左右。

We will have to wait for two hours.
我們將在這裡等上兩小時。

2 說明一個事件的「**開始時間**」，會用 since。since 後面會接「一個確切的時間」。

I have lifted weights since high school.
我從高中開始練舉重。

He's lived in Atlanta since 2015.
他從 2015 年開始，就住在亞特蘭大。

3 for 和 since 都常和現在完成式搭配，說明**事情持續了一段時間**。

Norton has been going to cram school for five months.
諾頓上補習班已經五個月了。

I've waited for you for two hours. Why are you so late? 我已經等你等了兩個小時了，你怎麼這麼晚才到？

Nancy has been at the cram school since 5:00. 南西從 5 點開始就一直在補習班。

I've waited for you since 4 p.m.
我從下午 4 點就開始等你了。

4 ago 是副詞，不是介系詞，用來說明「**在此之前**」，是從說話的當下往前推算。ago 只能用於過去簡單式，不能用於**完成式**。

The time is now 3:30 p.m., and Heidi left two hours ago. 現在時間是下午 3 點 30 分，而海蒂是兩個小時以前離開的。

✗ Franz has left three hours ago.
✓ Franz left three hours ago.
法藍茲是三小時前離開的。

5 ago 也常用於 how long ago 這樣的問句，來詢問「**多久以前**」。

How long ago did April start preparing for her wedding?
艾波多久以前開始準備她的婚禮？

How many years ago did you quit smoking? 你是幾年前開始戒菸的？

6 for 和 ago 雖然都具有「**多久**」的意義，但用法完全不同。

1 for 是「持續多久」，可以銜接「描述過去、現在或未來的任何一段時間」；

2 ago 是「多久之前」，一定是由「說話的時間往回推算」。

Simone was the top-ranked tennis player one year ago.
↳ 從現在往前推的一年前
一年前，席夢是排名頂尖的網球選手。

Simone was the top-ranked tennis player for one year.
↳ 過去某段時間，未必與現在銜接。
席夢曾有一年時間是排名頂尖的網球選手。

1

請以 for、since 或 ago 填空，完成句子。

1. Nat lived with his uncle _____ three years while he was a university student.

2. Ivan has been living in the faculty dorm _____ 1995.

3. Jamie graduated from the university one year _____.

4. How long _____ did Martina finish graduate school?

5. Next year Jake will be coming back for a visit _____ one month.

6. Wes has been staying in the haunted house _____ two days, and so far nothing has happened.

7. The reporter has been interviewing the actor _____ 2 p.m.

8. Sammi moved to Paris five months _____.

9. I have been thinking about the project _____ yesterday.

10. I have helped in my mom's restaurant _____ I was twelve.

2

請依據括弧提示回答問題。

1. How long have you been playing the piano? (fifteen years)
   → *I have been playing the piano for fifteen years.*
   _____

2. How long have you studied the history of art? (2005)
   → _____
   _____

3. How long ago did you start your YouTube channel? (three years)
   → _____
   _____

4. How long will you stay in Toronto? (six months)
   → _____
   _____

5. When did you arrive? (four hours)
   → _____
   _____

6. Since when have you been selling fried chicken in the night market?
   (last year)
   → _____
   _____

Part 18 Prepositions of Time
表示時間的介系詞

Unit **140**

Prepositions of Time: During (Compared With "In," "For," and "While")
表示「時間」的介系詞：
During（與 In、For、While 比較）

1 說明「介於某段時間之中」，可以用 in 或 during，意思相同。

Lily wore a chicken costume in/during the parade.
莉莉在遊行時穿著小雞的道具服。

The phone rang many times in/during the night. 電話一晚上響了很多次。

2 說明「在某個活動從頭到尾的完整期間」，要用 during，此時不能用 in。

✗ The dog had his head out of the window in the whole car ride.

✓ The dog had his head out of the window during the whole car ride.

在搭車這段時間，狗狗一直把頭伸出車窗外。

✗ We met the principal in our visit to the elementary school.

✓ We met the principal during our visit to the elementary school.

我們去小學參觀的時候，遇到了校長。

✗ In breakfast, we talked about our plans for the day.

✓ During breakfast, we talked about our plans for the day.

吃早餐的時候，我們談了當天的計畫。

3 during 和 for 雖然都指「一段時間」，但 during 是指「事情發生在某事件的期間」，經常接的是「一個事件」，for 是指「事情發生了多久」，要接「一段時間」。

❶ It rained during our vacation in Hawaii.
我們去夏威夷度假期間有下雨。

It rained for almost a week in Hawaii.
夏威夷下了快一星期的雨。

❷ We were in Mexico during the spring break. 春假的時候，我們人在墨西哥。

We were in Mexico for two weeks.
我們在墨西哥待了兩個星期。

4 during 和 while 的意義相同，都是「在……期間」，但 during 要接名詞，while 可以接子句。

❶ Marsha arrived during dinner time.
瑪莎在晚餐時抵達。

Cyrus arrived while we were eating dinner.
賽勒斯在我們吃晚餐的時候到達。

❷ Tiffany fell asleep during the opera.
蒂芬妮聽歌劇時睡著了。

Frankie fell asleep while he was watching the opera.
法藍奇去看歌劇的時候睡著了。

Practice

1

請勾選正確的答案。

1. My parents went to Sydney □ during □ while the winter.

2. Christina was at her office □ for □ in the whole day.

3. □ During □ In dinner we watched TV.

4. Marla was sleeping □ during □ for the morning.

5. Laura has scuba dived □ for □ during two hours.

6. □ During □ While the party, Alyssa lost her remote control for the TV.

7. Mary hid in her bedroom □ while □ during my in-laws were visiting.

8. Hillary was out of town □ for □ while ten days.

2 請將 A 欄句子和 B 欄的「介系詞片語」搭配，寫出完整的句子。

A

I burned my fingers

I had to go to the bank

I watched a basketball game

I ate a lot of ramen and pork chops

I've been busy with the bank merger

B

while my wife was taking a shower and getting ready to go

in the cooking class

during my lunch break

for the whole week

during my vacation in Tokyo

1. ....

2. ....

3. ....

4. ....

5. ....

Unit **141**

Prepositions of Time:
By, Until, From . . . To, From . . . Until,
Before, After
表示「時間」的介系詞：
By、Until、From . . . To、From . . .
Until、Before、After

1 by 意指「在某個時間之前」，不能晚於該時間。

I have to leave by 7 p.m.
↳ 最晚 7 點要離開。
我得在晚上 7 點以前離開。

I can finish proofreading the articles
by tomorrow afternoon.
我明天下午以前可以校對完這些文章。

2 until 或 till 意指「直到某個時候」，事件要到該時間才會結束。

I can work until/till 11 p.m.
我可以一直工作到晚上 11 點。

The engineer is checking the power
system. We won't have the power back
until/till 10 p.m. 工程師正在檢查電力系統，要到晚上 10 點才會恢復供電。

3 「from . . . to」和「from . . . until」的意義相同，都是「從一個時刻直到另一個時刻」。

I will need the car from 6:00 to 8:00 **this**
evening. 我今晚 6 點到 8 點要用車。
Can I use your truck from 3:00 until 5:00?
我 3 點到 5 點之間可以借用你的卡車嗎？

4 before 指「在某個時間或活動之前」。

Let's leave before 2:00.
我們 2 點之前出發吧。

We set off for the airport before dawn.
我們天亮之前就出發前往機場。

5 after 意指「在某個時間或活動之後」。

Do you want to come over after 3:00?
你要不要 3 點之後順道過來？

We walked along the coast after dinner.
晚飯之後，我們沿著海岸散步。

6 before 和 ago 都具有「之前」的意義，before 可以當作介系詞，也可以當作副詞，但 ago 只能當作副詞。

Tom arrived in Wellington two weeks
ago, **and Susan arrived in Wellington**
three days before **him.**
↳ Tom 從現在往前推的兩個星期前抵達；
　Susan 比 Tom 早三天抵達。
湯姆兩個星期前抵達威靈頓，而蘇珊又比他早三天到達。

Practice

1

請從框內選出適當的「介系詞」填空。

| by |
| until |
| from |
| to |
| before |
| after |

1. ＿＿＿＿＿ 1:00 ＿＿＿＿＿ 3:00 we are having an open house.

2. I'll stay at the house ＿＿＿＿＿ you come home.

3. I have to leave for the meeting ＿＿＿＿＿ 1:00 this afternoon.

4. We are busy ＿＿＿＿＿ December 1st ＿＿＿＿＿ December 10th.

5. This is our second visit. We were here once ＿＿＿＿＿.

6. We have to get to the airport ＿＿＿＿＿ 2 p.m.

7. We usually go for some snacks ＿＿＿＿＿ swimming.

8. I had a cup of coffee ＿＿＿＿＿ resuming my work.

9. I won't go home ＿＿＿＿＿ I finish these papers.

10. She has to get a job ＿＿＿＿＿ graduation.

2 請依圖示，同樣用上一題框內的「介系詞」填空，完成句子。

Bill got up early since he had to get to the office ＿＿＿＿＿ seven.

He had a quick breakfast ＿＿＿＿＿ he left for work.

He had an important meeting ＿＿＿＿＿ nine ＿＿＿＿＿ ten.

The meeting did not end ＿＿＿＿＿ twelve.

＿＿＿＿＿ the meeting, he went to the buffet next to his office for lunch.

He relaxed a little ＿＿＿＿＿ a hard day's work.

Part **19** Other Prepositions
其他介系詞

Unit **142**

Individual Usage of Prepositions:
With, By, In, On

一些介系詞的個別用法：
With、By、In、On

with

1 with 常用來描述「**某人或某物擁有的東西**」。

Melvin thinks he knows that guy with the briefcase.　↳ 那個男人有個公事包

梅爾文覺得他認識拿著公事包的那個男人。

April works for a company with two　↳ 那間公司有兩個海外分支
overseas subsidiaries.

艾波在一間有兩個海外分支的公司工作。

2 with 常用來描述「**做某事所使用的工具**」，此時不能用 **by**。

Open the wine bottle with the corkscrew.

用這個開瓶器開紅酒。

What are you going to buy with this money? 你打算用這筆錢買些什麼？

by

3 by 用來表示寫作、作曲、作畫的「**作者**」，此時不能用 **of**。

Hamlet is a famous play by Shakespeare.

《哈姆雷特》是莎士比亞的知名劇作。

"When I Have Fears That I May Cease to Be" is a poem by John Keats.

《每當我害怕》是約翰·濟慈的詩作。

This is a painting by an artist named Smith.

這幅畫是一名叫做史密斯的畫家所畫的。

in

4 說明書寫、作畫的「**方式**」要用 in。

in oils	in chalk	in ink	in watercolors
用油墨	用粉筆	用鋼筆	用水彩

Anita drew a picture in oils.

艾妮塔用油墨作了一幅畫。

May I fill in the form in pencil?

我可以用鉛筆填表嗎？

5 in 可以用來說明「**穿著**」。

Tammy looks great in her new shawl.

譚美穿著新披肩很好看。

Margaret has decided to go to the interview in her suit.

瑪格麗特決定穿著套裝去面談。

on

6 on 常常用來說明「**行程的目的**」。

- on a trip 旅遊
- on a journey 旅遊
- on (a) holiday 放假
- on business 洽公
- on a vacation〔美式〕/ on vacation〔英式〕度假

William will be away on business **for a week.**

威廉將出差一星期。

Practice

1

請從框內選出適當的「介系詞」填空。

> with
>
> by
>
> in

1. Do you want to go to a restaurant _____ private rooms?

2. Doris is going to the party _____ her new jeans.

3. Laurie knows the girl _____ the yellow umbrella.

4. Do you like oatmeal cookies _____ raisins?

5. The kids can go to the cram school _____ their uniforms.

6. I am reading a book _____ Charles Dickens.

7. Chop up these carrots _____ a chef's knife.

2

請依圖示，從框內選出適當的詞語，並搭配正確的「介系詞」填空。

> Andrew Lloyd Webber
> _____
> pen
> _____
> a gray scarf
> _____
> two garage doors
> _____
> (a) vacation
> _____
> the soap

Sign your name at the bottom
_____ .

My family went to Florida
_____ .

Cats is an opera _____
_____ .

That house
_____ belongs to the Simpsons.

Wash your hand thoroughly
_____ .

I don't recognize the woman
_____ .

Unit **143**

Individual Usage of Prepositions:
Like, As (Compared With "As If")
一些介系詞的個別用法:
Like、As（與連接詞 As If 比較）

like

1 like 可當作介系詞，用來說明兩種事物的相似性，此時後面要接名詞、代名詞或動名詞。

The woman looks just like you.
那個女人看起來和你很像。

She speaks like a native speaker of English.
她說話聽起來很像是英語的母語人士。

Talking to her is like talking to a diplomat.
跟她說話，就好像在跟外交官說話一樣。

2 like 經常用來「舉例」。

Darleen can cook gourmet food like soufflés and raspberry tortes.
達琳會烹飪精緻的食物，如舒芙蕾和覆盆子蛋糕。

as

3 as 可當作介系詞，用來說明「某人的工作」或「某物品的功能」。

When Louis was young, he worked as a draftsman. 路易斯年輕時，工作是繪圖員。

The little girl used the coffee table as a doll house. 這個小女孩把咖啡桌拿來當娃娃屋。

比較

as 和 like 都可能接「一個職業或功用」，但意義不同。使用 as 表示那是「真正的職業」，使用 like 表示「類似該職業，但其實不是」。

- **Amy works as an actress.** 艾美的工作是演員。
  ↳ 她真的是演員。
- **Amy looks like an actress.** 艾美看起來像演員。
  ↳ 她不是真的演員。

4 as 也可以表示「如同；像」，但多半屬於連接詞的用法，後面接子句為多。

The village was not as far away as we had expected to be.
村莊沒有我們想像中的遠。

as if

5 as if 屬於連接詞，但是它的用法常和 like 或 as 混淆。as if 後面要接子句。

Ron looks as if he is tired.
朗恩看起來很累。

The restaurant looks as if it will close soon.
這間餐廳看起來像是很快就要打烊了。

6 as if 經常用於「假設語氣」的句型，接過去簡單式來表示「與現在事實相反」，接過去完成式來表示「與過去事實相反」。

Barney orders us around as if he were our boss.
↳ 巴尼並不是老闆；在假設語氣中用 were 來取代 was，是更正式的用法。
巴尼不斷指揮我們，就好像他是老闆一樣。

Joan felt as if she had been transported back in time to her childhood. 瓊安覺得她彷彿被帶回過去，回到她的兒童時期。

7 **as if** 可以用 as though 取代。

The Senator says we have to address this evolving situation as though it were a matter of life and death.
參議員說，我們必須因應這個變化的情勢，彷彿這是什麼攸關生死的大事。

The house looked as though it hadn't changed in 40 years. 這房子看上去就好像四十年來從未改變過。

Practice

1

請用 like、as 或 as if 填空，完成句子。

1. Jerome's apartment is a lot _____ mine.

2. Gene has been promoted _____ I predicted.

3. This novel is so boring that it is _____ reading a phone book.

4. Sonny started his career in the hotel industry _____ a bellhop.

5. Willie looks _____ a professional athlete.

6. Jordan looks _____ he needs a strong cup of coffee.

7. Don't follow me around _____ you were a lost dog.

8. It looks _____ we will be going on the stage next.

9. James is good at many ball games _____ basketball and volleyball.

2

請勾選正確的答案。

1. Julia is working ☐ as ☐ like a secretary at our company.

2. Do you want to use this wood box ☐ like ☐ as a tea table?

3. Why is Lorelei dressed ☐ as if ☐ like an old lady?

4. He attended the conference ☐ as ☐ like the firm's representative.

5. You talk ☐ as ☐ as if you didn't know anything.

6. There was a big thunderstorm last night, but today everything is quiet and it seems as if nothing ☐ happened ☐ had happened.

7. Larry generously offered us the food and drinks ☐ as ☐ as though he were the host.

8. I can cook simple dishes ☐ as ☐ like fried rice and tomato salads.

9. He acted ☐ as ☐ like a professional performer.

10. Your ten-year-old car looks ☐ as if ☐ as it were new.

Unit **144**

Indirect Objects With or Without "To" and "For"

To 與 For 搭配間接受詞的用法

1 有些動詞如 give 和 buy，會同時有直接受詞和間接受詞。直接受詞通常是「物」，間接受詞通常是「人」，句型為「動詞 + 間接受詞 + 直接受詞」。

✗ Larry gave a gift Kate.

✓ Larry gave Kate a gift.
↳ 動詞要先接間接受詞（接受物品的人），再接直接動詞（物品）

賴瑞送給凱特一份禮物。

✗ Amanda is buying lunch Daniel.

✓ Amanda is buying Daniel lunch.
亞曼達在幫丹尼爾買午餐。

2 有些動詞如果先接**直接受詞**，要再加介系詞 to，才能接**間接受詞**，句型：

| 動詞 | + | 直接受詞 | + | to | + | 間接受詞 |

這類動詞有：

• bring	• pass	• read	• take
• give	• pay	• recommend	• tell
• lend	• post	• sell	• throw
• offer	• promise	• send	• write
• owe	• reach	• show	

Cliff gave the ring to **April**.
克里夫將戒指送給艾波。

Steven lent his notebook computer to **Lara.** 史蒂芬把他的筆記型電腦借給蘿拉了。

3 有些動詞若先接**直接受詞**，要再加介系詞 for，才能接**間接受詞**，句型：

| 動詞 | + | 直接受詞 | + | for | + | 間接受詞 |

這類動詞有：

• bring	• cook	• get	• prepare
• build	• do	• keep	• save
• buy	• fetch	• knit	
• change	• find	• make	
• choose	• fix	• order	

Belinda bought a ticket for **Diane**.
貝琳達買了一張票給黛安。

Belinda bought a ticket for **Diane, not Martha**.
↳ 在句中增加「否定子句」，可以更強調間接受詞。
貝琳達買了一張票給黛安，不是給瑪莎。

Jimmy is going to order wedding cakes for **Vera**. 吉米會幫薇拉訂購婚禮蛋糕。

She knitted a sweater for **herself**.
她為自己織了一件毛衣。

4 **直接受詞**如果是代名詞，則通常會放在**間接受詞**的前面。

✗ Eric gave **the guy it** at the door.

✓ Eric gave **it** to the guy at the door.
艾瑞克把它交給門口的那個人了。

There are many stories in this book. I used to read them **to my kids when they were little.** 這本書裡有很多故事，我在孩子還小時會唸給他們聽。

Practice

1 請將下列各句子改寫為「不用 to 或 for 的句子」。

1. Bella will give the letter to Trevor.
   → *Bella will give Trevor the letter.*

2. Phil will forward the email to Dave.
   → _____

3. John is going to buy a coat for Mindy.
   → _____

4. Mark bought the teapot for Rita.
   → _____

5. Can you read the news to Grandpa?
   → _____

6. I will show the ingredients to you.
   → _____

7. I am going to build a house for my parents.
   → _____

2 請將下列各句子改寫為「使用 to 或 for 的句子」。

1. Morris is going to bring Gabriel the paint.
   → *Morris is going to bring the paint to/for Gabriel.*

2. Gerald is going to pay Kate the money.
   → _____

3. Suzanne is going to read her son a book.
   → _____

4. Larry will recommend Gail a restaurant.
   → _____

5. I'll buy you lunch.
   → _____

Adjectives With Specific Prepositions (1)
形容詞所搭配的特定介系詞（Ⅰ）

about

- **excited about** 對……感到興奮
- **worried about** 對……感到擔心
- **nervous about** 對……感到緊張
- **angry about** 對……感到生氣
- **annoyed about** 對……感到惱怒
- **furious about** 對……感到憤怒
- **mad about** 對……感到著迷

Josephine is excited about visiting her family for a week.

要回去探望家人一星期，喬瑟芬感到很興奮。

Sophia is furious about her son's behavior at school. 蘇菲亞對她兒子的在校行為感到氣憤。

for

- **famous for** 以……聞名
- **well-known for** 以……聞名
- **responsible for** 對……負責

Sue is responsible for the purchase. 蘇負責採購。

This café is famous for chicory coffee and French crullers.

這家咖啡館的菊苣咖啡和法式甜甜圈很出名。

at

- **good at** 擅於
- **bad at** 不擅於
- **clever at** 擅於
- **hopeless at** 極不擅於
- **mad at** 對……生氣

Billy is good at ping pong.
比利很會打乒乓球。

John is hopeless at board games.

約翰對棋盤遊戲一竅不通。

- **surprised at/by** 對……感到驚訝
- **astonished at/by** 對……感到驚異
- **shocked at/by** 對……感到震驚
- **amazed at/by** 對……感到驚奇

Joan was surprised at receiving the full scholarship.
= Joan was surprised by the full scholarship she received.

瓊很驚訝能拿到全額獎學金。

We were all shocked at/by the news. 我們全都對這則新聞大為震驚。

with

- **pleased with** 對……感到滿意
- **bored with** 對……感到無聊
- **disappointed with** 對……感到失望
- **happy with** 對……感到開心
- **satisfied with** 對……感到滿意

The boss was pleased with your translation of the contract. 老闆對你翻譯的合約很滿意。

We were all bored with his speech. 我們都覺得他的演講很無聊。

- **angry/annoyed/ furious with** + *sb.* (**+ for** *sth.*) 為了某事生某人的氣

Don't be angry with your mother for overfeeding our kids when we go over to her house.

我們去你媽媽家的時候，你可別因為她餵孩子們吃太多就生氣。

Practice

請從框內選出適當的「介系詞」填空。

about

at

with

by

for

1. There is no reason to be worried _____ looking for a new job.

2. I hope you're good _____ hiding your job search effort from our boss.

3. You will be surprised _____ how many job offers you will get.

4. You are well-known _____ your research work in biology.

5. My wife would be unhappy _____ me if I took time off to relax and she still had to go to work every day.

6. Is Andy still mad _____ me?

7. Both my brother and I are mad _____ modern art.

8. My wife is hopeless _____ housework.

9. O. Henry's short stories are famous _____ clever and unexpected endings.

請依圖示從 A 框和 B 框中選出搭配的詞語填空完成句子。

A

amazed by

good at

nervous about

bored with

satisfied with

B

our teacher's long and uninformative speech

the dolphin show

solving a Rubik's cube

our son's English exam score

having dinner with my girlfriend's parents

1 We were _____ _____ at Ocean Park.

2 We were _____ _____.

3 We were _____ _____.

4 She is _____ _____.

5 I'm _____ _____.

Unit **146**

Adjectives With Specific Prepositions (2)
形容詞所搭配的特定介系詞（2）

to

- **engaged to** *sb.* 與某人訂婚
- **married to** *sb.* 嫁給某人
- **similar to** 與……相似

My brother is engaged to a charming woman.

我哥哥和一位迷人的女子訂婚了。

Fiona is getting married to Andy in June. 菲歐娜和安迪將於 6 月結婚。

- **nice to** *sb.* 對某人好
- **kind to** *sb.* 對某人好
- **good to** *sb.* 對某人好
- **friendly to** *sb.* 對某人友善
- **polite to** *sb.* 對某人有禮
- **rude to** *sb.* 對某人無禮

You should be nice to your little sister. 你應該對你妹妹好一點。

You shouldn't be rude to your classmates. 你不應該對同學無禮。

of

- **afraid of** 害怕
- **frightened of** 恐懼
- **scared of** 害怕
- **proud of** 驕傲
- **ashamed of** 羞愧
- **jealous of** 嫉妒
- **envious of** 羨慕
- **suspicious of** 懷疑
- **aware of** 注意到
- **conscious of** 意識到
- **capable of** 有能力
- **fond of** 喜愛
- **tired of** 厭倦
- **short of** 缺乏
- **full of** 充滿

Chester is afraid of being seen as a mama's boy.

切斯特怕被當成「媽寶」。

Alisa is fond of water skiing.

愛莉莎熱愛滑水。

others

- **different from/to** 與……不同

The house my grandparents live in has been remodeled and looks different from the way it looked twenty years ago.

我祖父母的家改造之後，看起來和二十年前很不一樣了。

The living room in your apartment looks different to mine. 你公寓的客廳看起來和我的不一樣。〔美式不用 to，英式可以用 to〕

- **nice of** *sb.* (to do . . .)
  某人很好心（做了某事）
- **kind of** *sb.* (to do . . .)
  某人很好心（做了某事）
- **good of** *sb.* (to do . . .)
  某人很好心（做了某事）
- **friendly of** *sb.* (to do . . .)
  某人很友善（做了某事）
- **polite of** *sb.* (to do . . .)
  某人很有禮貌（做了某事）
- **rude of** *sb.* (to do . . .)
  某人很無禮（做了某事）
- **stupid of** *sb.* (to do . . .)
  某人很愚蠢（做了某事）

It was nice of Ted to offer to pick you up at your house.

泰德提議到你家去接你，他人真好。

It was rude of you to push your little brother.

你那樣推你弟弟很粗魯。

- **interested in**
  對……有興趣

Are you interested in learning how to dance?

你有興趣學跳舞嗎？

- **keen on** 熱衷於

Archie is keen on Korean online games.

亞契很喜歡玩韓國的線上遊戲。

Practice

1

請用適當的「介系詞」填空，完成句子。

1. Looking for a job when you have experience is different _____ when you look for a job right after you graduate.

2. Only go for a job interview if you are seriously interested _____ the job with the company.

3. I'm capable _____ handling the customers' complaints, so I would be a good person for this job.

4. It is OK to be a little worried _____ what will happen if you leave your safe and secure job.

5. It was nice _____ you to ask for my advice on this matter.

6. I have never been keen _____ job hopping, but sometimes you have to do it.

7. I have been here so long that I'm practically married _____ my job.

8. I'm tired _____ making hundreds of phone calls every day.

9. It was kind _____ John to recommend me for the post, but I'm not looking for a new job at this time.

10. Louis is jealous _____ my being promoted.

11. I feel ashamed _____ what I've done to you.

12. His solution to this problem is different _____ yours.

2

請從圖片中選出適當的用語填空，完成句子。

try smoking	help the elderly	take a shortcut	yell at people

1. It was rude of you to _____.

2. It was kind of you to _____.

3. It was stupid of you to _____.

4. It was clever of you to _____.

Nouns With Specific Prepositions (1)
名詞所搭配的特定介系詞（1）

have difficulty with sb./sth.
與某人相處或做某事有困難

A rebellious teenager has difficulty with people of authority.

叛逆的青少年不易與權威人士相處。

answer to ……的答案

However, the answer to the problem is not buying more food from local restaurants. 然而，並不只是到本地市場多買一點食物就能解決問題。

demand for
對……的要求

The demand for housing is increasing.

住屋的需求逐漸增加。

example of ……的範例

As an example of her cooking difficulties, the young girl said making seaweed salad was especially hard.

為了說明她做飯的困難，這位年輕女士舉例說，做海帶沙拉就特別困難。

attitude toward/ towards 對……的態度

Many people's feelings and attitudes towards bullfighting are ambivalent.

許多人對鬥牛的觀感和態度是好壞參半。

difference between
（兩者之間的）不同

In terms of taste, there is no difference between fructose and sugar.

說到吃起來的味道，果糖和砂糖並沒有什麼不同。

fall in 在……方面的下降

There will be a fall in the price of bananas because of overproduction.

香蕉產量過剩的結果，造成售價下跌。

cause of ……的原因

The cause of the large-scale power outage is still unknown.

這次大規模的停電原因依舊不明。

difficulty (in) V-ing
在……方面的困難

The young girl had difficulty (in) cooking for her family when her mom became sick.

媽媽生病期間，那位年輕的女孩要為家人做飯是有困難的。

increase in
在……方面的增加

The elder women in the neighborhood have all noticed the increase in prices at the fruit stand.

這一帶年紀大一點的婦女都注意到水果攤的價格上升了。

decrease in
在……方面的減少

There was a decrease in the company's profit last year.

去年該公司的營收減少。

Practice

1

請從框內選出適當的
「介系詞」填空。

> to
> for
> of
> with
> between
> in
> toward

1. There are many differences _____ scooters and motorcycles.

2. There is a great demand _____ employees with language skills.

3. My son has difficulty _____ concentrating on his homework when the TV is blaring.

4. The new clerk in the accounting department has a bad attitude _____ me.

5. One of the answers _____ cheap and safe space travel is the building of space elevators.

6. I had difficulty _____ the language when I moved to Japan three years ago, but I can communicate without any big problems now.

7. There has been a fall _____ the country's industrial exports recently.

8. A recent policy allowed a small increase _____ the taxi fare.

2

請依圖示，從框內選
出適當的用語填空，
完成句子。

> difficulty in
> demand for
> example of
> decrease in
> causes of

1 The Pont du Gard is a good _____ _____ Roman architecture.

2 Toxic chemical substances are one of the _____ water pollution.

3 In the market there is a growing _____ _____ fresh and organically grown vegetables.

4 There has been a _____ the amount of ice in western Antarctica due to melting and the increased calving of icebergs.

5 Scientists are having _____ accurately predicting when and where an earthquake will occur.

Unit **148**

Nouns With Specific Prepositions (2)
名詞所搭配的特定介系詞（2）

---

invitation to
（到某活動的）邀請

Everyone in the office has received the invitation to her wedding.

辦公室裡的每一個人都收到她的喜帖。

---

need for 對……的需要

We have no need for a loan.

我們沒有貸款的需要。

---

picture/photograph of ……的圖片

I've uploaded the pictures of my trip to Malaysia to my web album.

我已經把我去馬來西亞旅遊的照片放上我的網路相簿了。

---

reaction to 對……的反應

What's their reaction to the new policy?

他們對新政策的反應如何？

---

reason for ……的理由

There is no reason for buying expensive clothing for kids when they outgrow their clothes so fast.

孩子們長那麼快，沒必要為他們買太貴的衣服。

---

relationship with 和……的關係

Elle has kept a close relationship with her college roommate.

艾兒一直和她的大學室友維持親近的關係。

---

relationship between （兩者或以上之間的）關係

The relationship between the three sisters has become complicated after they all got married.

三位姐妹結婚後，她們之間的關係就變得複雜起來了。

---

reply to 對……的回覆

You haven't provided a reply to my question.

你還沒有回覆我所提的問題。

---

rise in 在……方面的上升

The rise in unemployment needs to be dealt with.

失業率的攀升問題需要解決。

---

solution to ……的解決方式

The government was unable to implement any solution to inflation.

政府對於通貨膨脹的問題始終無法提出解決方案。

Practice

1

請從框內選出適當的「介系詞」填空。

to

for

of

with

between

in

1. Recently, there has been a steep rise _____ gasoline prices.

2. Roscoe was surprised when he received a photograph _____ his ex-girlfriend.

3. Vivian suggested a solution _____ the scheduling problem.

4. Helen has a good relationship _____ her husband's parents.

5. The reason _____ quitting a job differs from person to person.

6. The relationship _____ Tom and me is awful.

7. There's no urgent need _____ more doctors.

8. I haven't received any replies _____ my job applications.

2

請選出正確的答案。

_____ 1. The _____ sea level is linked to global warming.

 Ⓐ reaction to   Ⓑ rise in   Ⓒ reason for   Ⓓ solution to

_____ 2. The _____ a man and his father-in-law should be positive.

 Ⓐ relationship with   Ⓑ reply to
 Ⓒ relationship between   Ⓓ invitation to

_____ 3. Sulfur trioxide's _____ contact with water can be violent.

 Ⓐ reaction to   Ⓑ reply to   Ⓒ need for   Ⓓ rise in

_____ 4. You need to carefully maintain good _____ your family members and friends.

 Ⓐ relationships with   Ⓑ solution to
 Ⓒ relationships in   Ⓓ pictures of

_____ 5. Did you get an _____ Sue's birthday party this weekend?

 Ⓐ reply to   Ⓑ need for   Ⓒ rise in   Ⓓ invitation to

_____ 6. His _____ our request was astonishing.

 Ⓐ apply for   Ⓑ need for
 Ⓒ reply to   Ⓓ relationship with

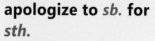

Verbs With Specific Prepositions
動詞所搭配的特定介系詞

「動詞 + 介系詞」的用法，其實屬於**片**
語動詞的一種，在 Units 85、86 當中已
經有詳細的範例。

在本單元裡，將把重點放在「**動詞 + 受**
詞 + 介系詞」，甚至受詞之前還要加介
系詞的習慣用法。

---

apologize to *sb.* for *sth.*
為了某事向某人道歉

Cody apologized to Miranda for being late.

寇帝為了遲到的事向米蘭達道歉。

---

accuse *sb.* of *sth.*
指控某人做了某事

Edgar claimed he didn't take Sophia's teddy bear, but Sophia accused him of not being honest.

艾加說他沒拿蘇菲亞的泰迪熊，但是蘇菲亞指控他不老實。

---

blame *sb.* for *sth.*
責怪某人做了某事

Don't blame me for losing that sale.

別因為失去那筆買賣而責怪我。

---

blame *sth.* on *sb.*
為某件事怪罪某人

Don't blame losing that sale on me.

別把失去那筆買賣算在我頭上。

---

borrow *sth.* from *sb.*
向某人借某物

George borrowed a truck from his brother to move our new furniture.

喬治向哥哥借了一輛卡車搬我們的新家具。

---

complain to *sb.* about *sth.*
向某人抱怨某事

My sister complained to me about her mother-in-law.

我妹妹對我抱怨她婆婆。

---

congratulate *sb.* on doing *sth.*
為了某件事恭喜某人

Trevor congratulated his neighbors on having a new baby.

崔弗恭喜鄰居誕育新生兒。

---

explain *sth.* to *sb.*
向某人解釋某事

Jeanette explained the city map to her son.

珍奈對兒子解說市區地圖。

---

invite *sb.* to *sth.*
邀請某人參加某活動

Malcolm is planning to invite his girlfriend's parents to dinner.

麥爾康打算邀請他女友的父母去吃晚餐。

---

remind *sb.* about *sth.*
提醒某人做某事

Miranda reminded Conrad about their plan to have dinner with the Harrisons.

米蘭達提醒康瑞德，他們要和哈里森一家人一起吃晚餐。

---

remind *sb.* of *sth.*
使某人回想起某事

Her story reminds me of a camping experience I once had.

她的故事讓我想起我曾有過的一次露營經驗。

---

tell *sb.* about *sth.*
告訴某人某事

Tell Oliver about the new manifests for shipping containers.

跟奧利佛說一下貨櫃箱的新貨單。

> ### warn someone about *sth./sb.* 警告某人提防某事／某人
>
> Tanya warned Chris about paying for their house insurance so it wouldn't lapse.
> 譚雅提醒克利斯要付房屋保險了，不然要過期限了。
>
> Sandra warned me about Mr. Parker.
> 珊卓提醒我要提防帕克先生這個人。

Practice

1

請從框內選出適當的「介系詞」填空。

of
for
from
to
about
on

1. The victim accused the tall man _____ snatching her purse.
2. Don't blame the bride _____ the groom's foolishness in drinking too much.
3. I borrowed a tuxedo _____ my brother for a friend's wedding.
4. Jack congratulated his boss _____ getting a promotion.
5. Sue explained _____ her mother how to create an Instagram story.
6. My neighbor invited me _____ a graduation party for his son.
7. The mother reminded her son _____ packing his recorder on the day he had music class.
8. Did you tell your teacher _____ your doctor's appointment tomorrow?
9. Sandy apologized _____ her brother _____ having used his car without asking him.
10. I can't agree with you if you're going to blame all this _____ me.
11. Will you explain your project _____ Mr. Robertson, please?

2

請從框內選出適當的用語，搭配括弧內的詞彙填空，完成句子。

remind of

warn about

blame for

congratulate on

borrow from

complain to . . . about . . .

1. Travis _____warned Marcia about the risk of buying stocks_____
(Marcia / the risk of buying stocks).
2. Warren _____
(a food processor / his sister).
3. You shouldn't _____
(her / spoil the children). You're the one who buys them new toys every week.
4. Andrea _____
_____ (her husband / his overloading the washing machine).
5. We held a dinner party to _____
_____ (Bernard / winning the award).
6. His story _____
(me / my childhood).

Unit **150**

Prepositional Phrases
慣用的介系詞片語

on time
準時（正好落在正確時間）

Dina always gets her work done on time.

蒂娜總是準時完成工作。

Jerry rarely turns in his reports on time.

傑瑞很少在規定的時間內交報告。

in time
及時（在規定的時間內）

She arrived home just in time for the Christmas dinner.

她剛好及時到家吃聖誕晚餐。

by credit card / check
用信用卡／支票

Lindsay is going to pay for the clothes by credit card.

琳賽要用信用卡支付買衣服的錢。

in cash 付現金

Bennett paid for his meal in cash.

班內特吃飯以現金付款。

at the end of
最終（表示事情結束）

At the end of the track meet, the medals were awarded to the winners.

田徑賽結束後，獎牌便頒發給得獎者。

The washer was making so much noise at the end of its rinse cycle that I was not surprised when it broke down.

洗衣機最後漂洗運轉的聲音那麼吵，我一點也不訝異它會壞掉。

in the end
終於（一段時間之後）

In the end, we chose some traditional wood furniture despite our initial indecision.

儘管難以決定，到頭來我們還是選了傳統的木製家具。

At first my mom didn't like the furniture, but in the end she grew to love it.

剛開始我媽媽不喜歡這些家具，但是過一陣子她漸漸開始喜歡了。

in someone's opinion
就某人的看法

In Wally's opinion, people are inherently good, but eventually some become corrupt.

華利認為人性本善，不過也有些人會受後天影響學壞。

for example 例如

Let's eat some healthy food for lunch, for example, a fruit salad.

我們午餐吃健康一點的食物吧，例如水果沙拉。

(fall) in love with
愛上

Nick is falling in love with Nancy. 尼克愛上了南西。

by mistake 不小心

Alison sent you the file by mistake.

艾莉森不小心把檔案寄給了你。

by accident/chance
意外地

I ran into Lisa by accident this afternoon.

我今天下午巧遇莉莎。

by chance 無意間

I saw this advertisement by chance.

我無意間看到這則廣告。

Practice

1

請勾選正確的答案。

1. Did you get the ticket ☐ in time ☐ on time to attend the basketball game?

2. Since the tickets didn't arrive either early or late, I guess you could say they arrived ☐ in time ☐ on time.

3. The buses are always late, and they never arrive ☐ in time ☐ on time.

4. We didn't arrive ☐ in time ☐ on time to see the pre-game show.

5. Helen is very punctual, and she always comes ☐ in time ☐ on time.

6. I hope my thank-you present arrives ☐ in time ☐ on time for you to take it with you when you leave.

7. In the beginning I disliked living in Caracas, but ☐ in the end ☐ at the end I didn't want to leave.

8. We are moving to Kuala Lumpur in Malaysia ☐ in the end ☐ at the end of the month.

9. At first Oscar didn't want to give up smoking, but ☐ in the end ☐ at the end he decided to give it a try.

10. I called every bookstore in the city, and ☐ in the end ☐ at the end I found exactly the right edition of the play.

11. Vince is starring in his first lead role ☐ in the end ☐ at the end of September.

12. Tony was barely able to walk or even stand ☐ in the end ☐ at the end of the 26.5 mile marathon.

2

請從框內選出適當的「介系詞」填空。

by
for
in

1. I forgot who I was calling and dialed your extension _____ accident.

2. I think I will pay _____ cash.

3. Seaweed, _____ example, often smells bad but tastes delicious.

4. Martin and Angela fell _____ love and got married.

5. _____ my girlfriend's opinion, we should get married right away.

1

請以正確的「介系詞」填空，完成句子。如果不需要介系詞，
請在空格內劃上「/」。

1. The team is meeting _____ the gym _____ Green Street _____ 7:00 _____ tomorrow morning.

2. We are looking for an apartment _____ Fukuoka.

3. Bonnie went for a drive _____ the countryside _____ Sunday afternoon.

4. I decided to take a taxi so that I could arrive _____ time for Sue's birthday party.

5. Marie is thinking _____ going to the art museum _____ Saturday. Are you interested _____ joining her?

6. Claude has been working _____ the design firm _____ Dresden _____ the last five years.

7. Ian had some difficulty _____ finding a place to live _____ the south of France.

8. The Harper family lives _____ 21 Beach Street. They live _____ the third floor.

9. Roger went to the Van Gogh Museum _____ his visit _____ Amsterdam two years ago.

10. _____ my opinion, there are too many commercials on TV.

11. Julia went _____ a vacation _____ the end of last month.

12. My parents have been staying _____ the Marriott Hotel _____ Broadway since they arrived _____ New York.

13. Kim has suffered _____ knee problems since she started to play on the tennis team.

14. At first Lou wanted to go home, but _____ the end he decided to go with everybody else to the pub.

15. I am reading a novel _____ Margaret Atwood.

16. Last summer Erica worked _____ a photographer _____ Africa _____ two months.

17. Alfred found an old coin _____ the floor _____ the desk _____ his grandfather's room.

18. Robbie is not very good _____ driving a motorcycle.

19. Howard and Cathy arranged to meet _____ the café on Tenth Street for a drink _____ 4:00 _____ Saturday afternoon.

20. Brigit has a good relationship _____ her boss.

21. There is an urgent need _____ better education in developing countries, as it is expected to improve local people's lives.

22. Joyce is very different _____ her mother but quite similar _____ her father.

23. Mona is looking for a new apartment _____ three bedrooms, two bathrooms, a kitchen, and a big living room.

24. The district attorney accused the defendant _____ filing a civil lawsuit for the sole purpose of harassment.

25. Do you know _____ a drink called coconut jelly tea?

26. Chicago is located _____ the southwestern tip of Lake Michigan _____ the Midwest of the United States. It is an industrial city _____ a population of about 2.7 million.

27. Is there any significant difference _____ these two kinds of flour?

28. Brook has always wanted his wife to be proud _____ her accomplishments.

29. The employees are happy _____ the increase _____ their year-end bonuses.

30. Sue complained _____ her sister _____ the smell _____ the downstairs where the tenant is always frying fish.

31. Last summer Sue went _____ Rome _____ a tourist trip _____ her husband.

32. I am a little bored _____ the job sometimes, but I am deeply committed to it.

33. What did you have _____ breakfast this morning?

Yes/No Questions
Yes/No 疑問句

1 所謂的「Yes/No 問句」，是要以「Yes.」或「No.」作為回答的問句。「Yes/No 問句」的構成，是將句中的 **be 動詞或助動詞**移到**句首**。

Monty is reading. 蒙提正在讀書。
→ Is Monty reading? 蒙提正在讀書嗎？
Virginia has finished her book.
維吉妮亞已經把書看完了。
→ Has Virginia finished her book?
維吉妮亞看完書了嗎？
Shelby can read one book a week.
莎碧每星期可以看一本書。
→ Can Shelby read one book a week?
莎碧每星期可以看一本書嗎？

2 句中**沒有 be 動詞或助動詞**時，就在句首加上 do、does、did，此時主要動詞要用原形動詞。

Airplanes fly over here. 這裡有飛機經過。
→ Do airplanes fly over here?
飛機會從這邊經過嗎？
Joe enjoyed flying over the mountains.
喬很享受飛過山岳的感覺。
→ Did Josephine enjoy flying over the mountains? 喬很享受飛過山岳的感覺嗎？

3 「Yes/No 問句」經常以**簡答**作為回應：

Yes, 主詞 + be 動詞／助動詞
No, 主詞 + be 動詞／助動詞 + not

Sue: Are you going out for breakfast?
Ann: Yes, I am. / No, I am not.
蘇： 你要出去吃早餐嗎？
安： 對，我要出去吃。／不，我不出去吃。

4 「Yes/No 問句」若回答時沒有明確的答案，有時會用 think、hope、expect、suppose、imagine、be afraid 等字來簡答，表達自己的想法，這些字的後面可以用 so 來表示肯定的簡答。

Jane: Is your daughter drawing a picture?
Mary: I think so.
(= Yes, I think she is drawing a picture.)
珍： 你的女兒在畫畫嗎？
瑪莉：應該是吧。
（對，我想她應該是在畫畫。）
Jane: Do you think it will be a good picture?
Mary: I expect so.
(= Yes, I expect it will be a good picture.)
珍： 你認為那會是一幅好畫嗎？
瑪莉：希望如此囉。（我希望那會是一幅好畫。）

5 think/expect/suppose/imagine 若要做**否定簡答**，是在這些字「前面」加上 don't。

Pete: Are you going to buy whiteboard markers?
Rene: I don't think so.
比特：你要去買白板筆嗎？
芮奈：沒有。

- I don't think so.
- I don't expect so.
- I don't suppose so.
- I don't imagine so.

6 hope 和 be afraid 的**否定簡答**，則是在後面加上 not。

Are you going to the meeting with the boss?
你要跟老闆一起去開會嗎？

I hope not.
希望不要。

Did they cancel the meeting?
他們取消會議了嗎？

I am afraid not.
恐怕沒有。

Lena: Do you have any money on you?
Stan: Yes, I do. / No, I don't.
莉娜： 你身上有錢嗎？
史丹： 對，我有。／不，我沒有。

Practice

1

寫出與下列各回答對應的「Yes/No 問句」。

1. This is a seaside spa.
   → Is this a seaside spa?

2. You can soak in the hot tub in your room.
   → _____

3. They have reserved two adjacent rooms for us.
   → _____

4. The hotel has been expecting our arrival.
   → _____

5. Connie likes spas with not much sulfur in the water.
   → _____

6. Andrew enjoyed the Japanese restaurant at the resort.
   → _____

2

請用「簡答」填空，完成句子。

1. "Can you drive?" "Yes, _____."

2. "Are you ready to start?" "Yes, _____."

3. "Have you got all the photocopies?" "No, _____."

4. "Have you been working on it?" "Yes, _____."

5. "Did you get all the books?" "No, _____."

6. "Is Susan late?" "Yes, _____."

3

請用括弧內的提示字寫出「簡答句」。

1. Is that a drawing of a bunny rabbit? (yes / think)
   → Yes, I think so.

2. Does that bunny rabbit have two ears? (yes / hope)
   → _____

3. Is that cute little bunny rabbit carrying a machine gun? (yes / afraid)
   → _____

4. Are you going to the meeting on Saturday? (no / think)
   → _____

5. Will the boss make me go? (no / expect)
   → _____

6. Are you going to have the weekend off? (no / afraid)
   → _____

Unit 153

Wh- Questions
Wh- 疑問句

1 Wh- 疑問句以字首為 wh- 的疑問詞開頭（how 也屬於這種疑問詞），同時句中的 **be** 動詞或助動詞也要移到**主詞前面**。

- who
- what
- where
- when
- why
- how
- which
- whose

❶ **Erica is thinking.** 艾瑞卡正在思考。

What **is Erica thinking about?**

艾瑞卡正在思考什麼？

❷ **Jerome has stopped.** 傑洛米停下來了。

Why **has Jerome stopped?**

傑洛米為什麼停下來了？

2 如果原句中**沒有 be** 動詞或助動詞，就要在疑問詞的後面加上 do、does、did。

❶ **Bill wants a new job.**

比爾想要新的工作。

Why does **Bill want a new job?**

比爾為什麼想要新的工作？

❷ **Tim needs a ride.**

提姆需要人載他一程。

When does **Tim need a ride?**

提姆什麼時候需要人載他？

❸ **Ruby bought a sandwich toaster.**

露比買了一台壓吐司機。

Where did **Ruby buy a sandwich toaster?**

露比在哪裡買了一台壓吐司機？

3 who 和 what 常用來詢問**主詞**，也就是「行為者為何」，此時可以直接以 **who** 或 **what** 當作主詞，不需要改變直述句的語序，也不需要另外加 do、does 或 did。

❶ **Stephanie loves Tom.** 史黛芬妮很愛湯姆。

Who **loves Tom?** 誰愛湯姆？ ↳ 語序不改

❷ **Bobby phoned Amy.** 鮑比打電話給愛咪。

Who **phoned Amy?** 誰打電話給愛咪？

❸ **James is helping Stella.**

詹姆斯正在幫史黛拉的忙。

Who **is helping Stella?**

誰正在幫史黛拉的忙？

4 who 和 what 也可以詢問**受詞**，也就是「動作的接受者為何」，此時 who 和 what 仍位於**句首**，但句子要使用**疑問句的語序**，並視情況加上 do、does 或 did。

❶ **Ruby loves his grandmother.**

露比很愛他祖母。

Who does **Ruby love?** ↳ 改疑問句語序

露比愛誰？

❷ **Christine phoned her boyfriend just now.**

克莉絲汀剛剛打電話給她男友。

Who did **Christine phone just now?**

克莉絲汀剛剛打電話給誰？

❸ **Margaret is helping her father.**

瑪格麗特正在幫她爸爸的忙。

Who **is Margaret helping?**

瑪格麗特正在幫誰的忙？

Practice

1

請依據提示的疑問詞，將右列各句子改寫為「疑問句」。

1. You are leaving.
   → When *are you leaving?*

2. Adrian will leave early.
   → Why _____

3. Woody can hide.
   → Where _____

4. Bryan is coming.
   → When _____

5. Rex has your hat.
   → Why _____

6. Susan has been taking photos.
   → Where _____

7. Mary wants to dance.
   → When _____

8. Herman went to an audition.
   → Why _____

2

請以 who 或 what 寫出詢問主詞或受詞的「疑問句」。

1. Ken likes somebody.
   → *Who does Ken like?*

2. Someone loves Buddy.
   → _____

3. Randy is playing something on his smartphone.
   → _____

4. Somebody called Lily.
   → _____

5. Bruce is cooking something.
   → _____

6. Something went wrong.
   → _____

7. Somebody is honking at Karla.
   → _____

8. Jack is waving at someone.
   → _____

Question Words: What, Who, Which, Whose
疑問詞：**What**、**Who**、**Which**、**Whose**

what

1 疑問詞 what 可以指「**人**」也可以指「**物**」，經常可以搭配名詞使用。

What **channel** are you watching?
你在看哪一台？

What **time** does this show end?
這個節目幾點結束？

What **musicians** do you like?
你喜歡哪些音樂家？

2 what 也可以**單獨使用**，不接**名詞**。

What **is Jordan doing tonight?**
喬登今晚要做什麼？

What **would you like to do tomorrow?**
你明天想要做什麼？

who

3 疑問詞 who 用來指「**人**」，通常**單獨使用**，不接**名詞**。

Who **is going to be awarded a prize?**
誰將會獲獎？

Who **picks the winner from the finalists?**
是誰從參加決賽的名單中選出贏家？

which

4 which 用來詢問「**選擇**」，可以指「**人**」也可以指「**物**」。which 可以**單獨使用**，也可以接名詞。

Which **living ex-president** should be sent to the ceremony? 應該派哪一位仍健在的前總裁去參加典禮呢？

Which **restaurant** in the food court at the mall do you prefer?
你比較喜歡購物中心美食街的哪一家餐廳？

Which **one of these black suitcases is yours?** 這些黑皮箱哪一個是你的？

Which **is your favorite, Chinese food or Japanese food?** 你最愛哪一國料理？中華料理還是日本料理？

whose

5 疑問詞 whose 用來詢問「**所有權**」，可以**單獨使用**，也可以接**名詞**。

Whose **toothbrushes are these in my coffee cup?**
我咖啡杯裡的這些是誰的牙刷呀？

Whose **are these pajamas on my bed?**
我床上這些睡衣是誰的？

Practice

1

請從框內選出適當的「疑問詞」填空，完成句子。

what

who

whose

which

1. _____ is that you are holding in your hand?

2. _____ is your all-time favorite singer?

3. _____ do you prefer, black tea or milk tea?

4. _____ books did you borrow from the library?

5. _____ house is that next to the post office?

6. _____ newspaper are you going to buy today, the *Daily News* or the *New York Post*?

7. _____ choice do I have for lunch?

8. _____ will the runners-up get?

9. _____ do you want, a tomato salad or a chicken salad?

2

請從框內選出適當的名詞，搭配 what、which 或 whose 填空，完成句子。

kind of tea

burger

magazine

toys

shoes

Ⓐ _____ are these in front of the door?

Ⓑ Those are Jane's. He dropped by for a coffee.

Ⓐ _____ do you want today?

Ⓑ I want the fish burger.

Ⓐ _____ are you reading?

Ⓑ It's a financial weekly. Would you like to take a look?

Ⓐ _____ did you order? It smells good.

Ⓑ It's Earl Grey.

Ⓐ _____ are those on the floor?

Ⓑ Those are mine.

Unit **155**

Question Words: Where, When, Why, How
疑問詞：**Where、When、Why、How**

where

1 疑問詞 where 用來詢問「**地點**」，通常**單獨使用**，不接**名詞**。

Where **is your sister?** 你姐姐在哪裡？

Where **does Lee work?** 李在哪裡工作？

when

2 疑問詞 when 用來詢問「**時間**」，通常**單獨使用**，不接**名詞**。

When **is the application due?**
申請什麼時候截止？

When **are they interviewing?**
他們什麼時候要面談？

why

3 疑問詞 why 用來詢問「**原因**」和「**目的**」，通常**單獨使用**，不接**名詞**。

Why **can't I read your comic book?**
為什麼我不能看你的漫畫書？

Why **are you so mean to me?**
你為什麼對我那麼壞？

how

4 疑問詞 how 用來詢問「**程序**」或「**方法**」，通常**單獨使用**，不接**名詞**。

How **do you make guacamole?**
你是如何製作鱷梨沙拉醬的？

How **can I chop onions without shedding tears?**
我要怎麼切洋蔥才不會流眼淚？

5 how 常用來「**打招呼**」、「**詢問對方健康狀況**」。

How **are you?** 你好嗎？

How **do you do? I'm Joseph. Nice to meet you.**
你好嗎？我是喬瑟夫，很高興認識你。

How **is your father doing? Is he still in the hospital?**
你父親現在好嗎？他還在住院嗎？

6 how 可以搭配形容詞或 many/much，來詢問「**程度**」。

How tall **are you?** 你多高？

How often **do you go to the library?**
你多常去圖書館？

How many **dance classes do you have each week?** 你每星期有幾堂舞蹈課？

How much **does a Nintendo Switch cost?**
任天堂 Switch 一台要多少錢？

Practice

1

請從框內選出適當的「疑問詞」填空，完成句子。

where

when

how

why

1. ＿＿＿＿＿＿ did you live when you were a child?

2. ＿＿＿＿＿＿ can you manage a team of 20 people so effectively?

3. ＿＿＿＿＿＿ did you decide to go after saying you wouldn't attend her wedding?

4. ＿＿＿＿＿＿ are you free to meet me for lunch?

5. ＿＿＿＿＿＿ are you taking the guitar class? Friday nights?

6. ＿＿＿＿＿＿ did you open that can? I gave up after I had tried five times.

7. ＿＿＿＿＿＿ are you saying this? It doesn't sound like you.

8. ＿＿＿＿＿＿ are you going scuba diving? I want to join you if I am free then.

2

請從框內選出適當的「疑問詞」填空，完成句子。

how often

how long

how early

how many

how much

1 ＿＿＿＿＿＿＿＿＿ do you get a haircut?

2 ＿＿＿＿＿＿＿＿＿ pairs of shoes do you have in your dressing room?

3 ＿＿＿＿＿＿＿＿＿ have you been married?

4 ＿＿＿＿＿＿＿＿＿ money did you pay for that wonderful two-piece suit?

5 ＿＿＿＿＿＿＿＿＿ do you get up for school every morning?

Unit 156

Negative Questions
否定疑問句

Form 形式

1 否定疑問句是以帶有 n't 的 be 動詞或助動詞開頭。

Aren't you ready to leave?
你還沒準備好要離開嗎？

Can't you sit still? 你就不能靜靜坐著嗎？

Haven't you been doing your homework?
你不是一直在做功課嗎？

2 句中**沒有 be 動詞或助動詞**的時候，則使用 don't、doesn't、didn't 構成否定疑問句。

Don't you know the time?
你不知道現在幾點嗎？

Doesn't your alarm clock work?
你的鬧鐘不是停掉了嗎？

Didn't you get up for school?
你沒有起床去上學嗎？

Doesn't she have a new car?
她不是有一輛新車嗎？

3 否定疑問句也可以不用 n't 的縮寫形式，而在**主詞後面**加上 not，但這種用法過於正式，比較少用。

Aren't you going? = Are you not going?
你沒有要走嗎？

Why didn't she return my calls?
= Why did she not return my calls?
為什麼她沒有回我電話？

Use 用法

4 否定疑問句可以用來表達「**驚訝**」、「**失望**」或「**憤怒**」。

驚訝 **Don't you live here anymore?**
你已經不住在這裡了嗎？

失望 **Haven't we been planning on this outing for a long time?**
我們不是已經計畫這次出遊很久了嗎？

憤怒 **Isn't there something more important that you should be doing?**
你不是還有一些更重要的事該做嗎？

5 否定疑問句經常用於「**感嘆句**」。

Isn't that a terrible waste of money?
那不是太浪費錢了嗎？

Isn't it an informative magazine?
這雜誌的內容不是很豐富嗎？

6 否定疑問句常用來「**確認一件已知的事情**」。

Aren't we meeting at 1:00 this afternoon?
我們不是約今天下午一點見面嗎？

Isn't this a departmental meeting everybody is supposed to attend?
這次的部門會議，不是大家都得參加嗎？

Practice

1 請將括弧內的詞組以「n't 的縮寫形式」改寫為「否定疑問句」，完成句子。

1. I sent you an email. _Didn't you receive it?_ (did you receive it)

2. You are not wearing a jacket. _____
(are you getting cold)

3. Just a minute ago you were carrying an umbrella, and now you're not.
_____ (is that your umbrella)

4. I am talking to you, and you are looking out of the window.
_____ (are you paying
attention to me)

5. I thought you liked ballet, not modern dance. _____
_____ (do you like ballet)

6. You have been eating for over an hour. _____
_____ (have you finished eating yet)

7. When will we arrive at Grandma's house?

_____

(have we been driving on this road too long)

2 請從框內選出適當的「否定助動詞」或「否定 be 動詞」，搭配括弧內的主詞和動詞填空，完成句子。

isn't
aren't
don't
doesn't
didn't
haven't
hasn't
won't

1. _____ (you / run) ten times around the
track already?

2. _____ (she) on business in New York
right now?

3. _____ (you / go) to the beach with us
tomorrow?

4. _____ (you / love) eating kiwi fruit?

5. _____ (he / graduate) from college yet?

6. _____ (this restaurant) the one you go
for dinner every Saturday?

7. _____ (you / call) me last night?

8. _____ (she / play) the kind queen
in the opera?

Unit 157

Tag Questions
附加問句

1 附加問句是在一個句子的最後，加上一個「簡短的疑問句」，形式為：
be 動詞／助動詞 + 人稱代名詞

That's a terrible TV show, *isn't it?*
那個電視節目真難看，不是嗎？

We can't catch the 7:55 train on time, *can we?*
我們趕不上 7 點 55 分的火車了，對吧？

That's about it, *isn't it?*
就這樣了，不是嗎？

You haven't taken a break, *have you?*
你到現在都還沒休息，對吧？

2 附加問句所使用的 be 動詞或助動詞，要與主要句子的動詞相同。

It is 2:00, isn't it? 現在時間是 2 點，對嗎？
You can jump high, can't you?
你可以跳很高，不是嗎？

You don't have the time to help me, do you?
你沒有時間可以幫我，是嗎？

He hasn't finished his homework, has he?
他還沒有完成他的家庭作業，對吧？

3 如果句子裡沒有 be 動詞或助動詞，那麼就要用 do、does、did 來構成附加問句。

You like cheese, don't you?
你喜歡起司，對吧？

He likes pizza, doesn't he?
他喜歡披薩，對吧？

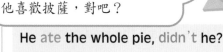

He ate the whole pie, didn't he?
他把整個派吃光了，是不是？

4 一般來說，**肯定句**要用否定的附加問句；**否定句**要用肯定的附加問句。

It is **hot today,** isn't it?
今天好熱，不是嗎？

He can **cook,** can't he?
他會做菜，不是嗎？

It isn't **cold today,** is it?
今天不冷，對吧？

He can't **drive a car,** can he?
他不會開車，對嗎？

5 「否定句 + 肯定附加問句」的句型，經常用來「提出要求」。

You don't **know where my sunglasses are,** do you?
↳ 其實想問對方太陽眼鏡在哪裡
你不知道我的太陽眼鏡在哪裡，對嗎？

6 附加問句的「語調」會影響意義：

■ 1 若語調「上揚」，表示「不太確定」；
■ 2 若語調「下降」，表示「非常肯定」，只是做確認。

You haven't finished reading my magazine, have you?
↳ 詢問對方是否已經看完
我那本雜誌你還沒看完，對嗎？

You haven't finished reading today's newspaper, have you?
↳ 確定對方並沒有看完
你還沒看完今天的報紙，是吧？

Practice

1

請在空格內填上正確的「附加問句」。

1. You aren't cooking curry, _____?

2. Melanie hasn't left yet, _____?

3. Linda can find the right bus, _____?

4. Because of the pollution, it's hard to see the mountains today, _____?

5. Randy doesn't have a map, _____?

6. Jerry hasn't been lost for very long, _____?

7. You like Switzerland, _____?

8. Sarah couldn't go with Tammy, _____?

9. You are a professional gambler, _____?

10. Joseph can't repair the computer, _____?

11. Claudia has taken out the garbage, _____?

12. It isn't my dad on the phone, _____?

13. He couldn't have saved so much money, _____?

14. You don't happen to have a stapler with you, _____?

15. Sandy loves parasailing, _____?

16. Ramon sent us a memorandum about the meeting yesterday, _____?

2

請依據「附加問句」的形式,寫出「主要問句」裡的正確動詞形式。

1. Sally _____ (sketch) portraits of people, can't she?

2. It _____ (be) unbelievable news, isn't it?

3. Kent _____ (speak) Japanese, could he?

4. You _____ (talk) with the vice president last week, didn't you?

5. She _____ (write) editorials for the newspaper, doesn't she?

6. You _____ (ask) for money, are you?

7. They _____ (translate) hundreds of finance articles, haven't they?

8. You wife _____ (cook) on weekdays, does she?

9. Tony _____ (go) for a walk last night, didn't he?

10. Susan _____ (have) a sports car, does she?

Tag Questions: Other Forms
特殊的附加問句形式

1 若**主要句子**以「I am」為首，附加問句要用「aren't I?」。

I am **going first**, aren't I?
我第一個出發，對吧？

I am **working the night shift today,**
aren't I? 我今天上晚班，對嗎？

2 若**主要子句**為「祈使句」，附加問句要用 will you、would you、can you 或 can't you，這時帶有「命令、要求」的意味。

Call **your brother,** will you?
打電話給你哥哥，好嗎？

Give **my suggestion some thought,** would you? 對我的提議表示一些想法，好嗎？

Buddy, sit down, can't you?
巴弟，你坐下行不行？

OK. 好吧。

3 在表示「邀約」的祈使句中，會使用 won't you 作為附加問句。

Come and join **us,** won't you?
來加入我們吧，好不好？

4 若**主要子句**是 there be 句型，附加問句也要用 there。

There aren't **any napkins,** are there?
一點餐巾紙都沒有了，對吧？

5 若**主要句子**以 Let's 開頭，附加問句要用「shall we?」。

Let's **go to the hot spring every weekend,** shall we?
我們每個週末都來泡溫泉，好嗎？

6 若**主要子句**的主詞是 nothing，附加問句則用 it 代替。

Nothing **is happening,** is it?
沒有事發生，對吧？

Nothing **mattered,** did it?
沒什麼大不了的吧，是不是？

7 **1** 若**主要子句**的動詞 have 是「行為動詞」，表示「做某事」，那麼附加問句要用 do/does/did；
2 如果 have 表示「擁有」，則附加問句可以用 do/does/did 也可以用 have。

You just **had lunch,** didn't you?
你剛吃過午餐，是嗎？

She **has a lot of work to do,** doesn't she?
= She **has a lot of work to do,** hasn't she?
她有很多工作要做，不是嗎？

1

請在空格內填上正確的「附加問句」。

1. I am right about everything I said, _____?

2. Let's forget all about our misunderstanding, _____?

3. There won't be any problems buying the spices, _____?

4. I am washing the dishes tonight, _____?

5. Drop in some time and have a cup of tea, _____?

6. There isn't any shower gel in the bathroom, _____?

7. Nothing is more important than your own health,

_____?

8. You had three cups of coffee, _____?

2

請勾選正確的答案。

1. It's a beautiful day, ☐ isn't it? ☐ isn't that?

2. ☐ Let's clean ☐ Clean the refrigerator this afternoon, shall we?

3. Turn off the computer and go to bed now, ☐ will you? ☐ don't you?

4. Let's take Ruby to the theme park this Sunday, ☐ don't we?
   ☐ shall we?

5. Say something constructive, ☐ won't you? ☐ can't you?

6. Move over a little, ☐ would you? ☐ aren't you?

7. There is some misunderstanding between us, ☐ isn't it? ☐ isn't there?

8. They don't have an elevator in their building, ☐ do they? ☐ don't they?

9. You just had an argument with your husband, ☐ haven't you?
   ☐ didn't you?

10. ☐ Put ☐ Let's put the bunny back on the shelf, would you?

11. ☐ Nothing ☐ No one matters anymore, does it?

Unit 159

Reply Questions
回應式疑問句

1 有時我們對於別人的陳述，會以**疑問句**來回應，這種回應式疑問句並不是真正的疑問句，反而是**感嘆句**，有時也暗示出**說話者的情緒**，例如感到有趣、同情、驚訝或憤怒。

I'm living in Soho now.
我現在住在蘇活區。

Are you? That is nice.
是嗎？那真不錯。

I moved last month.
我上個月搬家了。

Did you? I didn't hear about it.
是嗎？我沒聽說。

2 回應式疑問句的句型：
be 動詞／助動詞 + 人稱代名詞
這裡的 be 動詞和助動詞都要跟**原句一樣**。

Annie:	I am registering to vote.
Brad:	Are you? This is a big step for you.
安妮：	我正要登記去投票。
布萊德：	是嗎？這可是你的一大步。
Celine:	David has finished his painting.
Samuel:	Has he? Let's go and take a look at it.
席琳：	大衛的畫已經完成了。
山謬：	是嗎？我們去看看。
Vivian:	Roger isn't cutting the grass as you asked.
Laura:	Isn't he? Well, then, I need to have a word with him.
薇薇安：	羅傑沒有照你說的去剪草。
蘿拉：	沒有嗎？那我得和他談一談。

3 如果原句中**沒有 be 動詞或助動詞**，那麼回應式疑問句就要用 do、does 或 did。

Kelly:	I like buying lottery tickets.
Sue:	Do you? I never knew you liked gambling.
凱莉：	我喜歡買樂透彩券。
蘇：	是嗎？我都不知道你愛賭博。
Rita:	Morton bets on horses and plays cards.
Liz:	Does he? What does his wife say about that?
麗塔：	莫頓賭馬又打牌。
麗茲：	是嗎？那他的太太怎麼說？
Craig:	Jill won a jackpot the very first time she bought a lottery ticket.
Nick:	Did she? I am amazed. The odds of that happening are very small.
克雷格：	潔兒第一次買樂透彩券就中獎了。
尼克：	真的嗎？我太驚訝了，中獎的機率實在是很低。

4 原句是**肯定句**時，要以肯定疑問句回覆；原句是**否定句**時，就以否定疑問句回覆。

Grace can dance.
葛蕾絲會跳舞。

Can she? I never knew she could dance.
是嗎？我都不知道她會跳舞。

Helen doesn't like to drink alcohol.
海倫不喜歡喝酒。

Doesn't she? What does she drink when she goes to a pub?
是嗎？那她去酒吧都喝什麼？

5 唯有對原**肯定句**表達「**強烈同意**」時，會採用否定疑問句。

Tim:	It was a romantic restaurant.
Gill:	Wasn't it? It's a good place for a date.
提姆：	那是一間很浪漫的餐廳。
吉兒：	可不是嗎？那是個約會的好地方。

Practice

1

請以適當的「疑問句」填空，回應下列各句。

1. I'm leaving tomorrow for two weeks.

   → *Are you?*　Where are you going?

2. Pat can't remember his home address.

   → _____ That's unbelievable.

3. Daphne has just announced her engagement.

   → _____ That's good news.

4. Charles is tired of playing video games.

   → _____ I thought he enjoyed video games very much.

5. I have been raking the leaves in the yard.

   → _____ Mom will be pleased to hear that.

6. Bernard likes seaweed salad.

   → _____ I never knew he liked salad.

7. Yvonne went fishing with her brothers.

   → _____ That must have been fun.

8. Paula has a new hairdo.

   → _____ Does it look good?

2

連連看：請將 A 欄的「陳述句」與 B 欄的「回應式疑問句」組合成完整的句子。

A	B
____ 1. I went to a fortune teller last night.	A Did you? I thought you don't believe in fate.
____ 2. Johnny didn't win the match.	B Didn't he? But he plays so well.
____ 3. I haven't been home for two years.	C Did she? She doesn't look like a political radical.
____ 4. Connie joined the demonstration.	D Haven't you? You must miss your family.

Indirect Questions
間接問句

1 間接問句是在句子裡使用了「疑問詞所引導的附屬子句」。間接問句的主要子句,通常以下列句型開頭:

- Could you tell me . . . ?
- Do you know . . . ?
- Can you tell me . . . ?
- I know . . . .
- He asked . . . .

1 Where is Bourbon Street?
↳ 疑問句

波本街在哪裡?

Could you tell me where Bourbon Street is? ↳ 間接引述了 where 引導的疑問句,成為間接問句。

你能告訴我波本街在哪裡嗎?

2 When will the restaurant open?
↳ 疑問句

餐廳什麼時候開始營業?

Do you know when the restaurant will open? ↳ 間接引述了 when 引導的疑問句,成為間接問句。

你知不知道餐廳什麼時候開始營業?

2 間接問句裡頭,「疑問詞所引導的附屬子句」要使用**直述句**的語序,不用疑問句的語序。

Do you know what the time is?
↳ 不是用 what is the time。

你知不知道現在幾點?

I can't remember what the name of the restaurant is. ↳ 不是用 what is the name of the restaurant。

我不記得那間餐廳的名字了。

3 間接問句裡,不可使用**助動詞 do**、**does 或 did**,都要改成**直述句**。

1 What do you need?

你需要什麼?

Could you tell me what you need?

你能告訴我你需要什麼嗎?

2 When did Thomas arrive?

湯瑪士是什麼時候到的?

Do you know when Thomas arrived?

你知道湯瑪士是什麼時候到的嗎?

3 What did she say her name was?

她說她叫什麼名字?

Can you remember what she said her name was?

你記得她說她叫什麼名字嗎?

4 如果原疑問句沒有 **what**、**where** 等**疑問詞**,那麼間接問句就要用 if 或 whether。

1 Is Jenny free for lunch?

珍妮現在有空去吃午餐嗎?

Do you know if Jenny is free for lunch?

你知道珍妮現在是否有空去吃午餐嗎?

2 Did Hillary say she would meet us at the café?

希拉蕊說她要跟我們在咖啡館碰面嗎?

Could you tell me whether Hillary said she would meet us at the café?

你可不可以告訴我,希拉蕊是不是說她要跟我們在咖啡館碰面?

Practice

1

請將句子改寫為「間接問句」。

1. Where are the water boilers located?
   → Could you tell me *where the water boilers are located?*

2. How many liters can this water boiler hold?
   → Do you know _____
   _____

3. What other floor lamps do you have?
   → Could you show me _____
   _____

4. Where are programmable rice cookers sold?
   → Do you remember _____
   _____

5. Why can't this rice cooker be used to steam food?
   → Can you explain to me _____
   _____

6. When did the new rice cookers arrive?
   → Do you happen to know _____
   _____

7. Is this the only low-suds laundry soap you have in stock?
   → Do you know _____
   _____

8. Can I get this washing machine delivered tonight?
   → Do you have any idea _____
   _____

9. He asked, "Can I move to a small tropical island and go on with my writing?"
   → Did he ask _____
   _____

Short Replies With "So Do I," "Neither Do I," etc.

So Do I、Neither Do I 等簡答句型

1 「so + 助動詞 + 主詞」的倒裝句型，用來表示「某人也……」。

If you are having a drink, then so am I.
如果你要喝杯飲料，那我也要。

You can cook German food, and so can I.
你會做德國菜，我也會。

2 「neither + 助動詞 + 主詞」的倒裝句型，用來表示「某人也不……」。

If you are not drinking cocoa, then neither am I.

如果你不喝可可，那我也不要。

> 這種句型裡的 **neither** 也可以用 nor 取代。
>
> Mia:　We aren't ready to start.
> Lou:　Nor are we.
> 米雅：我們還沒準備好要開始。
> 盧：　我們也還沒。

You don't like pigs' knuckles, and neither do I.

你不喜歡豬腳，我也是。

3 上述兩種 so 和 neither 的**倒裝句**，經常用來做「簡答」。如果原句是**肯定句**，就用 so 的倒裝句簡答；如果原句是**否定句**，就用 neither 的倒裝句簡答。

Fay: I haven't eaten. 費：我還沒吃東西。

Kay: Neither have I. 凱：我也還沒。

Tony: I already ate. 東尼：我已經吃過了。

Tommy: So did I. 湯米：我也是。

4 so 和 neither 的倒裝句裡，使用的 **be** 動詞和助動詞要和原問句對應。

Helen:　Hal is ready to go dancing.
Marie:　So am I.
↳ 原句用 be 動詞，簡答句也用 be 動詞。

海倫：　哈爾已經準備好要去跳舞了。
瑪麗：　我也是。

Larry:　Jenny will not play volleyball this afternoon.
Sammi:　Neither will I.
↳ 原句用助動詞 will，簡答也用 will。

賴瑞：　珍妮今天下午不會去打排球。
珊米：　我也不會。

Sally:　Penny has got a new yellow highlighter.
Daniel:　So have I.
↳ 原句用助動詞 has，簡答句也用 have。

莎莉：　潘妮有一支新的黃色螢光筆。
丹尼爾：我也有。

5 如果原句裡**沒有 be** 動詞或助動詞，so 和 neither 的簡答句就要用 do、does、did。

Albert likes jogging.
亞伯特喜歡慢跑。

So do I.
我也是。

Pan doesn't eat shellfish.
潘不吃帶殼海鮮。

Neither does Ron.
榮恩也不吃。

Penelope loved the book.
潘妮洛普很愛這本書。

So did I.
我也是。

6 neither 或 nor 的句型，也可以用「not ... either」取代，此時就**不必倒裝**。

Yvonne:　I'm not sleeping in that dirty old hotel.
Marian:　I'm not either.
　　　　　(= Neither am I. = Nor am I.)

伊芳：　　我不要睡在那間又髒又舊的旅館。
瑪麗安：我也不要。

150

Practice

1

請用「so . . . I」和「neither . . . I」句型簡答，並在句中加上適當的 be 動詞或助動詞。

1. I am not interested in motorcycles.
   → *Neither am I.*

2. I like listening to early swing music.
   → _____

3. Roger has never been to Madagascar.
   → _____

4. Tina is a healthy and happy person.
   → _____

5. I don't like noisy bars and restaurants.
   → _____

6. George has been studying different Asian languages.
   → _____

7. My brother doesn't like to eat vegetables.
   → _____

8. I climbed Mount Jade last year.
   → _____

9. I don't believe in "happily ever after."
   → _____

2

請將括弧內的動詞以正確的形式填空，完成句子。

1. Sarah _____ (know) how to cook seafood, and so do I.

2. If Elvis _____ (join) the summer camp, then so am I.

3. If Luis _____ (agree) on the camping site, then neither do I.

4. Ashley _____ (play) tennis yesterday, and neither did I.

5. Michael _____ (skydive), and neither could I.

6. Kelly _____ (do) her part, and so have I.

7. Wendy _____ (finish) her meal, and neither have I.

8. Lindsay _____ (like) her job, nor do I.

9. Brad _____ (be) a baker, and so am I.

Unit 162

The Passive: Forms
被動語態的形式

1 英語可分為主動語態（active voice）與被動語態（passive voice）。當主詞是「**動作的執行者**」時，就用主動語態；當主詞是「**動作的接受者**」時，就用被動語態。

主動語態 Johnny turned off the air conditioner.
強尼關掉了冷氣。

被動語態 The air conditioner was turned off.
冷氣被關掉了。

2 被動語態的句型，是「be 動詞 + 過去分詞」。各種時態都可以用被動語態。

現在式 The coffee is brewed fresh every morning. 咖啡都是每天早上現煮的。

過去式 The café was cleaned from top to bottom yesterday.
昨天咖啡廳被徹底打掃得乾乾淨淨。

未來式 The performance will be held in the National Theater.
這場表演將於國家戲劇院登場。

3 被動語態也有「**進行式**」，句型是：「be + being + 過去分詞」。

The staff was being helped by the owner's wife.
工作人員當時一直受到老闆娘的幫助。

Cinnamon rolls are being baked in the oven.

肉桂捲現在正在烤箱中烘烤著。

4 被動語態也有「**完成式**」，句型是：「has/have/had + been + 過去分詞」。

His café has been expanded.
他的咖啡廳已經擴大營業了。

但是被動語態並沒有「**完成進行式**」。

✗ have/has/had + being been + 過去分詞

5 被動語態也有「不定詞」形式：「(to) be + 過去分詞」。在情態動詞 can、will 等或**特定動詞**的後面，都需要使用被動語態的不定詞。

The rabbit in the garden must be caught.
一定要捉到花園裡的兔子。

The carrots shouldn't be pulled up until they are bigger.
要等到紅蘿蔔再大一點才能採收。

The rice will be harvested next week.
稻米將於下週收成。

The rice field is going to be enlarged next month. 下個月起稻田將擴大範圍。

The irrigation system will have to be expanded. 灌溉系統將必須擴充。

That farmer wants to be phoned when his truck is repaired.
農人希望卡車修好時能電話通知他。

6 被動語態也有「**動名詞**」，也就是「being + 過去分詞」。當句子需要動名詞要做受詞，或任何需要使用動名詞的時候，就要用「being + 過去分詞」。

The line judges like being shown the instant replay.
↳ being shown 是被動式，當作動詞 like 的受詞，要用動名詞。

線審希望立刻觀看重播鏡頭。

Practice

1

請勾選正確的答案。
同時，若句子是「主
動語態」，請在空格
內填上 A（active），
若是「被動語態」，
請填上 P（passive）。

1. The construction company ☐ dug ☐ has been dug the hole for the foundation. → _____

2. The hole for the foundation ☐ dug ☐ has been dug by the construction company. → _____

3. The workers ☐ set up ☐ are set up the forms for the cement. → _____

4. The rebar ☐ has been wired ☐ wired together. → _____

5. The cement truck ☐ has been arrived ☐ has arrived. → _____

6. The cement ☐ is being poured ☐ poured. → _____

7. The masons ☐ have been working ☐ were being worked on the brick walls. → _____

8. The plumbers ☐ had told ☐ have been told to start to work next week. → _____

9. The sewer pipe ☐ was connecting ☐ was being connected. → _____

10. The carpenters ☐ are arriving ☐ have been arrived at the job site at this moment. → _____

2

請將右列主動語態句
子改寫為「被動語
態」。

1. That clerk ground those coffee beans.
   → *Those coffee beans were ground by that clerk.*

2. Father polished the leather shoes.
   → ....

3. Ariel is painting the house.
   → ....

4. Paul must have found the boar.
   → ....

5. We're going to close the shop.
   → ....

6. The boss is encouraging Ian.
   → ....

7. The scientists have discovered a supernova.
   → ....

8. Freddie planted a cactus in the garden.
   → ....

Unit **163**

The Passive: General Use
被動語態的一般用法

1 當我們要強調動作的「**接受者**」時，就可以用被動語態。

主動語態要改寫為被動語態時，只要將原本的受詞變成主詞。

Dad cooks dinner almost every night.
爸爸幾乎每天做晚餐。

Dinner is cooked almost every night by Dad. 每天的晚餐幾乎都是爸爸做的。

Most Canadians speak English.
大多數的加拿大人是說英語的。

English is spoken by most Canadians.
大多數的加拿大人都說英語。

2 當「**動作的肇始者不明**」，我們通常會用被動語態。

That library book was stolen.
↳ 主動語態是「Somebody stole that library book.」，我們不知道是誰偷了書的，通常用被動語態。

那本圖書館的書被偷了。

3 當「**事件發生的原因不重要**」時，也會用被動語態。

This library book has been damaged.
↳ 用被動語態比較不追究責任，表示對書被弄破的原因沒興趣，只強調「書已經破了」這樣一個事實。

這本圖書館的書被弄破了。

4 當「**我們不想追究事件的責任是誰的**」，通常可以用被動語態，巧妙地避免提到動作的執行者。

My son ripped a page out of the book.
↳ 用主動語態，提到了撕書的人。

我兒子把書撕了一頁下來。

A page has been ripped out of the book.
↳ 用被動語態，巧妙地不提是誰撕的。

書裡其中一頁被撕了下來。

5 另外還有一種比較不正式的被動語態，是以 get 代替 be 動詞，句型是「get + 過去分詞」。這種用法通常用於討論「**預料之外的偶發事件**」。

For some reason, the cat didn't get fed yesterday.
因為某個原因，
昨天沒有餵貓咪。

Even though Maureen was raising her hand, she didn't get chosen by the coach.
雖然瑪琳舉起了手，但是教練並沒有選她。

The thread in the sewing machine got stuck in the bobbin.
縫紉機上的線卡在捲軸上了。

Doug asked for a 7 a.m. wake-up call but he got called at 7 p.m.
道格要求上午 7 點打電話叫他起床，卻在晚上 7 點接到電話。

Practice

1

請將下列句子改寫為「被動語態」。

1. Someone must call the newspaper.
   → *The newspaper must be called.*

2. The TV station will send a cameraman and a reporter.
   → ⎯⎯⎯⎯⎯⎯⎯⎯⎯⎯⎯⎯⎯⎯⎯⎯⎯⎯⎯

3. The reporter is going to interview the store owner.
   → ⎯⎯⎯⎯⎯⎯⎯⎯⎯⎯⎯⎯⎯⎯⎯⎯⎯⎯⎯

4. The gang may have involved the store owner in their criminal activity.
   → ⎯⎯⎯⎯⎯⎯⎯⎯⎯⎯⎯⎯⎯⎯⎯⎯⎯⎯⎯

5. Someone should have called the reporter earlier.
   → ⎯⎯⎯⎯⎯⎯⎯⎯⎯⎯⎯⎯⎯⎯⎯⎯⎯⎯⎯

6. The store owner doesn't like the cameraman to videotape him.
   → ⎯⎯⎯⎯⎯⎯⎯⎯⎯⎯⎯⎯⎯⎯⎯⎯⎯⎯⎯

2

請用 get 與括號中的單字組成「過去被動式」，填空完成句子。

1. Mike said his pants ⎯⎯⎯⎯⎯⎯⎯ (tear) while he was climbing over a fence.

2. When Paul was playing in the garden, he ⎯⎯⎯⎯⎯⎯⎯ (sting) by a bee.

3. Allen tried to save some money, but it all ⎯⎯⎯⎯⎯⎯⎯ (spend) quickly.

4. Bessie ⎯⎯⎯⎯⎯⎯⎯ (lose) while looking for her friend's beach house.

5. Doris said she ⎯⎯⎯⎯⎯⎯⎯ (hurt) when she was moving a heavy bookcase.

6. Curtis ⎯⎯⎯⎯⎯⎯⎯ (elect) president of his class.

7. Little Kate ⎯⎯⎯⎯⎯⎯⎯ (kidnap) on her way to school.

8. The kidnapper ⎯⎯⎯⎯⎯⎯⎯ (catch) by the police when he was buying a beer at the grocery store.

Verbs With Two Objects and the Use of "By" and "With" in the Passive

雙受詞的動詞以及 By 與 With 在被動句裡的用法

1 擁有「**雙受詞**」的動詞，任一受詞都可於被動語態中扮演主詞的角色，因此有**兩種被動句型**。

The groom's parents bought *the new couple* a house.
↳ 句中的兩個受詞分別是 the new couple 和 a house。
新郎的父母幫這對新人買了一棟房子。

The new couple was bought a house by
↳ the new couple 當主詞。
the groom's parents.
這對新人的房子是新郎的父母買給他們的。

A house was bought *for the new couple*
↳ a house 當主詞。
by the groom's parents.
房子是新郎的父母買給這對新人的。

2 擁有「**雙受詞**」的動詞改寫為被動語態，以「人」當主詞的用法比較常見。

Tony offered *me* a sandwich.
湯尼給了我一個三明治。

常見 I was offered a sandwich by Tony.
罕見 A sandwich was offered *to me* by Tony.

3 這類經常接「**雙受詞**」的動詞有：

Lillian was sent a registered letter by her insurance carrier. 莉莉安收到一封保險公司寄給她的掛號信。

Theresa was shown a notice by the salesman that said she had to exchange the defective memory card.
泰瑞莎被業務員通知，她需要更換壞掉的記憶卡。

4 如果要在被動句裡提及**動作的執行者**，可以用 by，表明「**這件事是誰做的**」。

Sir Isaac Newton formulated the law of gravity. 艾薩克・牛頓爵士算出了地心引力。
↳ 主動句：動作的執行者 Sir Isaac Newton 是主詞。

The law of gravity was formulated by Sir Isaac Newton.
↳ 被動句：用 by 點出動作的執行者 Sir Isaac Newton。
地心引力是艾薩克・牛頓爵士算出來的。

Newton also created the branch of mathematics called calculus.
↳ 主動句
牛頓還發明數學的其中一個分支——微積分。

The branch of mathematics called calculus was also created by Newton.
↳ 被動句
數學的其中一個分支——微積分——也是牛頓發明的。

5 如果被動句裡面需要交代「**動作執行者所使用的工具**」，則可以用 with。

The garden is watered with an automated sprinkler system.
花園是用自動灑水系統澆水的。

The bulbs were planted with a trowel and the sweat of my brow. 這些球莖是用一個小鏟子和我額頭上的汗水所種出來的。

6 被動句裡，也可以用 with 來說明「**材料和成分**」。

The bread is made with flour, sugar, oranges, raisins, and walnuts. 這個麵包是用麵粉、糖、柳橙、葡萄乾和核桃做成的。

The bus was filled with peasants and chickens. 這輛巴士上載滿了農人與雞隻。

- send
- pay
- tell
- offer
- teach
- show
- promise

1

請用提示的主詞，及「過去簡單式的被動語態」改寫句子。

1. The thankful client sent Richard two ballet tickets.
   Richard _was sent two ballet tickets by the thankful client_ .

2. The sales representative offered Lauren a discount tour package.
   Lauren _____
   _____ .

3. The real estate agent showed Lucy the model home.
   Lucy _____ .

4. The advertising agency paid the baseball player about $1,000,000.
   The baseball player _____
   _____ .

5. The instructor taught the class four nights a week.
   The class _____
   _____ .

6. The sailor promised the woman a letter a day.
   The woman _____ .

7. Hazel bought me a digital watch.
   A digital watch _____ .

2

請用 by 或 with 填空，完成句子。

1. Brenda and Ronny were married _____ a priest.

2. The bowls are glazed _____ lead-free paint and varnish.

3. The hole for the swimming pool was dug _____ a backhoe.

4. The clouds on the ceiling were painted _____ Mike.

5. Christopher's house was purchased _____ his mother.

6. The tall fluted vases are made _____ a potter's wheel.

7. The windows in the car are tinted _____ a reflective silver coating.

8. Joan's teeth were examined _____ a dentist.

Unit 165

Some Common Passive Sentence Structures
常見的被動句型

1 被動句型經常用來「轉述他人的話」、「轉述他人認定的事情」。其中一種便是「It is said that . . .」的句型，表示「據說……」。

主動語態 People say that **Gloria** has perfect pitch.
人家說葛洛莉亞的音準奇佳。

被動語態 It is said that **Gloria** has perfect pitch.
據說葛洛莉亞的音準奇佳。

2 上述句型也可以用「人或物」當主詞，句型是：

somebody/something is said + 加 to 的不定詞

Gloria is said **to have** perfect pitch.
據說葛洛莉亞的音準奇佳。

Cheetahs are said **to run** faster than any other animal in the world.
據說獵豹是全世界跑得最快的動物。

3 這種被動句型常見於正式對話或寫作中，常用這種句型的動詞有：

It is expected that **the Prime Minister is** going to veto the resolution.
= The Prime Minister is expected **to veto** the resolution.
眾人預期總理將對該決議運用否決權。

It is believed that **our department head will start** the new program on August 1st.
= Our department head is believed to **start** the new program on August 1st.
大家相信，系主任將從 8 月 1 日起推行新課程。

- say
- think
- believe
- consider
- understand
- know
- report
- expect
- claim
- acknowledge

4 如果這裡所談論的事件是發生於「過去」，則「加 to 的不定詞」要使用完成式。

It is widely known that **the XY9 computer virus wreaked** havoc on the internet last week.
= The XY9 computer virus is widely known to have wreaked havoc on the internet last week.
大家都知道上星期的 XY9 電腦病毒造成網路一片混亂。

5 be supposed to 也常有「據說」的意味。

This cell phone is supposed to **be pretty good for such a low price.**
↳ 據說這是一支很不錯的手機。
以這麼低的價格來說，這應該算是一支很不錯的手機。

That smartphone was supposed to **have been on sale.**
↳ 用過去式，表示「據說手機有特價，但其實沒有。」
這支智慧型手機應該有特價才對。

6 be supposed to 也可以用來「提出質疑」。

Carrot cake is supposed to **be healthy, but I doubt it.**
紅蘿蔔蛋糕應該對健康有益，不過我很懷疑。

1

請分別用「it is said that . . .」和「. . . is said to . . .」改寫句子。

1. People believe that the number of school-age children will drop again this year.
   → *It is believed that the number of school-age children will drop again this year.*

   → *The number of school-age children is believed to drop again this year.*

2. People know that the secret negotiations started last week.
   →

   →

3. People think the sailors have been rescued.
   →

   →

4. People say that the pandemic completely changed how the world works.
   →

   →

2

請用 be supposed to 改寫句子。

1. People say that sitting too long is bad for your health.
   → *Sitting too long is supposed to be bad for your health.*

2. People say that watching TV is bad for kids.
   →

3. People say that drinking two liters of water a day is healthy.
   →

4. People say that quitting smoking is simply a matter of will power.
   →

5. People say that Doraemon is the most popular cat in the world.
   →

Have Something Done
Have Something Done 的用法

1 have 後面如果接的是「**事物**」，經常會用「**have ＋ 某物 ＋ 過去分詞**」的句型，表示「**讓某物接受某個動作**」，通常指「**安排他人完成某事**」，屬於被動用法的一種。

主動語態 Ben is cutting his own hair.
班正在幫自己剪頭髮。

被動語態 Ben is having his hair cut.
別人在幫班剪頭髮。

Martin is installing a hard drive in his
↳ 主動語態：馬丁自己安裝。

computer.
馬丁正在為他的電腦安裝硬碟。

Martin is having a hard drive installed in
↳ 被動語態：安排他人安裝。

his computer.
馬丁正在請人幫他安裝電腦硬碟。

Beverly had the battery in her watch replaced. 貝佛莉讓人給她的手錶換了電池。

How often do you have your car tuned up? 你多久保養一次車？

Are you going to have your eyes examined before you get new glasses?
你去配新眼鏡之前，會先去檢查眼睛嗎？

2 「**have ＋ 某物 ＋ 過去分詞**」也可以表達「**某人為某物做了某事**」。

Russell is having his sofa reupholstered.
羅素正在幫他的沙發換坐墊。

Sam has just had the oil changed in his car.
山姆剛剛才為他的車子換了機油。

Helen is having her legs waxed at the moment. 海倫此刻正在做腿部蜜蠟除毛。

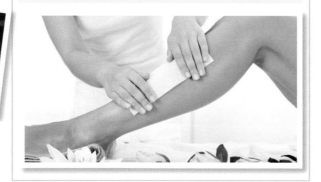

3 當某物發生「**始料未及、不愉快的事**」，或者是「**事情沒有安排好**」，也可以用這種句型。

Adrian had her glasses broken over the weekend. 雅德恩的眼鏡在週末時弄壞了。

Laura had her vacation cancelled because her replacement got sick.
蘿拉把假期取消了，因為她的職務代理人生病。

4 在非正式的對話中，可以用 get something done 取代 **have something done**。

Max needs to get his tickets reserved today. 麥斯今天一定得訂到票。

Gordon must get his son's birthday party set up right away.
戈登必須馬上把他兒子的生日派對準備好。

1

請用括號中的單字搭配 have something done 的句型填空，完成句子。

1. Janice must _____have her shoes repaired_____ (her shoes / repair).

2. Paul is going to _____ (his shoes / shine).

3. Where are you going to _____ (your skirt / dry clean)?

4. Are you going to _____ (that dress / alter)?

5. Last month the proud parents _____ (their daughter's baby shoes / bronze).

6. Last night Angela _____ (her dress / rip) when getting out of her car.

7. Bonnie _____ (the heel on her left shoe / break) early this morning.

8. Roger _____ (his briefcase / steal) on the train on his way to work this morning.

2

請將下列句子以 have something done 的句型改寫。

1. Ed is cutting the grass in his yard.
   → _____

2. Dennis is fixing the toilet.
   → _____

3. Rick just replaced three light bulbs.
   → _____

4. Wayne will change the sheets later.
   → _____

5. Eleanor is frying a steak on the stove.
   → _____

6. Claudia has ironed all the shirts.
   → _____

7. Ashley could switch a propane tank easily with this device.
   → _____

161

假設句型中，過去式的 be 動詞不分人稱都要用 were，不用 **was**。

- I wish Mike were here so I could congratulate him.

  我希望邁克人在這裡，我就可以當面恭喜他。

- If I were you, I wouldn't do that.

  如果我是你的話，我不會那麼做。

1 假設語氣用來表示「**假設、願望**」等，常使用假設語氣的用語有：wish、if only、if 等。

Tonya wishes she could fire her boss.
唐雅真希望她能開除老闆。

If only I hadn't sold my lovely dog. I miss him so much. 要是我沒把我的可愛狗狗賣掉就好了，我好想牠。

If I had been there, I would have stopped it. 如果我當時在場的話，我就能阻止這件事。

2 「wish + 過去式動詞」用來表示「**與現在或未來事實相反的願望**」、「**目前的悔恨**」，希望可以有不同的處理方式。

Tom wishes he had a job repairing cars.
↳ 用了假設語氣，表示他現在並沒有做修車工作。
湯姆希望可以做修車工作。

Ralph wishes he weren't working 50 hours a week.　　↳ 但是他得一週工作 50 小時。

雷夫希望他不用一週工作 50 個小時。

3 「wish + 過去完成式動詞（had + 過去分詞）」則表示「**與過去事實相反的願望**」、「**過去的遺憾**」。

I wish I had saved the business card Grace gave me.　　↳ 事實是：我並沒有把名片留下來。

真希望我當初有把葛麗絲給我的名片留下來。

I wish I hadn't given my tennis racquet to my brother. ↳ 事實是：我已經把網球拍送給弟弟了。

真希望我當初沒有把我的網球拍送給我弟弟。

4 if only 也用來表示「**願望**」，並且更強調個人感受。「if only + 過去式動詞」表示「**與現在或未來事實相反的願望**」。

If only Serena spoke Japanese, then she could sell more notebook computers. 要是瑟琳娜會說日語，她就能多賣幾台筆記型電腦了。

If only the committee were to decide, then we could write the amendment. 如果委員會做出決定，我們就可以撰寫修正案。

5 「if only + 過去完成式動詞（had + 過去分詞）」表示「**與過去事實相反的願望**」。

If only Ken hadn't closed that last sale, then Sylvia would have received a sales bonus.

要是肯沒有結束最後的拍賣，施薇亞就能拿到銷售紅利。

If only you had told me those were rare books before I sold them. 要是你在我賣書之前，有跟我說那些書很稀有就好了。

6 wish 和 if only 也可以接「would + 不加 to 的不定詞」，表示「**希望某事發生或不要發生**」。

Maybe Julia will sing. I wish she would.
說不定茱莉亞會唱歌，我希望她唱。

I wish you wouldn't feed the healthy food I made for you to your dog. 我希望你別把我為你準備的健康食物拿來餵你的狗。

If only he would come home soon.
希望他早日返家。

Practice

1 請從框內選出適當的動詞，依據提示搭配 wish 或 if only 填空，完成下列表示「假設」或「願望」的句子。

jog

lower

be watching

leave home

speak

bring

save

lock

come

1. Rick is out of breath while jogging.
   He said, "_____ *I wish I jogged* _____ more often." (wish)

2. Doug is going to be late for his dentist's appointment.
   He said, "_____ earlier." (wish)

3. Cynthia was scared while watching a horror movie in the movie theater.
   She messaged her mom, "_____ a comedy instead." (if only)

4. Sandy does not qualify for the job because she doesn't speak English.
   She said, "_____ English." (if only)

5. Harriet saw an expensive house for sale.
   She said, "_____ enough money to buy it." (wish)

6. Peggy wanted to bring her little brother to see the dinosaur bones, but the museum was closed.
   Her brother said, "_____ earlier." (wish)

7. Lorna and her boyfriend got soaking wet in a thunder storm. She said, "_____ our matching red raincoats." (if only)

8. Ron's scooter was stolen. He said, "_____ it with my U-bolt lock." (if only)

9. Mandy burned the pancakes.
   She said, "_____ the heat." (if only)

2 請從框內選出適當的動詞，依據提示搭配 wish 或 if only，以 would 或 wouldn't 的句型填空，完成句子。

talk

swim

sing

take off

1. Danny went to hear a female jazz singer.
   He said, "_____ more of her own songs." (wish)

2. Clay and his wife went to their son's graduation party.
   His wife said, "_____ to those young girls so much." (wish)

3. The warden put a new lock on the gate to keep the kids out.
   He said, "_____ in the reservoir." (if only)

4. Candy complained to her sister about the man next door.
   She said, "_____ his shoes when he brings us flowers." (if only)

"If" Sentences:
Real Present or Future Conditionals

If 子句：現在或未來可能發生的真實假設

1 if 子句是**條件子句**的一種，它可以放在**句首**或是**句尾**。當 if 子句位於句首時，要加逗號，與主要子句分開。

If you don't water your plants, they will wither and die.
= Your plants will wither and die if you don't water them.

你要是不幫植物澆水，它們會枯萎死亡。

2 當表示「**現在或未來有可能發生的事**」，不會使用假設語氣。此時，if 子句裡會使用現在簡單式，而**主要子句要用**未來簡單式 will。這種條件句被稱為**第一條件句**。

If Henry talks to Violet, he will learn about the photos.
↳ if 子句使用現在簡單式 talks；後面是主要子句，使用未來式 will learn。

如果亨利和薇麗交談，他就會得知照片的事。

If Eva leaves now, she will beat the rush hour traffic.
↳ 「現在」可能發生的事。

如果依芙現在出發，正好會碰上交通尖峰時刻。

If Frankie uses all his vacation days, he will go for almost a month.
↳ 「未來」可能發生的事。

如果法蘭基把假期一次休完，就可以去度假近一個月。

3 主要子句除了 will，也可以用 shall、can 或 may。

If we lose the case, we shall appeal.
要是我們輸了這場官司，我們將再上訴。

If we finish early, we can take a break.
如果我們早點完成，就可以休息一下。

If you're hungry, you may take some cookies from the plate.
如果你餓了，可以從盤子裡拿一些餅乾去吃。

4 主要子句也可以直接用祈使句。

If you are ready, let's go.
要是你已經準備好了，我們就出發吧！

If you don't want to quit, do the best you can. 如果你不想放棄，就盡力去做吧。

5 除了現在簡單式，if 子句也可以用其他現在式，如現在完成式或現在進行式。

If Herman has remembered to buy some pizzas, cheesecake, and ice cream, I would like you to dine with us tonight.
如果賀曼有記得去買一些披薩、起司蛋糕和冰淇淋的話，我今晚想請你過來和我們一起吃飯。

If Trudy is cooking dinner, would you join us as our guest? 如果楚蒂在準備晚餐，你願意加入我們，做我們的貴客嗎？

Practice

1

請將括弧內的動詞以正確形式填空，並從框內選出適當的用語填入第二個空格，完成句子。

will buy

can ride

will cool

will load

will be

will tell

tell her

will run

1. If I _____ (go) to the grocery store, I _____ paper towels for you.

2. If Tom _____ (go) jogging, I _____ with him.

3. If Archie _____ (have) enough space in his car, I _____ with him.

4. If Jan _____ (call), _____ I'm still waiting for her.

5. If Veronica _____ (have packed) all her boxes, I _____ them on the truck.

6. If Johanna _____ (be making) dinner, I _____ happy to come over.

7. If Willie _____ (turn) on the air conditioner, it _____ down the room.

8. If Sara _____ (call), I _____ her you are sick.

2

請依圖示，從框內選出適當的用語填空，完成句子。

go shopping

grow higher

keep eating

will make pudding

isn't working

doesn't rain

If the waves _____, we can go surfing.

We'll camp by the woods if it _____ tomorrow.

You'll get fat if you _____ like that.

If Emma is free this afternoon, she _____ for us.

If you can take this afternoon off, let's _____!

We'll go crazy if the air conditioner _____.

General Conditionals: Repeated Events or Truth
表示「習慣」或「真理」的條件句

1 在含有 if 子句的句子裡，**主要子句**如果描述的是「**習慣性**」的行為，會用現在簡單式。

If Nick **tells** me something, I always **believe** him.
↳ 一直都是這樣
只要尼克告訴我什麼，我都會相信。

If I **have** a little free time, I **take** a coffee break.
只要我一有點空，我就會喝咖啡小憩一下。

If Gerry **works** hard in the morning, he **naps** on the sofa after lunch.
如果傑瑞早上很認真工作，他午飯後會在沙發上睡一下。

2 在這種句型裡，if 相當於 **whenever**。

If / Whenever Walter **goes** drinking with his friends at night, the following day he **sleeps** all morning.
華特只要晚上和朋友一起出去喝一杯，第二天一定睡一整個上午。

If / Whenever it's the weekend, I always **spent** time watching sports on TV.
只要一到週末，我就會看電視上的運動比賽。

3 如果是 when 所引導的條件子句，也是屬於「某種條件下的習慣行為」，此時，**when** 子句和主要子句都會用現在簡單式。

When it's sunny, I **ride** my motorcycle to work. 晴天的時候我都騎摩托車上班。

When it's rainy, I **take** the subway to my office. 下雨的時候我會搭地鐵去公司。

4 主要子句如果描述的是「必然會發生的事」或「不變的真理」，則可以用現在簡單式，也可以用未來簡單式。

Egg yolks **solidify** when the temperature **reaches** 65 ˚C.
當溫度到達攝氏 65 度，蛋黃就開始凝固。

Oil will **wash** away if you **use** soap and hot water.
用肥皂和熱水沖洗，油汙就會洗掉了。

1

請用 if 或 when 填空，完成對話。

Son: Mom, ❶_____ I invite my friend Charley over, can he stay overnight?

Mom: Have you talked to Charley or Charley's mom?

Son: Not yet. ❷_____ I ask him, he will probably want to come.

Mom: ❸_____ you want to invite friends over, you always have to make plans ahead of time.

Son: ❹_____ you say it that way, I always know the answer.

Mom: ❺_____ you are so smart, tell me what I am going to say.

Son: You always say the same thing. ❻_____ you want to invite your friends over, you always have to make sure we call their parents.

Mom: ❼_____ we call Charley's mom right now, will she be home?

Son: I don't know. I will call.

Mom: ❽_____ you call to make plans, you always have to let me speak to the mom or dad.

Son: I know. Can I call now?

Mom: ❾_____ you know what to say, you can call.

2

請將括弧內的動詞以正確的形式填空，並從框內選出搭配的主要子句，連接起來。

he dresses up in his sharkskin suit

he takes Monday off

I give him the silent treatment

she knocks on wood three times

she listens to jazz music

we have to walk up to our 12th floor apartment

1. When Raymond _____ (work) on the weekend, _____.

2. When Sabrina _____ (see) a black cat, _____.

3. When the elevator _____ (not work), _____.

4. When Darren _____ (go) on a date, _____.

5. When my boyfriend _____ (not take) me out on Friday night, _____.

6. When Jess _____ (relax) at home, _____.

Part 22 Subjunctive Mood and Conditionals 假設語氣與條件句

Unit 170

"If" Sentences: Unreal Present or Future Conditionals
If 子句：與現在或未來事實相反的條件句

1 如果要表示「**與現在或未來事實相反的假設**」，就會使用假設語氣。此時 if 子句裡會使用過去式，而**主要子句**要用「would/could/might/should + 不加 to 的不定詞」，我們稱之為**第二條件句**。

If **Nancy** had **some extra money, she**'d (= would) go **traveling in Europe.**
↳ 事實是南西沒有閒錢去旅遊。

如果南西有閒錢，她就會去歐洲旅遊。

If **his travel agent** offered **tourist trips to the moon, Jim** would book **tickets right away.**
↳ 但是月球之旅目前是不可能的。

如果旅行社有提供月球之旅，吉姆一定會立刻訂票。

If **Antonia** spoke **Korean, she** would travel **to Seoul.**
↳ 可是她並不會說韓語。

如果安東妮雅會說韓語，她就會去首爾旅遊了。

2 如果談論的事情，雖然有可能發生，但是機會「**微乎其微**」，屬於「**現在或未來不太可能發生的事**」，也可使用假設語氣。

If **basketball players** were **all short, I** would be playing **in the NBA.**
↳ 但是籃球選手幾乎都很高，而我卻很矮。

要是打籃球的運動員都很矮，我就可以去 NBA 打籃球了。

If **Amy** went **to Patagonia next year, she** would see **some real penguins.**
↳ 但是她或許根本不會去。

如果艾咪明年前往巴塔哥尼亞，她就會看到真正的企鵝。

3 假設語氣裡，如果是「**非口語**」、「**正式用語**」，那麼 be 動詞不分人稱，都要使用 were，而不用 **was**。

If **Tonya** were **married, she would move to the suburbs.**

要是唐雅結婚，她就會搬到郊區。

Dean would propose marriage to Tonya if **he** were **more established in his career.**

要是迪恩的事業更穩定一點，他就會開口向唐雅求婚。

4 但是如果所談論的事情，是「**現在或未來有可能發生，只是機會微乎其微**」，那我們會在 if 子句裡用 should，在**主要子句**裡用未來簡單式 will。也就是不使用**假設語氣**，因為仍有發生的機會。

If **I** should hear **anything, I** will tell **you.**
↳ 我非常不確定會聽到。

要是我能聽到任何事，我就會告訴你。

Should **I** talk **to Tom, I** will explain **why you are angry with him.**
↳ should 用倒裝句型，更強調「可能性不高」。

要是我真能和湯姆談話，我就會向他解釋你為什麼生他的氣了。

1

請從框內選出適當的動詞組合，並以「假設語氣」填空，完成下列「現在或未來不可能發生或不太可能發生的事」的描述。

give / have

call / donate

hold / attend

change / inherit

be / give

1. If I _____ were _____ independently wealthy, I _____ would give _____ money to an art museum.

2. If my university _____, I _____ some stock.

3. If a fundraiser for starting a colony on Mars _____, I _____ the event.

4. What _____ in your life if you _____ a ton of money?

5. Who _____ you _____ money to if you _____ lots of money?

2

請勾選正確的答案。

1. When Nelson graduates, he ☐ will need ☐ would have needed a job.

2. If Nelson doesn't get a job, he ☐ wouldn't feel ☐ won't feel like an adult.

3. If Nelson wanted a job at the company where I work, I ☐ would ask ☐ always ask about openings for him.

4. If Nelson called me about his job hunting, I ☐ will discuss ☐ would discuss the possibilities with him.

5. If Nelson inquires about the job opening, I ☐ would be ☐ will be happy to tell him about it.

6. When Nelson contacts me at my office, I ☐ usually take ☐ would usually take his call.

7. If Nelson wanted advice about getting a job, I ☐ would have found ☐ would find time to talk to him.

8. If Nelson ☐ job-hunts ☐ job-hunted diligently, he will soon find the right job for him.

Unit **171**

"If" Sentences: Unreal Past Conditionals
If 子句：與過去事實相反的條件句

1 如果要表示「**與過去事實相反的假設**」，也會使用假設語氣。此時 if 子句裡會使用過去完成式，而**主要子句**要用「would/could/might/should + have + 過去分詞」，我們稱之為**第三條件句**。

If I had cut the grass, it would have been easy to find the ant hills.
↳ 事實是我當時沒有除草，不容易找到蟻丘。
如果我當時除了草，要找到蟻丘就很容易了。

If the traffic hadn't been so bad, the trip wouldn't have taken so long.
↳ 事實是當時交通很塞，旅程花了很長時間。
要不是交通那麼塞，這趟旅程也不用花那麼長的時間。

If Dave had made a higher offer on the house, he would have gotten it.
↳ 但是他出的價太低了。
要是當初戴維出更高價，他早就買到那棟房子了。

If our air conditioner had worked properly, we wouldn't have bought a new one.
↳ 但是它已經壞了，而且我們也已經又買了一台。
如果我們的冷氣還能正常運轉的話，我們也就不用再買一台新的了。

If Willie had contacted his office, he might have heard about the meeting.
↳ 事實是他沒有聯絡辦公室，錯過了會議。
如果威利當初有聯絡辦公室，他也許就會得知開會的事。

2 had 和 would 的縮寫都是「'd」，因此要仔細判斷句中的縮寫是哪一種。

If I'd (= had) called the store, I'd (= would) have discovered that it was closed.
如果我有先打電話去店裡，我就會知道他們已經關門了。

3 再來比較一次各種 if 假設句的用法：

現在或未來可能發生的事

If you find the time, I will meet you for lunch.
如果你能挪出時間，我會去找你吃午餐。
If you give me your shirts, I will iron them for you. 如果你把襯衫拿給我，我會幫你燙好。

與現在或未來事實相反，或不太可能發生的事

If you could find the time, I would meet you for lunch. 如果你挪得出時間，我就去找你吃午餐。
If you gave me your shirts, I would iron them for you. 如果你把襯衫拿給我，我會幫你燙好。

與過去事實相反的事

If you had found the time, I would have met you for lunch. 要是你當時有時間的話，我就會去找你吃午餐了。
If you had given me your shirts, I would have ironed them for you. 要是你之前把襯衫拿給我的話，我就會幫你燙好了。

Practice

1

請將括弧裡的動詞以正確的形式填空，完成右列「與過去事實相反」的句子。

1. If Donnie _____ (behave) properly, he _____ (not / embarrass) his family.

2. If Tara _____ (read) her horoscope, she _____ (know) Martin wasn't her celestial soul mate.

3. If Sharon _____ (buy) that dress, she _____ (not / worry) about what to wear to the wedding.

4. If Gary _____ (pay) his parking ticket, the police _____ (not / impound) his car.

5. If Michelle _____ (accept) Gordo's marriage proposal, she _____ (not / stay) single so long.

6. If Jeri _____ (mail) in the rebate form, she _____ (not / pay) full price.

2

請依據「if子句」的形式，將主要子句括弧內的動詞以正確的形式填空，完成句子。

1. If you look by the TV, you _____ (find) your magazine.

2. If you finish the milk, I _____ (buy) more tonight.

3. If you had some time for a movie, I _____ (meet) you at the multiplex.

4. If I were going to meet you, I _____ (leave) around 6 p.m.

5. If you had called, I _____ (know) all about it.

6. If my boss had told me she needed the report by noon, I _____ (finish) it this morning.

3

請依據主要子句的形式，將「if子句」括弧內的動詞以正確的形式填空，完成句子。

1. If Tammy _____ (want) me to go to see her, I will go right over.

2. If Sherry _____ (like) comic books, I would give her my old ones.

3. If Rhonda _____ (inquire) about the room, I would have rented it to her.

4. If Peter _____ (need) a ride, I will drive him to school.

5. If Matt _____ (study) a life saving course, he would improve his chances of getting a job at the swimming pool.

6. If Nelly _____ (wash) the lunch dishes earlier, she would have saved time in preparing dinner.

7. When Ned _____ (go) to the jazz club, he always invites me along.

Unit 172

Conditional Clauses Without "If"
不使用 If 的條件子句

1 unless 可構成條件子句，它的意義接近「**if . . . not**」（除非……否則）。

Unless you win the lottery, you can't quit your job. 除非你中了樂透，否則不能辭職。

I won't marry you unless you get down on one knee and propose.

除非你跪下來向我求婚，否則我不會嫁給你。

2 unless 常用來表示「**威脅**」和「**警告**」。

Unless you turn yourself in to the police, I will present evidence of your misconduct to the newspapers. 你要是不自己向警察自首，我就把你行為不當的證據交給報社。

Unless Tom names his source for this story, the owner of the newspaper is going to fire him.

除非湯姆能說出這篇報導來源，否則報社老闆就要開除他。

3 unless 和 if 都可以用來表示「**條件**」，但是 if 具有**正面意義**，unless 具有**負面意義**。

If you buy a ticket, then you can go in.
如果你買了票，就可以進去。

Unless you buy a ticket, then you can't go in.
除非你買票，否則不能進去。

The store will be closed if you get there after 9 p.m. 如果你晚上 9 點以後才到，店就打烊了。

The store will be closed unless you get there before 9 p.m.

除非你晚上 9 點以前到，不然店就打烊了。

4 as long as 和 so long as 可以用於條件子句，意義為「只要」（**so long as** 不太常用）。

You can go camping with your friends as long as you finish your homework.
只要你把功課做完，就可以和朋友一起去露營。

You can borrow my tent as long as you clean and dry it before you put it back with my outdoor gear.
我可以把帳篷借給你，只要你把它清理晾乾，和其他露營用具一起放回原處就好。

5 provided that 和 providing that 可用於條件子句，意義也是「只要」。

Amber says she will go on the camping trip provided that she doesn't have to climb any mountains.
安柏說只要不爬山，她就願意去參加露營。

Providing that John can bring his dog, he will come along. 只要約翰能帶他的狗，他就會來。

6 在表示「**與事實相反的假設**」時，suppose 和 supposing 也可以用於條件子句，取代 **if** 的位置。

Suppose/Supposing you were offered a promotion, but it involved moving to Malaysia, would you take the offer?
↳ 假設子句裡使用過去式 were offered 和 involved，主要子句使用「would + 不加 to 的不定詞」，是假設語氣的用法

假設你升職了，但是得到馬來西亞工作，你會接受嗎？

Suppose I gave you some plant fertilizer, would you use it?

假如我給你一些肥料，你會用嗎？

Practice

1

請勾選正確的用語。

1. ☐ Unless ☐ Providing you call now, it will be too late to call tonight.

2. ☐ Supposing ☐ As long as you call her before her birthday, it doesn't matter whether it's tonight or tomorrow.

3. ☐ Providing that ☐ Unless the gift you sent her gets there in time, you can call a little later.

4. You don't have to call your aunt ☐ so long as ☐ suppose you send her a birthday card.

5. Unless Nelson spends less time on the sofa, he ☐ would have turned ☐ will turn into a couch potato.

6. ☐ Suppose ☐ As long as you gave your mother a trip to Bali as a gift, would she take it?

7. ☐ Unless ☐ If you put your potted plants inside your house, you will have to cover them with blankets because it's going to freeze tonight.

8. As long as Paul keeps looking for a job, his father ☐ gave ☐ will give him an allowance.

9. Suppose Bob didn't need a job, what ☐ would have he done ☐ would he do?

2

請用括弧裡的詞語改寫句子。

1. You must pass the driving test before you can drive on the road. (unless)
   → _Unless you pass the driving test, you can't drive on the road._

2. You can improve your reading comprehension by reading every day. (unless)
   → _____

3. I will forgive you if you apologize sincerely. (as long as)
   → _____

4. He will come to the dinner, but you must not mention his divorce. (provided that)
   → _____

5. I can write a recommendation for you. Will it help? (suppose)
   → _____

Unit 173

"It's Time" in Subjunctive Mood and "And/Or" in Conditionals
It's Time 的假設用法與
And/Or 表示「條件」的用法

it's time

1 「it's time + 加 to 的不定詞」的句型，常用來「叫某人做某事」。

It's time to eat **your dinner**.
你該吃晚餐了。

It's time **for you** to buy **a new car.**
你該換一輛新車了。

2 但如果是「暗示某人去做某事」，經常用「it's time + (that) 子句」，that 子句用**過去式動詞**。

這是假設語氣，並不是在講過去的事，而是「**現在或未來該做的事**」。

Don't you think it's time **Marian** fixed the crack in the living room wall?
你不認為瑪麗安現在應該把客廳牆上的裂縫補一補了嗎？

It's time **you** cleaned **your ears.**
你該清清耳朵了。

3 it's about time 和 it's high time 的用法，和 **it's time** 相同。

It's about time to pick up **Katie**.
差不多到時間去接凱蒂了。

Don't you think it's about time to return **the books to your aunt?**
你不覺得現在差不多該還你阿姨書了嗎？

It's high time **you** called **your mother.**
你真該打電話給你母親了。

and/or

4 and 常用來連結兩個「**互為條件、因果**」的句子，雖不是假設語氣或條件子句的用法，但意義相同。

Get there early and **you will avoid the line.**
↳ 只要早點到那裡，你就能避開排隊的人潮。
早點到那兒，才能避開排隊的人潮。

Work hard and **you will succeed.**
↳ 如果你努力，你就會成功。
努力就能成功。

5 or (else) 也可用來連結兩個「**互為條件、因果**」的句子，表示「**不然、否則**」。

它也不是假設語氣或條件子句的用法，但意義類似。

Be there before 7:00 p.m. when the first act starts or (else) **you won't get a seat.**
↳ 你要是 7 點以前沒到，就會沒有位子坐。
你得在晚上 7 點鐘第一幕開演前抵達，不然會沒有位子。

Practice

1

請將括弧內的動詞以「it's time + somebody + did something」的句型填空，完成句子。

1. Let's go get Jimmy. We need to go now. School gets out at 12:00. It's 11:55. _It's time we left_ (leave) to get Jimmy.

2. You said you were going to fix the air conditioner last month. Now it's the middle of the summer. It's so hot in here. _____ (fix) the air conditioner.

3. Keith should have picked up his package at the post office last week. This attempted delivery notice says he has ten days to claim it. Today is the last day. _____ (pick up) his package.

4. Penny wants Tom to design a new ad campaign. Penny has asked him several times to talk about the new ads. The plan for the new ads needs to be made right away. _____ (design) the new advertisements.

2

請從框內選出適當的子句，完成句子。

her feelings will get hurt	you'll get sun burned
swallow the cough medicine	listen to the expert

1 You need to wish her happy birthday or else _____.

2 You should put on sunblock or else _____.

3 _____ and you'll stop coughing in a few minutes.

4 _____ and you will learn how to do it right.

Unit 174

Direct and Reported Speech
直接引述與間接引述

1 引述他人說過的話有兩種方法，分別是**直接引述**和**間接引述**。

直接引述是**一字不改地說出某人說過的話**，這種句型裡，引述句要放在引號（"..."）裡。

Billy said, "Let's get a little wild tonight."

比利說：「我們今晚瘋狂一下吧！」

Mia reminded Billy, "Let's not get too wild. Last time you got 'a little wild,' I had to get you out jail."

米雅提醒比利：「也別太瘋狂了。上回你不過『瘋狂一下』，我就得把你從警局保出來。」

2 而間接引述句是**將別人講過的話，透過我們自己的口吻、釋義來轉述出來**。這種句型裡，不需要加**引號**。

I have Jason on the phone and he says he can't go out with us tonight.

我在和傑森講電話，他說今晚不能跟我們一起出去了。

I asked if he was sure. He said not tonight.

我問他確定不去了嗎，他說今晚不行。

3 引導引述句的動詞，稱為**引述動詞**，常見的引述動詞有：

Glenn said he would be busy next week.

葛倫說他下個星期會很忙。

He stated that he did not do anything wrong.

他說他沒有做錯任何事。

- say
- tell
- state
- report

4 **引述動詞**和**間接引述句**之間，可以加 that 也可以省略，加了 that 較為正式。

Victor said (that) he was being called to testify before the commission.

維克多說他正被召至委員會前作證。

Margery told me (that) she was attending a board meeting.

瑪格莉對我說，她要去參加董事會議。

5 say 和 tell 是常見的引述動詞。在**間接引述**中，say 後面可以直接加「**一件事**」，或者先加上「to somebody」，再接要講的事。

I said I was going to take a break.

我說我要休息一下。

Margo says she wants to take a day off.

瑪歌說她想休息一天。

I said to Jacob that we were all going to the break room.

我對雅各說我們全都要去休息室。

6 tell 要先接「**人**」當作受詞，再接所要講的事。

I told Roger I was going to take a break.

我跟羅傑說我要休息一下。

Margo tells us she wants to take a day off. 瑪歌跟我們說她想休息一天。

7 tell 和某些詞連用時，可以不需要加「**人**」做受詞。

tell a story 說故事
tell the time 說出時間
tell the truth 說實話
tell a lie 說謊
tell a tale 說故事
tell a joke 說笑話
tell a secret 說祕密
tell the answer 說出答案

Practice

1

在「直接引述句」前面寫上 D（**direct**），「間接引述句」前面寫上 R（**reported**）。

.... 1. Ruth says, "I want to go to the science museum."

.... 2. Ruth says she wants to go to the science museum.

.... 3. Julius said he preferred to see the aquarium.

.... 4. Last week Angela said, "I have to work tomorrow."

.... 5. Lillie says that she wishes she could go with you.

.... 6. Yesterday Ted said, "I already went there."

.... 7. Last night Philip said, "I want to visit to the planetarium."

.... 8. Janet said she had been to Mexico three times.

.... 9. This morning Susan told me she's going to quit the job.

2

請用 **say** 或 **tell** 的正確形式填空，完成句子。

1. Yesterday Robert ...., "Let's go to a pub on Friday night."

2. Last night Bernie .... me he was going out with Robert to a pub.

3. Have you .... Julie we are going out tonight?

4. Last week Julie .... she would be working late on Friday.

5. Just now Alice .... to me that it is a dark and dirty pub.

6. Johnny ...., "I don't think Jade would lie to me."

7. Sandy .... to her boss, "Why not try the new technology to achieve better efficiency?"

8. Could you .... me the name and phone number of the piano teacher?

3

tell 常和哪些非「人」的受詞連用？請勾選出正確用法。

☐ tell tales   ☐ tell a dream

☐ tell love   ☐ tell the truth

☐ tell a joke   ☐ tell a report

☐ tell a fortune   ☐ tell a news

☐ tell the year   ☐ tell a lie

☐ tell the time   ☐ tell a book

Reported Speech: Verb Forms
間接引述的一般動詞時態

1 要將**直接引述句**改為**間接引述句**時，需要注意句子的「**時態**」。

如果**引述動詞**是現在式或未來式，那麼**間接引述句**的時態就和**直接引述句**相同，不需要改變。

Rene says, "I'm in a mood to go dancing tonight."

= Rene says she is in a mood to go dancing tonight. 芮奈說她今晚想去跳舞。

↳ 引述動詞 says 是現在式，直接引述句是**現在式**，則間接引述也用**現在式**。

2 **引述動詞**是過去式時，那麼**直接引述句**改為**間接引述句**，就需要改變動詞時態。

如果**直接引述句**是現在式，**間接引述句**就要改為過去式。

❶ Zane said, "I love surfing the Internet."

贊恩說：「我喜歡上網。」

Zane said he loved surfing the Internet.
↳ 現在式要變成過去式。

贊恩說他喜歡上網。

❷ Dorothy said, "I don't like online games."

桃樂絲說：「我不喜歡線上遊戲。」

Dorothy said she didn't like online games.

桃樂絲說她不喜歡線上遊戲。

❸ Michelle said, "I'm going to an Internet café." 蜜雪兒說：「我要去網咖。」

Michelle said she was going to an Internet
現在進行式要變成過去進行式。↵

café. 蜜雪兒說她要去網咖。

❹ Bruce said, "Louise has downloaded hundreds of songs."

布魯斯說：「露意絲下載了數百首歌曲。」

Bruce said Louise had downloaded
現在完成式要變成過去完成式。↵

hundreds of songs.

布魯斯說露意絲下載了數百首歌曲。

3 **引述動詞**是過去式時，如果**直接引述句**是過去式，**間接引述句**就要改為過去完成式。但有時也可以維持過去式。

❶ Bob said, "I bought a wireless LAN for my house."

鮑伯說：「我在家裡裝了無線網路。」

Bob said he had bought a wireless LAN for his house.

= Bob said he bought a wireless LAN for his house.

鮑伯說他在家裡裝了無線網路。

❷ Francine said, "Bob bought more computer gizmos."

法蘭辛說：「鮑伯買了更多電腦零件。」

Francine said Bob had bought more computer gizmos.

= Francine said Bob bought more computer gizmos.

法蘭辛說鮑伯買了更多電腦零件。

4 如果**直接引述句**是過去完成式，**間接引述句**仍然維持過去完成式。

Amy said, "Bob had forgotten to buy a USB cable until I reminded him with a message."

愛咪說：「我發訊息提醒鮑伯，他才想起要買 USB 線。」

Amy said Bob had forgotten to buy a USB cable until she reminded him with a message.

愛咪說她發訊息提醒鮑伯，他才想起要買 USB 線。

Practice

1

請將右列句子改寫為
「間接引述句」。

1. Kathy said, "I am going out to dinner."

   → ....

2. Abby said, "I spoke to the Director."

   → ....

3. Sam said, "I saw a car accident on my way to the store."

   → ....

4. Scott said, "I have listened to that song thousands of times."

   → ....

5. Sarah said, "I am in a taxi with my mom."

   → ....

6. Tina said, "I had finished my homework long before my mom came back home."

   → ....

2

請依圖示，從框內選
出適當的詞語填空，
完成右列「間接引述
句」。

| had bought him the watch | everyone has gone to work |
| wanted to enjoy the sea breeze | the pizza had already arrived |

1

Liz said Huck ....

.... for twenty more minutes.

2

Puca says ....

.... and he is so bored.

3

Anna said ....

....

4

Steve said Lisa ....

.... as his birthday gift.

Unit 176

Reported Speech: Modal Verb Forms
間接引述的情態動詞時態

1 如果**引述動詞**是**過去式**，**間接引述句**要改變動詞時態，情態動詞也一樣。當**直接引述句**裡面使用了**現在式**的情態動詞，改寫為**間接引述句**時要改為**過去式**的情態動詞。

will → would
can → could
shall → should
may → might

❶ Bob said, "I can upgrade my computer myself." 鮑伯說：「我自己會升級電腦。」
Bob said he could upgrade his computer himself. 鮑伯說他自己會升級電腦。

❷ Tony said, "Bob will install a Linux operating system."
湯尼說：「鮑伯要安裝 Linux 作業系統。」
Tony said Bob would install a Linux operating system.
湯尼說鮑伯要安裝 Linux 作業系統。

2 但如果**直接引述句**中的情態動詞是過去式，則**間接引述句**仍然沿用過去式，不需要改變。直接引述句中的情態動詞 should，在間接引述句中也不用改變。

❶ Howard said, "Bob should use a firewall on his PC at home." 霍華說：「鮑伯應該在他家裡的電腦上設置防火牆。」
Howard said Bob should use a firewall on his PC at home. 霍華說鮑伯應該在他家裡的電腦上設置防火牆。

❷ Eleanor said, "I might buy an iPhone someday." 愛麗諾說：「有一天或許我會買 iPhone。」
Eleanor said she might buy an iPhone someday. 愛麗諾說有一天或許她會買 iPhone。

3 如果**直接引述句**中使用的情態動詞是 must，則在**間接引述句**裡可以用 must 或 had to。

Sam said, "I must learn Python in my MIS class." 山姆說：「我在資訊管理系統課，得學 Python 程式語言。」
Sam said he must learn Python in his MIS class.
= Sam said he had to learn Python in his MIS class.
山姆說他在資訊管理系統課上，得學 Python 程式語言。

4 如果「**引述內容從過去到現在都是事實**」，那麼即使**引述動詞**是過去式，**直接引述句**改寫為**間接引述句**時，通常**不改變**原本的動詞時態，但如果為了強調時態一致，也可以改變。

❶ Mia said, "Linux is a free operating system."
麥雅說：「Linux 是一種免費的作業系統。」
Mia said Linux is a free operating system.
= Mia said Linux was a free operating system.
麥雅說 Linux 是一種免費的作業系統。

❷ Joe said, "Many versions of Linux are free to download from the internet."
喬說：「Linux 有很多版本都可以從網路上免費下載。」
Joe said many versions of Linux are free to download from the internet.
= Joe said many versions of Linux were free to download from the internet.
喬說 Linux 有很多版本都可以從網路上免費下載。

當然如果當初所說的事實，到了現在已經改變，那麼動詞時態還是要改變。

• Elle said, "All versions of Linux are free."
艾兒說：「Linux 系統的所有版本都是免費的。」
• Elle said all versions of Linux were free, but in fact many companies sell their own versions of Linux.
艾兒說 Linux 系統的所有版本都是免費的，但實際上許多公司都有販售他們自己的 Linux 版本。

Practice

1

請將粗體動詞改以正確的時態填空，完成改寫的句子。

1. Dina said, "I **can handle** the job."
   → Dina said she _____ the job.

2. Ivan said, "I **must get** home before 9:00."
   → Ivan said he _____ home before 9:00.

3. Gwen said, "Mount Everest **is** the tallest mountain in the world."
   → Gwen said Mount Everest _____ the tallest mountain in the world.

4. Jake said, "Taipei 101 **is** the tallest building in the world."
   → Jake said Taipei 101 _____ the tallest building in the world, but it has been surpassed by Burj Khalifa.

5. Ann said, "We **shall arrive** in a minute."
   → Ann said they _____ in a minute.

6. Anita said, "Uncle Bob **may drop by** some time."
   → Anita said Uncle Bob _____ some time.

7. Rudolph said, "You **should come** and see it."
   → Rudolph said I _____ and see it.

8. Father said, "I **must cook** dinner before your mom gets home."
   → Father said he _____ dinner before Mom got home.

9. Larry said, "Pirating a book **is** illegal."
   → Larry said pirating a book _____ illegal.

10. The weather forecast said, "It **will rain** tomorrow."
    → The weather forecast said it _____ tomorrow.

11. Johnny said, "The teacher **is going to punish** us."
    → John said the teacher _____ us, but in fact, the teacher has forgiven us.

12. Frances said, "I **can speak** three languages."
    → Frances said she _____ three languages.

Unit **177**

Reported Speech: Changes of Pronouns, Adjectives, and Adverbs
間接引述的代名詞、形容詞與副詞的變化

1 直接敘述句中的代名詞和所有格形容詞，到了引述句中要改變人稱，例如 **I** 可能要改成 **he/she**，而 **my** 可能要改成 **his/her**。

Norman said he was at the zoo with his daughter, and they were looking at the baby elephant.

諾曼說他和他女兒在動物園，他們在看大象寶寶。

Norman said, "I am at the zoo with my daughter, and we are looking at the baby elephant."

諾曼說：「我和我女兒在動物園，我們在看大象寶寶。」

2 直接引述句中的時間副詞或地方副詞到了間接引述句中也往往需要改變。

here → there
now → then
right now → right away
today → that day
tonight → that night
tomorrow → the next day / the following day
yesterday → the day before / the previous day
next Friday → the following Friday
last Sunday → the previous Sunday

Tom said, "I'm here." 湯姆說：「我在這裡」。
Tom said he was there. 湯姆說他在那裡。
Jane said, "I will visit Mr. Lee tomorrow."
珍說：「我明天會去拜訪李先生。」
Jane said she would visit Mr. Lee the next day.
珍說她隔天會去拜訪李先生。

3 另外有些動詞和指示詞，也會視需要改變。

come → go
this → that/the

Peter said, "I want you to come to my birthday party."

彼德說：「我希望你來參加我的慶生會。」

Peter said he wanted me to go to his birthday party.

彼德說他希望我去參加他的慶生會。

引述別人說的話時，到底要對原句做哪些改變，**視情況而定**。

例如在不同日期使用 tomorrow 這個字，就代表不同的時間。

如果你在昨天用 tomorrow 這個字，時間其實是今天（today）；如果 tomorrow 是你在一星期前提的，那麼那時候的「明天」早就已經過了。

tomorrow 這個字是指說話當時的明天，因此在引述句中是否要修改，其實要視該敘述句是何時說出而定。

1

請將下列「直接引述句」改寫為「間接引述句」。

1. Yesterday Elmore said, "I will call you tomorrow."

   → ......

2. Hans said, "You should wash your hands before meals."

   → ......

3. Ann said, "I want you to come here right now."

   → ......

4. Bruce said, "I bought this watch from a vendor in the night market."

   → ......

   ......

5. Bernie said, "I'm going to have tuna for lunch today."

   → ......

   ......

6. Kayla said, "I'll stay here until noon."

   → ......

7. Charlotte said, "My brother went camping yesterday."

   → ......

   ......

8. Amy said, "I don't know where Tom was last week."

   → ......

   ......

9. Steve said, "I'll be out of town for a couple of days."

   → ......

   ......

10. Bella said, "I'll go to your place this afternoon," but she never showed up.

    → ......

    ......

Reported Questions
間接引述疑問句

1 當**引述動詞**是「**提問**」的動詞，如 ask、inquire 等，就可以構成引述疑問句。

在間接引述疑問句中，要用**直述句**的語序，而不用疑問句的語序。句末也不用問號而用「**句號**」。

直接引述疑問句 **1** My friend asked me, "What are you listening to?"

我朋友問：「你在聽什麼？」

間接引述疑問句 My friend asked me what I was listening to.

↳ 不用疑問句的語序 what was I listening to，而用直述句的語序 what I was listening to；句尾用句號。

我朋友問我在聽什麼。

直接引述疑問句 **2** My sister asked me, "When is the concert?"

我妹妹問我：「音樂會是什麼時候？」

間接引述疑問句 My sister asked me when the concert was.

我妹妹問我音樂會是什麼時候。

2 間接引述疑問句中，也不能使用**助動詞 do/does/did**。

1 I asked him, "What do you think of this song?"

我問他：「你覺得這首歌如何？」

I asked him what he thought of this song.

↳ 原本句子裡使用了助動詞 do，但間接引述疑問句裡要用直述句的語序，因此不需要助動詞。

我問我朋友他覺得這首歌如何。

2 I asked, "Where did you get the ticket?"

我問：「你從哪裡得到這張門票的？」

I asked where he got the ticket.

我問他從哪裡得到這這張門票的。

3 如果**直接引述疑問句**裡並沒有使用到 what、why 等 wh 開頭的疑問詞，是一般的 **Yes/No** 問句，那麼改寫成間接引述疑問句時，就要加上 if 或 whether。

1 I asked my girlfriend, "Do you like reggae and ska?" 我問我的女友：「你喜歡聽雷鬼和斯卡音樂嗎？」

I asked my girlfriend if she liked reggae and ska.

↳ 原句是 Yes/No 問句，改寫成間接引述句時，須使用 if 或 whether。

我問我女友是否喜歡雷鬼斯卡音樂。

2 I asked my boyfriend, "Can you dance and hold your soda at the same time?"

我問我男友：「你能夠拿著汽水跳舞嗎？」

I asked my boyfriend whether he could dance and hold his soda at the same time.

↳ 原句是 Yes/No 問句，改寫成間接引述句時，須使用 if 或 whether。

我問我男友是否能夠拿著汽水跳舞。

4 有些間接引述疑問句，如果引述動詞 ask 後面直接加 wh- 疑問詞的話，可以接「**加 to 的不定詞**」。

1 Rene asked, "How do I use the video chat on the cell phone?"

芮奈問：「這支手機的視訊功能要怎麼用？」

Rene asked how to use the video chat on the cell phone.

芮奈問這支手機的視訊功能要怎麼用。

2 Sunny asked, "What should we do next?"

桑尼問：「我們接下來要做什麼？」

Sunny asked what to do next.

桑尼問接下來要做什麼。

Practice

1

請從框內找出與各題目人物吻合的問句，並改為「間接引述疑問句」填空，完成句子。

Do you like ballet?

Do you have an affordable health insurance plan?

How do you get enough protein and calcium?

What type of music do you play?

Have you ever felt nervous when flying?

How many cows do you have?

1. I asked the dancer _if he/she liked ballet._

2. I asked the vegetarian _____

3. I asked the musician _____

4. I asked the dairy farmer _____

5. I asked the airline pilot _____
   _____

6. I asked the insurance sales representative _____
   _____

2

請將右列各「直接引述疑問句」改寫為「間接引述疑問句」。

1. Pete asked his boss Annie, "Would you like to see the file?"
   → _____

2. Annie asked Pete, "What kind of file is it?"
   → _____

3. Pete asked, "Where shall I put the file?"
   → _____

4. Pete asked Annie, "Can I get a pay raise?"
   → _____

5. Annie asked Pete, "Why should I give you a pay raise?"
   → _____

6. Pete asked, "Aren't I working hard enough?"
   → _____

7. Annie asked Pete, "Do you want a pay raise or a nicer office?"
   → _____

Reported Speech Using the "To Infinitive"
使用不定詞的間接引述句

1 引述「**命令、要求、警告、建議和邀請**」的句子，經常使用「引述動詞 + 受詞 + 加 to 的不定詞」的句型。這類的**引述動詞**有：

- tell
- ask
- order
- request
- warn
- advise
- invite
- beg

❶ **The brother ordered, "Put the Hello Kitty magnet back on the shelf right now."** 哥哥命令說：「現在就把凱蒂貓的磁鐵放回架子上。」
The brother ordered **his sister** to put **the Hello Kitty magnet back on the shelf right away.** 哥哥命令妹妹現在就把凱蒂貓的磁鐵放回架子上。

❷ **Amy requested, "Tom, could you pick up the marbles?"** 愛咪要求說：「湯姆，請把彈珠撿起來好嗎？」
Amy requested **Tom** to pick up **the marbles.** 愛咪要求湯姆把彈珠撿起來。

❸ **My mom warned me, "Avoid walking on the kitchen floor."**
母親警告我說：「別踩廚房的地板。」
My mom warned **me** to avoid **walking on the kitchen floor.**
母親警告我別踩廚房的地板。

❹ **He advised, "Lily, you should tell your dad about what happened."**
他建議：「莉莉，你應該告訴你爸爸發生了什麼事。」
He advised **Lily** to tell **her dad about what had happened.**
他建議莉莉告訴她爸爸發生了什麼事。

2 引述「**提供幫助或物品、承諾和威脅**」的句子，則不加**受詞**，會使用「引述**動詞** + 加 to 的不定詞」句型。這類的**動詞**常用：

- offer
- promise
- threaten

❶ **Mom asked, "Can I get you some milk?"**
媽媽說：「我倒點牛奶給你喝好嗎？」
Mom offered to get **me some milk.**
媽媽說要倒點牛奶給我喝。

❷ **Her son promised, "I will take my vitamin pill."** 她兒子答應說：「我會吃維他命。」
Her son promised to take **his vitamin pill.**
她兒子答應要吃維他命。

❸ **His father threatened, "I will take away your robot."**
他父親威脅道：「我要把你的機器人沒收。」
His father threatened to take away **the robot.** 他父親威脅要把機器人沒收。

3 上述兩種**間接引述句型**，如果是**否定句**，句型是：
引述動詞（＋受詞）＋ not ＋加 to 的不定詞

❶ **My mother warned, "Don't throw the ball in the house."**
我媽媽警告說：「不准在家裡玩球。」
My mother warned **me** not to throw **the ball in the house.**
我媽媽警告我不准在家裡玩球。

❷ **He promised, "I won't climb on the furniture."**
他保證說：「我不會爬到家具上」。
He promised not to climb **on the furniture.** 他保證不會爬到家具上。

Practice

1

請使用「不定詞」，將右列的「直接引述句」改寫為「間接引述句」。

1. Dan offered, "I will do the dishes."
   → *Dan offered to do the dishes.*

2. Mom ordered me, "Get your feet off the coffee table."
   → _____

3. My neighbor warned me, "Stay away from that dog."
   → _____

4. Tom asked me, "Would you like to go to a karaoke with us?"
   → _____

5. My husband offered, "Can I help you move the sofa?"
   → _____

6. The painter promised, "I will be careful up on the ladder."
   → _____

2

右列為一名求職者記錄他與餐廳老闆的對話。請將這些「直接引述句」改寫為「間接引述句」，描述他們的對話。

1. "I want a new job," I told him.
   → *I told him (that) I wanted a new job.*

2. "Are you a chef?" he asked me.
   → _____

3. "I have a job opening," he told me.
   → _____

4. "Don't touch the mushrooms," he warned me.
   → _____

5. "I was in the south digging truffles," he told me.
   → _____

6. "Maybe you can cook truffles for me." he said.
   → _____

7. "I have never cooked truffles before," I said.
   → _____

8. "You should never overcook truffles," he told me.
   → _____

9. "I won't overcook the truffles," I promised.
   → _____

10. "Can you start working here on Monday?" he asked me.
    → _____

Unit 180

Restrictive and Non-restrictive Relative Clauses
「限定關係子句」與「非限定關係子句」

1 關係子句是以關係代名詞 what、who、that、which 等引導的附屬子句。多用來修飾**名詞**或**代名詞**，因此屬於形容詞子句。

Do you know the guy who **is dressed in blue?**
↳ 關係子句，修飾名詞 the guy。

你認識那個穿藍衣服的人嗎？

I think this is the bag which **Jay was looking for.**
↳ 關係子句，修飾名詞 the bag。

我認為這就是杰在找的袋子。

2 限定關係子句用於**界定名詞**，**說明人物、地點或事物**。它是句中**不可或缺**的部分，也就是說，刪除它之後，語意會不完整。

That is the man who **started this company.**
↳ 用來界定那個人是什麼人，如果刪除後，句子將不知所云。

那位就是創辦這間公司的人。

The coin which **I found yesterday is about 150 years old.**
↳ 用於界定硬幣是「我找到的硬幣」，如果刪除，讀者將不知道是哪個硬幣。

我昨天找到的硬幣將近有一百五十年的歷史。

3 非限定關係子句不是用來「指定」人事物，而是**對已知的人物、地點或事物「提供更多相關訊息」**，就算刪除，語意還是完整。

Barbie's boyfriend, who **is a licensed pilot, owns two aircraft.**
↳ 並非用來界定是何人，因為我們已知句中提到的是芭比男朋友，只是用來補充說明芭比男朋友是一位機師。

芭比的男朋友是位執照機師，他有兩架飛機。

4 非限定關係子句可以位於**句中**，也可以位於**句尾**，通常會用逗號和**主要子句**隔開，傳達附屬的訊息。

> 限定子句則不需要加**逗號**。

My mother sent me a box, which **still hasn't arrived.**

我媽媽寄了一個包裹給我，但是還沒送達。

My wife, who **loves kids, has decided to open a daycare center.**

我太太很愛小孩，所以決定要開一家托兒所。

5 **that** 不能用於非限定關係子句。

✗ Betty has a really inexpensive apartment, that is an illegal rooftop structure.

✓ Betty has a really inexpensive apartment, which is an illegal rooftop structure.

貝蒂有一間非常便宜的公寓，是一棟違建的屋頂建築物。

6 在非限定關係子句中，「**不能省略**」關係代名詞 who(m) 或 which。（關係代名詞在限定關係子句的省略，請見 Unit 182。）

✗ Carey, I met in France, speaks excellent French.

✓ Carey, whom I met in France, speaks excellent French.

我在法國認識凱瑞，她說得一口流利法文。

✗ Jacob bought me a fountain pen, I carry all the time.

✓ Jacob bought me a fountain pen, which I carry all the time.

雅各買了一支鋼筆給我，我隨時都帶著。

The house **on the corner,** which **has been empty for years, is said to be haunted.**
↳ 並沒有界定是哪一棟房子，因為我們已經知道是位在角落的房子。

位於轉角的房子已經空在那兒好多年了，聽說鬧鬼。

Practice

1 請判斷下列句子中的關係子句是「限定子句」還是「非限定子句」。
請在「限定子句」前面寫上 R，「非限定子句」前面寫上 N。

.... 1. My sister, who is 16 years old, is a pest.

.... 2. The sale, which started today, will continue for two weeks.

.... 3. The girl who is sniffling has a cold.

.... 4. The used car, which I bought yesterday, runs pretty well.

.... 5. I spoke to the mechanic that fixed my car.

.... 6. The flu medicine, which I always buy, is on sale.

2 請從框內的「關係子句」中，選出與圖片呼應的用語填入空格中，完成句子。

> Ⓐ who is tasting the wine?
>
> Ⓑ who is holding a cup of coffee in his hand.
>
> Ⓒ which I've been carrying with me for years.
>
> Ⓓ that has mud around its nose
>
> Ⓔ who is sitting on the bench and using a laptop?
>
> Ⓕ which leads to my house.
>
> Ⓖ that serves organic salads?

Do you know the woman
........A........

This is the pocket watch
....

Do you know the woman
....

Look at the guy ....

Have you been to the
restaurant ....

Don't you think the pig
.... is adorable?

This is the shortcut ....

Unit 181

Restrictive Relative Clauses With "Who,"
"Which," and "That"

以 Who、Which、That 引導的限定關係子句

that

who

1 who 指「人」，常用於限定關係子句。
如果拆成兩個句子，who 就相當於代名詞的地位。

Robin called the person. He placed the ad in the newspaper.
↳ 第一個句子不是完整句子。
→ Robin called the person who placed the ad in the newspaper.
羅賓打電話給在報紙上登廣告的人。

I talked to the man. He owns the house.
→ I talked to the man who owns the house.
我跟這房子的屋主談過。

The man is talking to the agent. She is showing the house.
→ The man is talking to the agent who is showing the house.
那個男人跟正在展示這間房子的仲介說話。

which

2 which 指「事物」，常用於限定關係子句。

Did you see the phone bill? I paid it yesterday.
→ Did you see the phone bill which I paid yesterday?
你有看到我昨天付的電話帳單嗎？

The money is for your school lunches. I put it on the table.
→ The money which I put on the table is for your school lunches.
我放在桌上的錢是給你到學校吃午餐的。

Shirley wants to see the apartment. It is being advertised in the newspaper.
→ Shirley wants to see the apartment which is being advertised in the newspaper.
雪莉想要看看報紙廣告上的那間公寓。

3 that 可以在限定關係子句中指
「人」，也可以指「物」。

I like the bag. I bought it in Tokyo.
→ I like the bag that I bought in Tokyo.
我喜歡那個我在東京買的包包。

Did you see the picture frame? It was on top of the TV.
→ Did you see the picture frame that was on top of the TV?
你有沒有看到電視機上面的相框？

Try the cherry tomatoes. They are on the table.
→ Try the cherry tomatoes that are on the table.
吃吃看那些放在桌上的小番茄。

4 關係代名詞和人稱代名詞不可並用。

✗ Janet asked the man who he was standing in the middle of the path to step aside.
✓ Janet asked the man who was standing in the middle of the path to step aside.
珍妮特要那擋在路中央的人靠邊一點。

✗ I took some boxes that they were on the shelf.
✓ I took some boxes that were on the shelf.
我從架子上拿了一些盒子。

1

請用「關係代名詞 who、that」連接各題的兩個句子，改寫為帶有「限定關係子句」的句型。

1. I called the woman with a German accent. She had left a message on my answering machine.
   → *I called the woman with a German accent who/that had left a message on my answering machine.*

2. Did you see the woman? She was sitting by me on the bus.
   → _____

3. The guy was cool. He talked to me while I was having my iced tea.
   → _____

4. Have you seen the water bottle? It was by the door.
   → _____

5. I tripped over the slippers. They were in the hallway.
   → _____

6. The hat was on the coat tree when I left home this morning. It is now on the floor.
   → _____

2

請將右列錯誤的句子改寫為正確的句子。

1. Did you see the blue backpack who I bought yesterday?
   → *Did you see the blue backpack which/that I bought yesterday?*

2. Could you please pass me the pepper who is on the counter?
   → _____

3. I called the history teacher who I met him at the party last night.
   → _____

4. I went to the new restaurant which it opened last Sunday.
   → _____

5. I didn't recognize the tall woman which talked to me at the bank yesterday.
   → _____

6. Jack said the woman, that he had dinner with last night, was his ex-wife.
   → _____

Unit 182

Leaving out Objective Relative Pronouns in Restrictive Relative Clauses
限定關係子句中受詞關係代名詞的省略

1 在限定關係子句中，關係代名詞 who、which、that 可以當作**主詞**，也可以當作**受詞**。

Amy is the waitress. She served us at the restaurant yesterday.

→ Amy is the waitress who served us at the restaurant yesterday. ↳ who 是主詞。

愛咪就是昨天餐廳為我們服務的服務生。

Emily is the woman. We talked with her at the restaurant last night.

→ Emily is the woman who we talked with at the restaurant last night.

↳ who 是 talked with 的受詞。

艾蜜莉就是昨晚我們在餐廳講話的那位女子。

2 當 who、which、that 在限定關係子句中當作**主詞**的時候，**不可以省略**。

✗ Colin is the accountant called about your tax refund.

✓ Colin is the accountant who called about your tax refund.

柯林就是打電話通知你退稅的那位會計師。

✗ Have you paid the electricity bill is due today?

✓ Have you paid the electricity bill which is due today?

你付了今天到期的電費帳單嗎？

3 當 who、which、that 在限定關係子句中當作**受詞**的時候，**可以省略**。

Barcelona is the city we went to on our last vacation.

= Barcelona is the city that we went to on our last vacation. ↳ that 是 went to 的受詞，可以省略。

巴塞隆納就是我們上次度假去的那個城市。

I really liked the laptop I saw in the computer shop last Sunday.

= I really liked the laptop which I saw in the computer shop last Sunday.

↳ which 是 saw 的受詞，可以省略。

我很喜歡我上星期日在電腦店看到的那台筆電。

4 who 當作受詞時，正式的用法是用 whom。但是 whom 聽起來太過正式，現在多用 who 或 that。

Stefan met an old friend whom he knew from college. ↳ 較正式

→ Stefan met an old friend (who) he knew from college.

→ Stefan met an old friend (that) he knew from college.

史蒂芬遇到了一位大學時期的老朋友。

Practice

1

請以 who 指「人」、that 指「物」做適當的填空，並將可以省略的「關係代名詞」加上括弧。

1. Mr. Roberts is the guy ＿＿＿＿＿＿ sold us the painting.

2. Mrs. Stevens is the woman ＿＿＿＿＿＿ we talked to about the auction.

3. Have you seen the auction house catalog ＿＿＿＿＿＿ I received in the mail?

4. Check the reference number ＿＿＿＿＿＿ was marked on the side.

5. I saw a large bronze statue of a ballet dancer ＿＿＿＿＿＿ I liked.

6. Mr. Stone introduced me to a Russian woman ＿＿＿＿＿＿ said she knew you.

2

請將下列句子以「省略關係代名詞的關係子句」句型改寫，合併為一個句子。

1

Guam is the island. We went to Guam for our honeymoon.

→ ＿＿＿＿＿＿＿＿＿＿＿＿＿＿＿＿＿＿＿＿＿＿＿＿＿＿＿＿＿＿＿＿＿＿

＿＿＿＿＿＿＿＿＿＿＿＿＿＿＿＿＿＿＿＿＿＿＿＿＿＿＿＿＿＿＿＿＿＿

2

Sophia is the student. I mentioned her yesterday.

→ ＿＿＿＿＿＿＿＿＿＿＿＿＿＿＿＿＿＿＿＿＿＿＿＿＿＿＿＿＿＿＿＿＿＿

＿＿＿＿＿＿＿＿＿＿＿＿＿＿＿＿＿＿＿＿＿＿＿＿＿＿＿＿＿＿＿＿＿＿

3

The roast duck was the dish. Patricia recommended the dish in this restaurant.

→ ＿＿＿＿＿＿＿＿＿＿＿＿＿＿＿＿＿＿＿＿＿＿＿＿＿＿＿＿＿＿＿＿＿＿

＿＿＿＿＿＿＿＿＿＿＿＿＿＿＿＿＿＿＿＿＿＿＿＿＿＿＿＿＿＿＿＿＿＿

4

This is the house. Janet sold the house in two days.

→ ＿＿＿＿＿＿＿＿＿＿＿＿＿＿＿＿＿＿＿＿＿＿＿＿＿＿＿＿＿＿＿＿＿＿

＿＿＿＿＿＿＿＿＿＿＿＿＿＿＿＿＿＿＿＿＿＿＿＿＿＿＿＿＿＿＿＿＿＿

Unit 183

Restrictive Relative Clauses With "Whose," "Where," "When," and "Why/That"

以 Whose、Where、When、Why/That 引導的限定關係子句

whose

1 whose 表示「**所有權**」，可以用於限定關係子句，相當於**所有格代名詞 his、her** 等。

I have an uncle. His daughter is getting married.
→ I have an uncle whose daughter is getting married.
我有一個即將嫁女兒的叔叔。

That is the family. Their neighbor is a famous general.
→ That is the family whose neighbor is a famous general.
他們是那個鄰居為知名將軍的家庭。

2 whose 和 who's 很容易混淆，whose 是**所有格**，而 who's 則是 **who is** 或 **who has** 的縮寫，不是所有格。

✗ My brother is married to a woman who's family comes from Russia.
✓ My brother is married to a woman whose family comes from Russia.
我哥哥娶了一名來自俄國的女子。

where

3 where 指「**地點**」，可以用於限定關係子句。

The city in Russia where Natasha comes from is Vladivostok.
娜塔莎來自的城市是俄國的海參崴。

4 where 在限定關係子句當中通常**不能省略**，但如果先行詞是 somewhere、anywhere、everywhere、nowhere、place 等字，通常可以省略。

The place (where) I learned to dive is said to have sharks around.
我以前學潛水的地方，現在據說有鯊魚出沒。

Last summer the hotel where we stayed was very noisy.
我們去年夏天住的飯店非常吵。

when

5 when 指「**時間**」，可以用於限定關係子句，也可以省略。

Lena didn't speak any other language other than Russian. She arrived in America on that day.
→ Lena didn't speak any other language other than Russian the day (when) she arrived in America.
莉娜剛來美國的時候，除了俄語，不會說別的語言。

Can you set a time? We can meet at that time.
→ Can you set a time (when) we can meet?
你可以定一個我們會面的時間嗎？

Is there a good time (when) we can play ping pong on Sunday?   ↳ when 可以省略。
我們星期日有合適的時間打乒乓球嗎？

why / that

6 why 表示「**理由**」，可以引導限定關係子句，但只搭配先行詞 reason 使用。這種句型也可以用 that。why 和 that 在這裡都**可以省略**。

What is the reason (why) she left Russia?
她離開俄國的原因是什麼？

Having no chance of promoting is the reason (that) he left the company.
缺乏升遷管道是他離開這間公司的原因。

Practice

1

whose

where

when

why/that

請從框內選出適當的「關係代名詞」填空，並將可以省略的加上括弧。

1. What is the reason <u>(why/that)</u> Terry wants to buy such an old house?

2. Joseph is the man ＿＿＿＿＿＿＿ brother just returned from Patagonia.

3. This is the bakery ＿＿＿＿＿＿＿ I always buy rye bread.

4. This meeting is as boring as yesterday's meeting ＿＿＿＿＿＿＿ the boss fell asleep.

5. I knew he was my true love at the moment ＿＿＿＿＿＿＿ I met him.

6. The bus stops next to a waterfall ＿＿＿＿＿＿＿ you can take pictures.

7. Is there a reason ＿＿＿＿＿＿＿ you want to put your money into gold?

8. Judy and Frank are the couple ＿＿＿＿＿＿＿ picture was in yesterday's newspaper.

2

請用適當的「關係代名詞」合併各題的兩個句子。

1. I remember the day. We first met on that day.
   → <u>I remember the day when we first met.</u>

2. We go to the city for a shopping trip every year. The city is Bangkok.
   → ＿＿＿＿＿＿＿＿＿＿＿＿＿＿＿＿＿＿＿＿＿＿＿

3. I know a guy. His father owns a company with two thousand employees.
   → ＿＿＿＿＿＿＿＿＿＿＿＿＿＿＿＿＿＿＿＿＿＿＿

4. He hasn't spoken to me for a week. I don't know the reason.
   → ＿＿＿＿＿＿＿＿＿＿＿＿＿＿＿＿＿＿＿＿＿＿＿

5. I need the address. I can send this parcel to the address.
   → ＿＿＿＿＿＿＿＿＿＿＿＿＿＿＿＿＿＿＿＿＿＿＿

6. The rain came at a time. The peasants needed it most.
   → ＿＿＿＿＿＿＿＿＿＿＿＿＿＿＿＿＿＿＿＿＿＿＿

Unit 184

Non-restrictive Relative Clauses
非限定關係子句

唯有 *that* 不可用於非限定關係子句。

1 who 可以引導非限定關係子句，用來指「人」。

I called the police, who arrived at my apartment in five minutes. 我打電話報警，警察五分鐘後來到我的公寓。

The tall man with gray hair, who is wearing a pair of sunglasses, must be Professor Jones. 那個頭髮灰白、戴著墨鏡的高個子男人，一定是瓊斯教授。

2 which 可以引導非限定關係子句，用來指「物」。

I am going to sell this watch, which has increased in value.
這支錶已經增值了，我打算出售它。

3 which 可以用來代替「前面的句子」。

Mr. Brown grows his fruit completely without pesticides, which means it is organic.   ↳ which 用來代替前面整個句子
布朗先生種水果完全不用農藥，意味著是有機栽培。

4 whom 可以引導非限定關係子句，用來指「人」，但只能在關係子句裡當受詞。當受詞時，whom 也可以用 who 代替。

Senator John Brown, who(m) we met at the fundraiser, has called to ask for a donation. 我們在募款會上遇到的約翰·布朗參議員，打電話來要求募捐。

5 whose 可以引導非限定關係子句，補充說明「所有權」。

The woman at the bakery, whose dog weighed 25 kilograms, was buying a birthday cake for her daughter.
麵包店裡那位女士有一隻重 25 公斤的狗，她那時正在為她的女兒買生日蛋糕。

The woman at the coffee shop, whose hair is gray, has a cute dog with white fur.

咖啡店那位灰白頭髮的女士，有一隻全身白毛、非常可愛的狗。

6 where 可以引導非限定關係子句，表示「地點」。

The bakery at the corner of Park Street and Vine Avenue, where I saw the woman with the cute dog, sells organic snacks.

在公園街和藤蔓大道轉角那家烘焙坊有賣有機點心，我在那裡看到過一位女士帶著一隻可愛的狗。

7 when 可以引導非限定關係子句，表示「時間」。

Today is my 18th birthday, when I am finally eligible to take the test for my driver's license.

今天是我 18 歲的生日，我終於有資格去考駕照了。

Practice

1

請從框內選出適當的
詞彙填空，完成句子。

who

which

whose

where

when

1. Lindsay, _____ brother is a friend of mine, wants to come with us.

2. My son, _____ you just met, wants me to drive him to baseball practice.

3. The bus stopped in front of the junior college, _____ I once took a welding course.

4. That awful bus accident happened in the fall, right before my birthday, _____ the leaves were changing colors.

5. We are going to the water park, _____ we held our wedding last year.

6. That is the school my son attends, and it's _____ I bring him every morning.

7. This is my son, _____ you met when he was little, is now a pilot.

2

請依圖示，從框內選
出適當的描述用語，
搭配正確的 who、
which、whose、
where 填空，完成句
子。

car has a flat fire	lies in the South America
is sitting here reading a newspaper	the Emperor Penguins live

The Amazon, _____ _____, is the largest river in the world.

Jennifer, _____ _____, always enjoys her morning break with a cup of coffee.

The Antarctica, _____ _____, is mostly covered by ice.

I think we should help the woman over there, _____ _____.

197

Part 24 Relative Clauses 關係子句

Unit 185

Relative Clauses With Prepositions
搭配介系詞的關係子句

1 關係代名詞可在**關係子句**中當作**介系詞的受詞**。當關係代名詞是 which 或 whom 時，介系詞可放在 which 或 whom 的**前面**。

That is the building. Daniel works in it.
→ That is the building in which Daniel works.
ㄴ which 代替 it，是介系詞 in 的受詞。
那就是丹尼爾工作的大樓。

The application is from the Indian with a big beard. We know very little about him.
→ The application is from the Indian man with a big beard about whom we know very little.
ㄴ whom 代替 him，是介系詞 about 的受詞。
這張申請表，是來自那位我們不太熟悉、留著大鬍子的印度人。

2 在**非正式的用法**裡，介系詞可位於**子句動詞的後面**，不和關係代名詞連在一起。這種情況下，關係代名詞可以是 who、which、whom 或 that，並且**可以省略**。

That is the pot (which) I put the soup in.
那個就是我用來盛湯的鍋子。

The people (who) I work with are very nice. 和我一起工作的人都非常好。

This is the corkscrew (that) I open wine bottles with. 這是我用來開酒瓶的開瓶器。

3 因此，當關係代名詞是 which 或 whom 時，介系詞可以有兩種位置，意義都相同。

That is the company I own stock in.
→ That is the company in which I own stock.
那就是我擁有股票的公司。

4 在正式的非限定關係子句裡，介系詞一樣可以放在 **which 或 whom** 的前面，這種用法很常見。

This is my pet mouse's favorite book, at which she can look for hours.
這是我的寵物鼠最愛的書，她可以盯著看好幾個小時。

This necklace was purchased by my wife, on whom it looks splendid.
這副項鍊是我太太買的，她戴上時光彩奪目。

5 在非正式的非限定關係子句裡，介系詞比較常放在**動詞後面**，不與關係代名詞連用。同時，多以 who 代替 **whom**。

Those are the songs from the early 1900s, which I listened to a lot as I grew up. 這是 1900 年代早期的歌曲，我在成長時期聽了很多。

Max and Lily, who I just talked with, are old friends of mine. 剛剛跟我講話的麥斯和莉莉，都是我的老朋友了。

6 在非限定關係子句裡，可以用一些 of 的詞組來表達「**數量**」。

- some of
- much of
- all of
- many of
- none of
- two of

Cliff owns three houses, all of which cost big bucks.
克里夫擁有三棟房子，全都價值不菲。

Miffy has three sisters, none of whom are married. 米菲有三個姐妹，全都未婚。

Mr. Tanner is the man I work for.
→ Mr. Tanner is the man for whom I work.
坦納先生就是我老闆。

Practice

1

請用括弧裡提示的介系詞，搭配適當的「關係代名詞」填空，完成句子。

1. That is the university _____ (in) Dave is enrolled.

2. Wendy, _____ (with) you can speak privately, is our top attorney in this field of law.

3. The band _____ (in) I used to play is now on tour in Europe.

4. That is the armchair _____ (in) she was sitting half an hour ago.

5. Mary is an interior designer, _____ (about) I know very little.

2

請依圖示，從框內選出適當的用語填空，完成句子；再用「介系詞放在動詞後面的句型」，將各個句子改寫成另一種關係子句。

about whom

in which

for whom

with which

This is Mia's favorite toy, _with which_ she can play for hours.

= _This is Mia's favorite toy, which she can play with for hours._

That woman is our new manager, _____ I've heard a lot.

= _____

This is Lulu's favorite pool, _____ she often swims for a long time.

= _____

That pretty woman is my wife, _____ I make a cup of rooibos tea every day.

= _____

Let's See
Grammar Intermediate 2

彩圖初級英文文法 三版

作　　者	Alex Rath Ph.D.
審　　訂	Dennis Le Boeuf／Liming Jing
譯　　者	羅竹君／丁宥榆
校　　對	梁立芳／樊志虹／吳佳芬
編　　輯	張盛傑／丁宥榆
主　　編	丁宥暄
內文設計	洪伊珊／林書玉
內文排版	洪伊珊／蔡怡柔
封面設計	林書玉
圖片協力	周演音
製程管理	洪巧玲
出 版 者	寂天文化事業股份有限公司
發 行 人	周均亮
電　　話	+886-(0)2-2365-9739
傳　　真	+886-(0)2-2365-9835
網　　址	www.icosmos.com.tw
讀者服務	onlineservice@icosmos.com.tw
出版日期	2021 年 5 月 三版一刷

國家圖書館出版品預行編目 (CIP) 資料

Let's See Grammar：彩圖中級英文文法 intermediate 2
/ Alex Rath 著 . -- 三版 . -- [臺北市]：寂天文化事業股份
有限公司 , 2021.05
面；　公分
ISBN 978-626-300-011-7　（第 1 冊：菊 8K 平裝）
ISBN 978-626-300-012-4　（第 2 冊：菊 8K 平裝）
1. 英語　2. 語法
805.16　　　　　　　　　　　110006247